Murder in
Plein Air

Murder in Plein Air

KAREN LEIGH CHARLES

WINDING ROAD STORIES

NEW YORK   LOS ANGELES

Jacket design by Rejenne Pavon

Jacket Copyright 2022 by Winding Road Stories

Interior book design by A Raven Design

ISBN#: 979-8-9866043-1-2 (pbk)
ISBN#: 979-8-9866043-2-9 (ebook)

Published by Winding Road Stories

www.windingroadstories.com

For my husband, Charles F. Smithson, and my sister, Patricia A. Neary

plein air *[French]*
adjective \ple-'ner

1. Taking place in the open air, outdoors: *plein air dining*
2. Of or relating to painting in outdoor daylight

CHAPTER ONE

My morning run along the outskirts of town had been uneventful, but I had a gut feeling that was about to change. The air tingled with tension the closer I got to Pix's lingerie shop. I hastened my pace, recalling the murderous looks in some of the shopkeepers' eyes during those hot-tempered Merchant Association meetings. All because they didn't believe thongs, brassieres, teddies, and peekaboo nighties belonged on our quaint, historic Main Street.

I pushed the thoughts away as I jogged past my office and glanced at the "purrs" sitting in the window—Caspurr, Coppurr, and Jaspurr. My three cats. I didn't stop to greet them by tapping on the glass, knowing they'd break into plaintive cries urging me to feed them. They're always ready for food, hungry or not. But they'd already eaten breakfast and washed down the kibble with water streaming from their kitty fountain.

Besides, I was anxious to stop by Pix's shop, Treasure's Trove of Lingerie, where the filming would already be in full swing. The level of hostility targeted at Pix remains a mystery since she possesses a sizeable collection of antique undergarments, and her most cherished pieces are displayed in her storefront window.

1

During the heated debates of whether to allow Pix's business to stand alongside the numerous antique shops, galleries, bookstores, and restaurants that line the street, Dolly Evans, the proprietor of the Tea Pot Shoppe wanted to run her out of town, while Chuck Stetson, the owner of the Chocolate Box, became her champion. The controversy finally dropped to a low simmer but had been newly resurrected by the hubbub surrounding the news of her lingerie shop being featured on *Lingerie Exposed*, a national TV show. The prospect of Hollywood invading the town caused both a thrill of excitement and a new resurgence of resentment toward Pix.

Or was it plain jealousy?

Who thought there'd be enough interest in women's underwear to produce a TV series, let alone a reality show? But apparently, the Hurrah Channel detected the void and obligingly filled it. The concept turned out to be spot on and caused a viewing sensation no one, I'm sure, ever imagined. Viewers couldn't wait to cast votes for their favorite lingerie shop to determine the series grand winner. A couple of months ago, a producer contacted Pix about showcasing her lingerie assortment on the program after reading her blog, *Sexy Nights in Victorian America*.

I slowed to a stop, shocked to see a crowd standing five deep and overflowing into the road that had been blocked off to vehicular traffic. I edged closer and caught a glimpse of Pix gesturing toward her window display. A bright-eyed blonde stood next to her. I wiggled through the cluster of onlookers ignoring the flicks of irritation springing to their faces. Chuck stood front and center. I guess he sensed the commotion, glanced in my direction, threw out his arm like a lifeline, and pulled me up front.

I'd seen the lingerie program a couple of times after Pix received the news of her upcoming segment and wondered if maybe her favorites, mainly historical pieces, would fit in with the show's usual Frederick's of Hollywood fare. I tapped my foot, a habit that rose from impatience, as I scrutinized the immaculately arrayed host. Her tightly-fit designer suit, her dewy make-up, and her shiny blonde hair upswept into a stylish chignon. Her voice, however, didn't match her appearance with its low, droning quality lacking even the smallest tidbit of fervor, or even interest, I suspected narrowing my eyes. I chewed my lip, trying to recall her name, but for the life of me, it'd totally slipped my mind. Continuing my assessment, she stood shorter than I'd imagined. If we stood side by side, I'd tower over her. But Pix and the host paired nicely, standing nearly at eye level. Hence my friend's nickname, Pix, short for Pixie. Treasure is a mouthful of a name, and I thought her sobriquet suited her perfectly.

"Obviously, lingerie is your passion. But why this old-fashioned stuff?" Lines wrinkled the interviewer's flawless forehead.

Pix frowned, but then her face brightened. "Once you take a closer look, I bet you'll become a fan too. I love them because of the fine workmanship, the lush, sensual feel of the fabrics, and of course for the mystique that maybe those Victorians weren't as uptight as we envision."

"But it isn't exactly daring, now, is it?"

"Not by our standards," Pix said. "I have plenty of daring for you to see inside the shop. But these exquisite examples, dating from before the Industrial Revolution, get my heart pounding."

The confusion crossing the blonde's face told me she wasn't the sharpest. Pix didn't seem to notice as she chattered on. "About five years ago, when I was still in art school, I saw my first old time-hot time nighty, as I refer to them." A slight blush of color rose to her cheeks. "It was then the collecting bug bit me, and I was hooked. I spent hours searching dusty attic trunks and musty basements, auction houses, and antique stores—clear across the country—to build my one-of-a-kind collection of eighteenth to early twentieth-century unmentionables." She made a pair of air quotes.

"Sounds like an unusual kind of treasure hunt."

"An intriguing search for examples of nearly forgotten women's under apparel. And I learned a lot. For example, bone-framed corsets not only trained the female form but acted as back supports. Centuries ago, household chores were grueling. Lugging buckets of water from wells, churning butter, and scrubbing floors took a toll on the body. Corsets helped alleviate shoulder and back pain. Before the 16th-century, women wore corsets from childhood until their wedding night. The groom would undo up to fifty tight laces to demonstrate self-control before consummating the marriage."

"Hmm." The host narrowed her eyes.

"I have an amazing collection of Victorian underclothing. Under their frocks, women wore chemises, knee-length drawers, corsets, stockings, corset covers, short horse-haired crinolines, and three or more ankle-length petticoats." Pix motioned toward a lacy garment that resembled a frilly summer top with a line of buttons down the front. "The Victorian lady who owned this corset cover must've had plenty of leisure time to embroider tiny rosettes in a matching ivory-colored thread. The purpose of the corset cover—"

"Thanks for the history lesson, but my viewers are interested in today's lingerie."

"Of course."

I noticed a flick of irritation cross Pix's face. She could go on for hours about her collection and didn't like being interrupted.

"The corset evolved into the bra, girdle, and body shaper," Pix continued. "And interestingly enough, the corset is making a comeback today," Pix continued. "My aim was to display my antiques juxtaposed with current lingerie. But I had no idea where to showcase my treasures. My BFF suggested I set up shop here."

I swallowed hard. Pix wasn't going to place the blame on me. Not on national TV.

"Then quite a brouhaha developed," the host said. She raised her neatly arched eyebrows as a smile tugged at the corners of her mouth.

"I should've seen it coming. Instead, I was blindsided. Bayleys Landing was founded in 1772, so I thought there couldn't be a more ideal location for my business. But a lingerie boutique didn't align with some of the merchants' narrow attitudes." For a split second, she glared at Dolly Evans, who pressed against me. But then Pix's face lit up.

"Becca!" Pix stepped toward me. "This is my friend who encouraged me to share my eclectic assortment of lingerie with the public."

The cameraman turned in my direction.

"No." I shrieked. "I've been running. I'm a mess."

"Don't be ridiculous," the host said. "Most women would sacrifice their first-born to look like you after jogging."

I opened my mouth to object, but before I could utter a sound, she continued.

"I've got a fantastic idea." She pointed her well-manicured hand in my direction. "I want you to go to the corner and jog toward us." The blonde pursed her lips for a second. "Wait a minute. Do you have one of those bicycles with a wicker basket attached to the handlebars? And a puppy. A puppy in the basket. That'll be the perfect prop to create a homey, small-town effect."

"I have a mountain bike. And cats. Three of them."

"Oh, no. That won't do. Let's stick with the original plan." The host glanced at a man standing next to the guy with the camera. "The jogger has opened up a new angle I'd like to pursue."

He shrugged and then half-nodded.

"Wait a minute," I protested. "I don't think so. No." If I was ever going to be on television, I'd insist on, at the very least, a smattering of lip gloss and a cute outfit—not a pair of smelly sweats.

"Come on, Becca. It'll be fun. Plus, you'll be able to put in a plug for your businesses. A nationwide plug." Pix paused a second. "Please?"

"Oh, all right." I surrendered against my better judgment and marched down the street.

When I reached the corner about twenty-five feet away, I began to run toward them.

"Whoa. Wait for the signal." I heard a male voice yell in my direction.

As I hustled back to the corner, I remembered the interviewer's name. Mindy Marks . . . a.k.a. Mostly Mechanical, for the way she drones on like a machine. Proud of my clever observation, I smirked, shifting from one foot to the other, waiting for a woman with flaming red hair to finish primping Ms. Marks. With one last swipe of the powder puff, the make-up lady slipped away, and Mindy refocused on Pix. I strained to hear what they were saying but couldn't make out a single word.

"Cut," a booming voice sounded. I guessed it belonged to the director. He moved toward me with his hands waving and his bald head reflecting the shine from the early morning sun. "You missed your cue. Pay attention. We're gonna have to retake the scene."

"Sorry," I mumbled as my face grew hot. I didn't know the first thing about cues and retakes. "This wasn't my idea. How 'bout I just bow out." I pressed my lips together, remembering how important this opportunity was for Pix. If the shoe was on the other foot, she'd do it with a big smile and not a word of protest. "Won't happen again."

This time I kept my eyes peeled on the director. When he pointed at me, I took off. I gradually slowed as I approached the two women.

"Mindy, look who's here. My friend Rebecca Flynn. If it wasn't for her, Treasure's Trove of Lingerie would still be a pipedream." Pix pointed to the gold letters stenciled on the shop's window. "By the way, her business is right down the street. Flynn Investigations and Photography Studio."

"An unusual combination." Mindy shook her pert head.

"Not really," I said. "You'd be surprised how important a good photographer is in this field. As a private investigator—"

"There's a bit of detecting I'm interested in." Mindy pinned me with a pair of skeptical green eyes. "I bet you're wearing hot, sexy lingerie underneath that sweatsuit. Why don't we step inside and take a peek?"

CHAPTER TWO

An hour after the lingerie shoot wrapped up for the day, I waited for Pix at the work table in her store's backroom while she prepared tea in the adjoining kitchenette. It would've been hard to ignore the crystal vase stocked full of long-stemmed yellow roses in the middle of the table. Without a second thought, I lifted the florist card lying on top of a stack of invoices. I recognized the elegant hand, distinctive with its great flourish of curly cues. Chuck Stetson offered her sincere wishes that she'd break a leg. I couldn't help but chuckle seeing the smiley face he'd added under his name. That man has it hard for her, I thought with a shake of my head. I replaced the card as Pix entered, carrying a bamboo tray holding a ceramic tea pot, two mugs, and a plate of gingersnaps.

"Sorry I took so long." She set the tray down and filled the cups with green tea. "Peter called." She withdrew her cellphone from the back pocket of her black, skinny jeans and placed it on the table.

It still startled me that Pix calls her parents by their first names. "So, what's the news from Beverly Hills?"

"Montecito. They sold the Beverly Hills house last year to a

7

movie director." Pix said with a shrug. "Peter invited me to spend a few weeks at the commune he started when he was a hippie."

"A hippie?"

"I thought for sure I'd told you about that?"

"Peter being a hippie, I would've remembered."

"It wasn't that unusual. Back then, a lot of kids, not only rich ones, turned their backs on the establishment. It was all about love and peace. But to Peter's credit, Harmony Vista is still a thriving organic farming commune. My parents used to take me there during the summers when I was a kid. It was fun—that is until I got bored with the whole thing. Plus, the place is crawling with bugs. Worms, bees, flies, gnats, ants, mosquitos." She scrunched up her face. "Mosquitos are the worst."

"Is that where he met your mom?"

She shook her head. "That happened after he started up EnviroTech."

"Your mom always looks great. Brenda can't be as old as your—"

"No. Peter's a lot older. When they got married at HV, Harmony Vista, he was forty-seven, and Brenda was twenty-three. I was four."

"Whoa. Your mom was nineteen when you were born?"

"Yeah. A teen-age mother. But Peter hired a nanny to help her out."

"Do you remember the wedding?"

"If it wasn't for the DVD, I probably wouldn't. I watched it the last time I was home. It wasn't a typical wedding. Definitely New Age."

"Oh?"

"For starters, a shaman performed the ceremony. He knotted Peter and Brenda's hands together with a red velvet ribbon, symbolizing their love would always remain passionate. The guests sat around the three of us in a circle as sage sticks burned and filled the air with the smell of burning weed." Pix wrinkled her nose. "But, I guess, burning the herb was important. The sage ritual cleansed my parents from all their past relationships."

I nodded, pretending I understood.

"I'll never forget now beautiful my mother looked with her blonde hair flowing around her shoulders and a braided ring of flowers encircling her head. Her pure silk, A-line dress was pale blue, soft and creamy." A hint of a smile crossed her face. "Brenda had slipped her lucky crystal into her bustier before the ceremony and told me that was to be our little secret."

"Lucky crystal?"

"You know how Brenda is into spiritual energy."

"Uh-huh." I wasn't surprised by Pix's description of her parents' wedding. Their spirituality was based on ecology, the environment, flora and fauna—whatever you wanted to call it—and at times, they came across as a bit unconventional. And being a typical child, as Pix searched for her own identity, she'd rejected most of their nonconformist outlook.

"Brenda and I had a long talk the other night," Pix said. "She was able to calm my nerves about the interview. And all along, she was right that I'd do fine. But I guess all moms know how to make their kids feel better."

"I guess," I said under my breath.

"My parents are looking forward to getting back to nature, if only for a little while. Brenda is thrilled about teaching the HV residents yoga and meditation. That's her passion."

"You're going with them?"

"I'm tempted. But the thought of all those mosquitos." She narrowed her eyes. "It's so basic there. I doubt there's even Wi-Fi."

"All the more reason. You'd be able to spend quality time with your folks."

"I'd have a better time with them at their chalet in Switzerland. The skiing there is phenomenal."

"You're nothing but a spoiled rich girl."

Pix frowned.

"I'm only kidding."

She waved the air in front of her face.

"Look," I said, "We're close as sisters. I know when

something's wrong." I couldn't resist, so I blurted, "What's bugging you?" I figured that would bring a smile but instead, she frowned again.

"It's the thin man. He was here during the filming." She lifted a gingersnap, took a bite, and chewed slowly.

I tried not to but couldn't help rolling my eyes. Ever since she started hanging around the small group of volunteer guides who conduct evening ghost tours, she'd become convinced the ghost of Robert Sullivan, a Union soldier who went AWOL during the Battle of Fredericksburg, has a thing for her.

His ghost supposedly roams the doorsteps and front porches of Main Street because he'd been shot to death in a botched escape from the provost marshals who were escorting him to a court-martial hearing. Shot on the staircase of the Old Railroad Hotel, circa 1847, that now houses Anna's Antiques.

Even if it's true, and I'm certainly not sold on the idea, could a ghost have a crush on a living, breathing, vivacious young entrepreneur? Namely Pix?

Or is it, I considered, that Pix needs constant male attention including dead guys. Isn't it enough that just about every man in town is gaga over her? It might be catty, but I think Pix isn't happy unless some guy has the hots for her so she can string him along with her constant flirting—only to drop him like a hot potato.

I took a long sip of tea as I eyed her. I've known Pix for nearly eight years since rooming together at the Maryland Institute College of Art. She'd been a fiber major, and I doubled majored in painting and photography. Enrolling there had been the best decision I ever made. It offered me the chance to not only develop my art skills but sort out my mess of a life.

Directly out of high school, I'd impulsively married the first guy who paid attention to me. Drop-dead handsome with startling blue eyes you could lose yourself in, he was older, had been married before, and worked—occasionally. Down on the docks. But dammit, he was magnetic. Could charm the skin off a snake and promised me the world. What I got was three years of breaking my neck trying to make a home for us while I waitressed at Hooters. I became suspicious about how he was spending his jobless days. So I started following him. The funny thing, he never suspected I was on his tail, snapping pictures of him with his numerous lovers. That's when I got a germ of an idea that I'd make a crackerjack PI.

I left him and started the divorce process but never followed through. I couldn't face up to my failings of choosing a loser for a husband. In the end, it didn't matter. A couple of years later, the cops fished his body out of the harbor. Probably pissed off a jealous husband.

Where I'd struggled to make ends meet waitressing and working at an art supply store, Pix suffered no financial angst due to the generosity of her ultra-rich parents. Despite her privileged life and the age difference (I'm nearly thirty and she's twenty-five) we clicked and have been best buds since our first meeting.

I cleared my throat. "It's hard to swallow that a hundred-and fifty-year-old ghost is infatuated with you. Or any ghost, for that matter."

"Can I help it if men are drawn to me? Even dead ones."

I sighed. Men found Pix irresistible. Doe-like eyes, pouty lips, perfect figure, and her sexy walk wasn't the only reason men fell for her. She had the talent to make them feel they were the most important person in the world. As is every word slipping through their teeth was a revelation. "I think it's high time we get to the bottom of this. I am a private investigator, after all."

The tension touching Pix's jaw faded as she tucked a strand of long, golden hair behind her ear.

"Tell me about him, um, this Civil War deserter, Robert Sullivan."

"You already know I've nicknamed him the thin man because there doesn't seem to be much to him. He's like . . . like transparent, but I can't see through him. It's kinda hard to explain since I'm no ghost expert. After all, Robert Sullivan is the first one I've ever seen. But he's not like the typical ghost you hear about dressed in white. In fact, his clothing is dark.

A blue jacket with red piping, two military stripes, brass

buttons, and a cream-colored collarless shirt. The pants look felted. Must be wool."

I wasn't the least surprised that Pix had focused foremost on the types of fabrics used for the ghost's ensemble.

"He has wavy, almost curly ebony hair, and he's beardless but has a thick stubble like he hasn't shaved for a couple of days. It's his eyes that strike me the most. They're cerulean blue and look sad."

"Hmmm. Sad eyes." I reached into my oversized leather tote and pulled out a notebook. I unhooked the pen, flipped to a clean sheet of paper, and jotted down Pix's depiction of Robert Sullivan. I knew full well the description could've belonged to an actor she saw last night on the classic movie channel. Old movies were another of Pix's passions.

"You saw him today during the filming."

"Uh-huh." She reached for another gingersnap but let her hand drop. "I caught a glimpse of him when I was showing Mindy that slinky tiger-print teddy. It's hard to believe it's synthetic." She shrugged. "Anyway, he was in his usual spot by the door staring at me with those sad eyes."

"I'll ask around town. Maybe someone else has seen him." I closed the notebook and dropped it into my bag.

"If you happen to dig up a medium, please, have that person give the thin man a message—leave me the hell alone."

"What did you think of Mindy?" I said, changing the conversation as I reached for a cookie and took a bite. It crumbled onto my lap. I scooped up the pieces and placed them onto a paper napkin.

"If she really loves lingerie, I can't imagine why she wasn't blown away by my antique collection."

"I never get tired of looking at your corsets. Thank God we don't have to wear those torturous body shapers. Give me spandex any day." I lifted the tea pot and topped off my mug. "Mindy did perk up a little when you showed her that see-through lace teddy."

"It still amazes me the show's a hit with a host like Mindy Marks," Pix said.

"That credit probably belongs to the production crew and editors who must do a ton of revising. Not Mindy."

"Probably considers it a stepping stone to something bigger. But I doubt Mindy's gonna go far with that deadpan personality of hers."

"I was thinking the same thing." I raised my cup and took a quick sip. "Mindy better make sure they delete that crack she made about what I was wearing under my sweats."

"If she had actually taken a peek, she would've been disappointed."

"Can I help it if I'm practical?" I ran a hand over my lap and smoothed a wrinkle from my faded jeans.

"One day you'll find the man of your dreams. Then I won't be able to keep you out of my store."

I didn't want to go there. My relationships with men since my ill-fated marriage had left something to be desired.

I chewed my lip, hating my unnerving habit of being attracted to the same kind of man as my ex. All good looks and empty promises. *Mister Right won't be all about himself but will appreciate my talents and consider me an equal partner—oh, and of course, love me. But where to find a guy like that?*

I chased the thought away by focusing on Pix. "Speaking of your store, I think she was more impressed with your decorating skills than the lingerie. But who wouldn't be since your showroom resembles a room taken straight from a royal palace."

Pix shrugged. "I've ordered a magnificent chandelier. It's supposed to be delivered in a few days." She placed her mug on top of the table and glanced at the Rolex encircling her wrist.

"Oh, my gosh. If I don't get going, I'll be late for dinner."

"With Chuck?"

"The cute camera guy. Nick Rizzo. Didn't you notice him?"

"I noticed him. But aren't you and Chuck on for your usual Monday, karaoke night, at the pub?"

"I can do something else if I want to. It's not written in stone that I have to be with Chuck every Monday night. We're not a couple, after all." She raised her eyebrows.

"He's crazy about you." I gestured to the roses.

"You know how I always keep things light—airy—no commitments. Chuck knows that, too. Besides, I think you're reading way too much into it."

I doubted Chuck looked at their relationship that way. Unlike the Main Street guys who worn their hearts on the sleeves around Pix, Chuck's interest in her seemed grounded. Real in fact.

"I'd hate to disappoint him, though. Maybe you can take my place?" She pressed her lips together. "Nick is headed to Miami tomorrow, and tonight is the only time we can hook up."

I spied the pleading look filling her eyes. "Oh, all right."

"You're a lifesaver." Pix jumped up and grabbed her cellphone from the table. "I'll call Chuck and tell him I'm worn out from all the show stuff. That I'm not up to singing." She tapped the phone's screen. "By the way, Nick and I are dining at the Tiber Bistro so don't stop there for a late-night supper."

"I draw the line at karaoke. Tell him to come over here for dinner. Chuck likes my cooking. I baked lasagna last night and have plenty of leftovers."

"Thanks, Becca. You're the best."

"Yeah, yeah," I said under my breath. But if Pix was serious about them being only buddies, that left the field open for me. After all, there has to be some truth in the old proverb that the best way to a man's heart is through his stomach. And lucky for me, I'm a damn good cook.

CHAPTER THREE

The cats greeted Chuck as he stepped into my apartment. They brushed around his legs, their little voices squeaking with pleasure. He stared straight ahead, didn't stoop to pat them or reach into his pocket, as usual, to drop a handful of their favorite treats onto the floor. In fact, his shoulders slumped, his ever-ready smile hadn't surfaced, and the sparkle was missing from his eyes. Something major must've happened. My first inclination was that sales at the Chocolate Box had slackened. But that couldn't be since his patronage continues to be robust ever since opening his doors three years ago. Then it hit me. Pix. She was the cause of his dampened spirit and glum mood.

"Thanks for inviting me to dinner. But really, it wasn't necessary," he said.

"Don't be silly. Come in and take a load off."

He handed me the bottle that had been nestled in the crook of his arm.

I noticed the label. "Perfect choice for Italian."

Chuck attempted a smile. His lips turned upward, but then fell flat. I grabbed his arm and walked him through my tiny entrance into the living area. I left him by the sofa where Jaspurr had jumped with his bushy tail high like a flag, his eyes bright, and his purr motoring. The long-haired red and white cat has always been his favorite. I suspected Chuck would drop onto the couch and give Jaspurr a good belly rub. I didn't stop to watch but continued to the kitchen at the end of the room.

I don't live in one of those trendy, open-space lofts, all airy and light-filled. Truth is, I reside in a four hundred and seventy-five-square-foot studio apartment. Everything is in one room—including my bed, a Murphy that lifts up into the wall. Faux cabinets camouflage the closed-up bed and offer the illusion of a generous amount of storage space. A large window above the kitchen sink is the main source of natural light and provides a view of lush greenery thanks to the assortment of locust, beech, and oak trees beyond the Tiber's rock-laden stream.

But instead of schmoozing with Jaspurr, Chuck followed and pulled out one of my dinette chairs. He plopped down and folded his hands on the table's Formica top.

"Dinner should be ready in a jiff." The aroma of garlic bread, still warming in the oven, filled the air as I ripped a piece of romaine into bite-size pieces. "I think an O's game is on TV. If you want to watch it while I finish up in here, be my guest."

"Becca. I want you to be completely honest."

The serious tone of his usual breezy voice startled me. I dropped the lettuce leaf and faced him.

"What's wrong with me?" A forlorn look covered his face.

"Wrong?"

"On my way to Bacchus Wines, I walked past the Tiber Bistro. I saw Pix with some guy all cozy at the table in the window."

Dammit. I bit my lip, trying to come up with something. I decided to try the truth.

"Oh, him. He's the cameraman with the lingerie show."

"Don't tell me, she wanted to discuss if he'd captured her in just the right light?"

"Of course not." I couldn't believe he was acting like a hurt little boy instead of grown man around my age. I reached into an upper cabinet and removed two wine glasses. I placed them on my fake wood countertop and took a step closer to him. "I would've guessed by now you figured out that Pix is an insatiable flirt. In all the time I've known her, she's only had one significant relationship and that, well—"

"She has to know I'm serious about her."

"She likes you."

"I supported her. Fought that rabid pack at the Bayleys Landing Merchant Association." "She appreciates all you've done."

"Then why isn't she interested in a relationship?"

I was stumped. Not only was Chuck Stetson outgoing, thoughtful, and funny; he was a total hottie. Tall, jet-black hair, and worked out in the gym almost every day. I often reminded myself that he was a chocolatier, not a model for Jockey underwear.

"In all honesty, I don't know." The timer buzzed, signaling the bread was ready. I stepped over to the oven, grabbed a potholder, and removed the sheet tray. Then I slipped the foil-covered Pyrex dish stuffed with lasagna inside.

When I turned back to Chuck, I noticed Jaspurr had nestled into his lap. He combed his long fingers through the cat's fur.

"That Nick person doesn't mean anything to Pix. I think she just wants to be hospitable, you know, to a fellow Californian."

Good God, did I really say that?

"The most I've ever gotten from Pix is a quick peck on the cheek. Am I doing something wrong?"

"Of course not." I cracked open the oven door and guessed the lasagna needed at least twenty-five minutes to warm. I slammed the door shut, set the timer, and moved back to the salad. "I know you're going to hate this, but Pix considers you a friend—well, more like the big brother she never had." I dumped the Tupperware containers filled with chunks of tomatoes, red pepper, and onion on top of the romaine. "The way you stood up against all those negative forces and defended her—she looks up to you—admires you." After a quick sprinkle of Italian dressing, I tossed the colorful mixture. "Sometimes friendship can be better than a romance. Usually lasts longer," I said, facing Chuck."

"My intentions aren't brotherly."

The little voice in my head told me I'd said enough. I didn't want to spend the entire evening talking about Chuck's hurt feelings or Pix's intentions. Why in heaven's name wasn't he interested in me? *What am I anyway, a piece of chopped liver? Mirrors don't crack when I look into them.* I pressed my lips together, determined to shift the subject away from my fickle friend and maybe spark his interest—in me.

"I can't wait to tell you about the cat show last weekend. Your little pal there"—I jutted my chin at the cat in his lap—"placed best in show." I pulled apart the foil-covered bread and arranged half of the loaf inside a napkin-lined basket. With the bread in one hand the salad bowl in the other, I walked toward Chuck.

He rose, took the salad bowl from me, and placed it in the center of the table. I handed him the breadbasket and proceeded to chat about a cute incident from the cat show as I laid the place settings and poured the wine. "You would've died laughing the way Jaspurr was trying to get the judge's attention. Every time she paused in front of his cage, he poked out his paw and tapped her. It was hilarious. He couldn't wait to get on the judging bench and show off. That's what earned him that," I motioned toward the wall where I'd hung Jaspurr's latest satin ribbon rosette. I hoped to get a chuckle from him and, at the very least, a smile. But no.

"You know, Becca, sometimes I wish to God, we were a couple."

I held my breath.

"You're talented—an amazing painter. And a huge sports fan. Your job isn't easy, but you work hard to uncover the truth—no matter what obstacles are in your way. Those are just a few of the things I admire about you. You're a terrific woman."

Is he hinting that we should start dating?

"I get it that you don't want me to get my hopes up about Pix," he said. "But no matter how unrealistic my quest to capture Pix's love might be—I can't give up. I'm crazy about her."

I exhaled.

"Look, Chuck," I said. "You'll feel a heck of a lot better once you've eaten. Then we can relax and catch the end of the ballgame. I've got plenty of snacks, and there's beer in the fridge."

"That's what I mean. You're real. Authentic. Nothing like that stuck-up host of *Lingerie Exposed.* You're the best buddy a guy like me could ask for." He scooped up a plateful of salad.

"Plus, you're the best cook I know."

Great, I thought. *So much for romance.*

CHAPTER FOUR

As I hustled along Main Street, it seemed crazy that I planned to interview my fellow business associates about a ghost. Before even attempting to begin such an idiotic pursuit, I needed a strong cup of coffee. The best place to get one was at the Hot and Chilly Bean, renowned for their piping hot brew as well as their array of flavored iced coffees. As I raced eastward, I paused at Pix's shop window and wondered how her date had turned out last night.

"Rebecca."

I glanced away from the familiar window display and settled on the pastor of St. Paul the Apostle Church. In an attempt to offer the sixtyish, gray-headed priest a smile, I wound up frowning instead. This ghost thing was starting to bug me. "Father McCarthy. Good morning."

"Sure to be another glorious April day."

I noticed a well-worn theology book wedged under his arm and a Styrofoam cup from the Hot and Chilly Bean in his hand. I cleared my throat. "Lots of sunshine, I understand." I paused long enough to make a split-second decision. "There's something I've been wondering about and hoped, um, well, ah . . ." As I hemmed

21

and hawed, his smile faded, and concern filled his warm, brown eyes. "What exactly is the Church's take on ghosts?"

"Ghosts. Why do you ask?"

I waved my hand, gesturing to the buildings lining the street. "I've heard stories. I'd really appreciate an authoritative spin on the whole idea of disembodied spirits."

He pointed toward the nearby pocket park. "The way I see it, people want to believe in ghosts for a simple reason. They provide proof of the immortality of the human soul." We neared the small pedestrian bridge that spanned the Tiber Creek and stopped at a bench dappled with spots of shade cast by the budding foliage of an old oak tree.

"It's all wishful thinking then?"

"Church teaching doesn't rule out the possibility of ghosts or that we might be allowed to see them." He sat down on the park bench. "Of course, the Bible offers some clues." He took a quick sip from the cup then placed it on the bench. "In fact, I recently read something that might help satisfy your curiosity on the subject."

Father McCarthy freed the book and began to thumb through the pages browned with age. I sat on the bench's edge.

"Now, where is that passage?" He spoke as if talking to himself, so I remained silent.

"Ah, here it is." He tapped the page with his index finger. "This insight is from one of the most influential theologians of the twentieth century. Karl Rahner, S.J."

My interest piqued by the possibility that a Jesuit scholar could be an expert in the realm of ghosts.

Father McCarthy took another sip of coffee, cleared his throat, and began reading. "*The great mistake of many people is to imagine that those whom death has taken, leave us. They do not leave us. They remain! Where are they?*" He glanced from the page and swept his hand through the air separating us. "*In the darkness? Oh, no.*" He shook his head. "Now, this is the important piece. *It is we who are in the darkness. We do not see them, but they see us. Their eyes radiant with glory, are fixed upon our eyes.*" He paused long enough to fix his eyes on me and then continued reading. *"Though invisible to us, our dead are not absent. They are living near us transfigured into light and power and love."* He said the last sentence without looking at the printed words. "So, Rebecca. There's no reason to be concerned about spirits roaming our quaint Main Street. No reason, at all."

The idea of dead people, no matter how transformed with their eyes glued on me, creeped me out. That was until I thought of my parents, and I could almost feel their presence surrounding me with love. Though they had been gone for sixteen years, died when their sailboat capsized in the Chesapeake after being hit by a rogue wave during a squall, I still mourned the loss of them.

"Thank you, Father. You've been a big help." I hesitated a second. "It is possible for people to see ghosts, isn't it?"

He ran his fingers through his thick, wavy hair and shrugged. "Perhaps."

I chewed my lip, wondering if I should ask him the niggling question in the back of my mind. After a quick breath, I let the words escape through my lips, "I guess it would be unusual for a ghost to have romantic feelings like, um—a crush on somebody who is living."

Father McCarthy closed his book. A smile began to form, but he pressed his lips together, squelching it. "That would be highly unlikely. Impossible, I think." He stood and brushed a speck of lint off his black suit coat. "Don't forget about Friday's fish dinner in the church hall. I hope to see you and Treasure there. We can always use an extra couple of volunteers in the kitchen."

"Haven't missed one yet. We'll be there."

With a quick nod, he stood and sauntered through the park toward Tiber Alley. I leaned back on the bench and closed my eyes. I guess there'd be no harm investigating this mysterious ghost of Robert Sullivan. That is until I get a real job. I sighed, hoping it would be soon because I'd just mailed off my undercover surveillance notes and photos for a suspected adultery case that hadn't turned out the way the husband hoped. His wife was guilty as sin. He'd been my most recent client, and except for a scheduled photoshoot of the upcoming historic Designer House, I was plumb out of assignments.

Determined to get to the bottom of this ghost business, I stood and stepped away from the bench. There was no better place to start than at the source of the original crime. I stopped at the corner of Laureate Avenue, where I had a bird's eye view of the Old Railroad Hotel. It stood a solid rectangle, four stories high, with its blue-gray granite façade made from blocks of stone for which Bayleys Landing was famous. Black wooden shutters flanked each window.

I waited for the traffic to thin as vehicles crawled along, no doubt, trying to spy a vacant parking space on the narrow street. A town built in the mid-eighteenth century had no need for parking areas and multi-leveled garages. The two parking lots, the most popular one sat behind the firehouse, were small and usually filled up by nine in the morning. I stepped off the curb, and after checking both directions, jogged across the street. After only a second of hesitation, I pulled open the door of the former hotel and stepped into the antique shop.

"Good morning." Anna Fischer looked up from her desk with a smile that faded when she saw me. "Can I help you find something, Becca?"

"They're gorgeous." I pointed to a pair of Chinese vases.

"Nineteenth-century Cantonese. Priced to sell at seven thousand dollars. Are you interested?"

I swallowed hard. "I'd love to buy them, but—"

"I see." Anna focused on the opened magazine on her desk.

"I stopped by to ask you some questions. About the ghost."

Anna jerked her head up with narrowed eyes. "Ghost?"

"Robert Sullivan." I noticed the muscle along her jaw tighten. "Pix, um, Treasure Winslow has noticed him outside her shop."

"She does have a magnificent collection of Civil War-era undergarments displayed in her window. Perhaps they remind him of his wife."

"There really is a ghost?"

"Of course there is." She nodded, and the tight silver curls framing her plump face bounced.

"You haven't told him to leave?"

"Why would I do that? After all, we're famous for our ghosts. People flock to Bayleys Landing because of the ghosts, and once they arrive, well, they shop for antiques. I have no qualms with Robert Sullivan or any of the other spirits that roam along our lanes and byways." She paused a second. "They're good for business."

"Have you seen him?"

"Not exactly. No."

"Then how do you know he exists?"

"Does that really matter? As long as people believe he exists is what counts." Anna rose and stepped next to an occasional table with a marquetry inlay. She ran her fingertips along its polished surface. "As you said, Treasure has seen him. That proves it."

My right temple began to throb. I really needed that cup of coffee.

"Now," Anna said, brushing an imaginary speck from her floral printed blouse, "is there anything I can show you?"

I shook my head and edged toward the door. "Thanks," I mumbled and exited.

With quick strides, I hurried to the coffee shop. I pulled open the door, and a riot of aromas pervaded my nostrils—smoky, nutty, herbal, and fruity—truly an olfactory celebration. I moved to the counter and considered my options. I couldn't make up my mind between the house blend and the spiced chocolate espresso. So, I decided on hot chocolate with whipped cream.

The shop could only accommodate eight rectangular tables with seating arrangements of four matching chairs. To my surprise, there was one empty table. With my eyes focused on the mug, determined not to spill a single drop, I pulled out a chair and eased into it. I stirred the rich cream into the velvety smooth chocolate and took a swallow. A rush of comforting warmth engulfed me as the creamy liquid slid down my throat. *Ambrosia.* I raised the cup again. This time I took only a sip, deciding to nurse the drink as I tried to figure out my next move. The longer I sat, the more I realized apprehending a ghost would be like trying to pour the ocean into a child's sand pail. It didn't really matter what Anna Fischer said. She'd agree that Spiderman lived in her storeroom if it would sell more of her antiques. Robert Sullivan is most likely a shadow or a reflection on the glass window.

Giving up on the tiny sips, I gulped a couple mouthfuls of the chocolatey liquid. I glanced into the chunky mug, and the remains of the drink barely covered the bottom. I considered buying another but nixed the idea. I certainly didn't need the extra calories. I'm not overweight or even a bit pudgy, but I understand my weaknesses, which include every imaginable type of simple carb and sugar, primarily in the form of chocolate. Candy, frostings, cake, ice cream, puddings, pies—dark, milk, or white—it doesn't matter as long as it's chocolate.

I did my best to drain the cup by pulling my head back so far that I was staring at the *fleur de lis* ceiling. I placed the empty mug on the table, but I lingered to study the plafond. The burnt caramel and gold pressed tin tiles seemed to belong to an earlier time, and I wondered if the ceiling was original to the shop's Victorian structure. Or added later because of its cool design. I shrugged, crumpled my napkin, and dropped it into the empty mug.

A chair bumped into the back of mine. I scooted closer to the table, but the chair hit me again, this time only harder. Usually, I don't pay attention because of the close quarters in the coffee shop but banging into my chair twice seemed too much. I was about to turn and say something rude but pressed my lips together, knowing I'd regret the angry words later.

I stood and was about to leave when a testy, irritated voice rose above the shop's steady hum of conversation. A voice I recognized. Dolly Evans. I dropped back into my seat, glanced over my shoulder, and spotted the back of her head. I hadn't noticed her entering the shop and figured she'd slipped inside when I was focused on the ceiling's intricate design. I leaned closer and did what came naturally. I eavesdropped.

"I don't know what the devil's gotten into Chuck Stetson," Dolly's voice rang. "He was always *so* personable, *so* polite, and the Chocolate Box his signature pride and joy. Until she showed up with her trashy lingerie and mothy, musty relics. Her vulgar collection of underthings doesn't belong here. And quite frankly, I'm willing to do almost anything to run her out-of-town lock, stock, and barrel."

Though I strained, I couldn't detect the response to Dolly's not so veiled threat. I reached deep into my tote bag and pulled out a compact, flipped it open, and positioned the mirror so I could see who else sat at the table. It took some doing since it's not as easy as they make it out to be in the movies. After a bit of shifting in my seat, I caught a glimpse of Dolly's tablemate. You could've knocked me over with a feather. It was Mindy Marks.

CHAPTER FIVE

I f possible, Mindy's polished look had taken on a higher gloss. I studied her from my new spot on the coffee shop's window seat as I clutched the latest edition of the Bayleys Landing Gazette and peeked over the top edge of the paper. Dressed in a pair of midnight blue silk crepe trousers and a satiny fuchsia blouse, her hair bounced around her shoulders. The blouse's bright color heightened her creamy, porcelain complexion. With a flash of jealousy, I took in her high-cheekbones, luminous wide-set eyes, and full pouty lips. No doubts about it. Mindy Marks was a bona fide, dyed in the wool, beauty. I forced myself to cease my appraisal of the lingerie host and frowned in mystification, wondering how she and Dolly Evans had become chummy overnight.

I glanced at my watch. Nearly half-past ten. Pix was sure to breeze into the Hot and Chilly Bean any minute. A notorious late riser, she always started her day with a latte at the counter where she could flirt with whichever young man happened to be working.

I gulped a mouthful of air and headed to the table occupied by the two women. As I approached, Dolly glanced in my direction. The half-smile playing on her lips went cold, as did her sky-blue eyes.

"So, you're the one responsible for bringing that underwear hawker into our lovely community. That tacky lingerie shop is all your fault."

Before I could utter a sound, Mindy began to add her two cents worth.

"Now, Dolly, don't get worked up. You can't expect a lady PI to realize that a lingerie shop could threaten the businesses on Main Street. First a lingerie shop, and before you know it, tattoo parlors will be springing up on every corner.

Dolly nodded in agreement.

That's ridiculous," I said.

I wouldn't be too sure about that," Mindy said, riveting her eyes on me. "Dolly is the president of the Merchants Association. It's her job to keep lowlife businesses out of Bayleys Landing."

Dolly thrust out her chin with a nod.

"And I understand," Mindy continued, "your little detective agency was only admitted because your office is located off Main Street." She raised a bottle of Perrier and emptied it into a glass. "I found your friend's shop interesting with its over-the-top decor, but even with that collection of old-timey underthings, maybe it isn't right for the town." Mindy's lips curled devilishly upward.

What in heaven's name has Dolly been feeding her? A boatload of horse manure, for sure.

"I should've been updated on the situation earlier," Mindy said. "Of course, I was aware of the opposing viewpoints about your friend's shop. But not how it has torn the town apart." She raised her glass and took a quick sip. "It's a good thing Dolly tracked me down after yesterday's shoot and gave me a full report on the ongoing crisis. This delicious bit of controversy will put a new spin on that rather boring segment. It'll add a much-needed bit of fireworks to the show."

"What do you mean?" I pulled out a chair and sat next to Dolly.

"Treasure hasn't told you?" Dolly twisted her stout body and fixed her eyes on me.

"Told me what?"

"Miss Winslow should be arriving any minute," Mindy said. "We'll be heading to the Tea Pot Shoppe for a debate about the possibility of shutting down Treasure's Trove of Lingerie for good. As the moderator, I'll keep things from getting too out of hand. We know how catty we woman can be when provoked." Mindy's eyes seemed to shine. "Who would've thought that lingerie could stir up an entire business community? It's just fantastic."

I glanced over Mindy's shoulder the moment Pix entered the coffee shop. She stepped next to the counter and offered a few words to Ralphie, the barista, before facing our table. She moved closer, and I noted she looked classy dressed in her favorite suit—the handmade one—and a hundred percent virgin wool. Her long hair was swept up into a sophisticated chignon, and her flawless makeup appeared natural and perfect as usual.

I jumped up and met her halfway. "What the heck is going on?"

"That old biddy, Dolly Evans, is what's going on. She's trying to turn a fluffy lingerie show into a battleground. She wants to air her hatred for me on national television."

"Maybe you should've said no." As the words slipped out, I realized my stupid comment wouldn't even register. Pix never—in all the time I've known her, at least—backed down from a dispute. Whether it be over receiving poor service to a slur about her favored political candidates or the extreme scenario of somebody trying to tell her how to live her life. With this recent hullabaloo, she'd been able to charm the local businessmen with her beauty and the women with her open and guileless personality. Well, a few of them. It was Chuck who basically won over the female business owners who opposed Treasure's Trove of Lingerie. All but Dolly Evans, that is. And now Mindy Marks, as Dolly's eager assistant, is salivating in anticipation of resurrecting the once hostile feud. But to what end? Pix has already been voted into the business community.

There was absolutely nothing Dolly could do about it, even if the disagreement was presented on a national scale.

"I know how to handle Mindy," Pix said. "Last night, Nick shared all the things that irritate her big time during an interview, like not kowtowing and definitely disagreeing with her.

Anyway, I think it's kind of stupid to rehash it. It's water under the bridge." She marched to the table leaving me standing quite alone in the middle of the now nearly deserted coffee shop.

~

I DECIDED, invited or not, to tag along. Pix needed the moral support. The walk to the Tea Pot Shoppe was icy silent, but mercifully short since the store is only two doors up from the Hot and Chilly Bean, wedged between the Tiber Bistro and the Hour of Roses, a florist shop. I checked my watch. I had planned to drop by the gallery where I'd recently had a one-woman show of my mostly plein air landscapes. That would have to wait. Being there for Pix was more important than an update on my sales.

Dolly stepped inside the Tea Pot Shoppe, followed by Mindy. Pix hesitated only a second, but long enough for me to squeeze her hand and offer a quick word of encouragement. Once inside, anticipation filled the air amid the displays of tea pots and delicate matching cups and saucers. Near the back wall a group of wrought iron tables and chairs sat adorned with lacy tablecloths and dainty bud vases, sprouting long-stemmed red roses. Every day between two and four, Dolly provides afternoon tea to her patrons. It was at one of these tables that the discussion between Pix and Dolly was to take place.

The store looked more like a Hollywood set with lights and camera in place. The only thing needed was for someone to shout, "Action." Except, I sensed something seemed off. The director and Mindy had their heads together, and their voices were so low I couldn't make out a single word.

I watched Dolly disappear into the small kitchen located off of the tiny tearoom area.

"Where's Nick?" Pix said, turning around in a tight circle.

"Nick?" I glanced at the camera stationed by the interview table.

"During dinner, he got a phone call from Mindy. She explained they were staying over for another half-day. That their flight had been rescheduled."

I scanned the store, a bit surprised that I hadn't noticed the cameraman was missing.

"I'd turned my phone off," Pix continued, "but after Nick told me about the change in plans, I checked my messages. Mindy had texted me. So, I contacted her and agreed to the interview."

"Seems like she was pretty certain that you'd agree—making new arrangements without consulting you."

"She betted on the fact that I'd want to defend my business. And she was right on target."

Dolly reemerged with a tray holding a bone china tea pot decorated with hand-painted cherry blossoms and a platter of scones. While in the kitchen, she'd popped on a wide-brimmed burgundy hat reminiscent of something the Queen of England would wear. Prim, proper, and precisely Dolly. The hat even matched the color of her rather stuffy dress with a lace ruffle around the neckline and wrists. With what seemed a welcoming smile, even though I honestly couldn't ever remember seeing her smile, Dolly announced that she was ready to begin the debate.

Mindy glanced at her for a second before turning back to the director, who had a cell phone pressed against his ear.

"We don't want the tea to get cold." Dolly moved near us. Not receiving a response, she narrowed her eyes and crossed her arms against her chest. She turned to me. "What's happening?"

I shrugged.

"And you call yourself an investigator." She huffed and moved next to Mindy.

I rolled my eyes.

Pix, now seated at the table, poured a cup of tea. Dolly frowned and waddled toward Pix. Obviously, the tea pot aficionado had her heart set on playing hostess.

The piercing siren of a police cruiser flying down the street startled me. I peered out of the gingham curtained window and watched two more patrol cars whizz by. Unlike nearby Baltimore, our little community was virtually crime-free. But when something did happen, the police were only too eager to respond, as if itching for something big to happen. Usually turned out to be nothing more than teenage mischief or a cat up a tree.

"There's a problem," Mindy said. "The cameraman hasn't arrived. David," she said pointing at the director, "is going to the inn where the production team spent the night to fetch Nick. Should take only a few minutes."

Though she tried to sound nonchalant, I picked up on her annoyance, which caused her brows to form a frown. The director hurried outside and headed westward toward the Candlestick Inn located on upper Main Street, about a half-mile away.

"Well then, there's no use wasting a good pot of tea," Dolly said. She hurried us to the back of the store like a mother hen.

Dolly and Mindy sat at the table with Pix, who held her half-full cup by its dainty handle. As the two women spoke in muted tones, Pix slammed the teacup onto its saucer. The clatter startled Dolly, who almost jumped out of her seat and didn't try to hide the scowl slashing her pudgy face. Pix grabbed one of the freshly baked strawberry scones and sashayed to the far end of the large room. I offered the perturbed women a shrug before joining Pix.

Antics like this that reminded me that Pix, an only child, had enjoyed a privileged upbringing and was used to getting her way. But she didn't usually act like a spoiled brat about to have a temper tantrum. Something bothered her beyond Dolly's stab at sabotage. Most likely, the tardy cameraman.

Pix nibbled at the confection with her eyes glued to the window. "Nick knew about this interview last night," she whispered, taking a step closer to me. "We even cut our date short because he wanted a good night's sleep. And he's not irresponsible or unreliable as those two are implying," she said, tossing her head in the direction of the tearoom. "He's really quite wonderful—

good looking—sexy actually, with a fun personality, and he loves his job. Nick, not being here doesn't make sense."

As the minutes ticked by, we kept a vigil by the window until David stepped through the doorway. "Nick's not there. The innkeeper said he didn't see him come in last night. He doesn't keep tabs on his customers, so we went to Nick's room. Hadn't been slept in."

"What?" Pix cried. "He headed back to the Candlestick around eight forty-five. We said goodnight at the upper parking lot before I left for home."

"You were with Nick last night?" Mindy jumped up from her seat and clutched her tiny waist.

"We had a date."

Mindy's lips thinned as she moved closer to Pix. "He knows he's not supposed to fraternize with the show's guests. God Almighty, I thought he was a professional, but instead, he's just a man who wants to get some."

"Wait a minute." Pix's voice rose. "Nick's not like that. I'm worried about him."

"Worried? Well, I'm worried too, since he's costing us plenty of money with his shenanigans. We would've had the interview wrapped up by now." Mindy glowered, checking her watch. "Our flight leaves in two hours. We have that shoot tomorrow in Miami."

"Mindy's right. We've gotta get going," David said.

"What about Nick?" A trace of confusion filled Pix's voice.

"I wouldn't be surprised if he's already at the airport. Probably forgot about this change in the schedule. Truthfully, he is a bit anal. Not very flexible."

The director scratched his bald head. I could tell he wasn't buying into Mindy's explanation.

Mindy faced Dolly and grabbed her hand. "Too bad we couldn't have our little debate.

I'll do my damnedest to reschedule it soon. Ta." She headed to the exit, but before she reached it the door flew open.

Chuck burst inside. His shirt and shorts were soaked, his shoes muddy, and bits of twigs clung to clothing. His eyes rested on me.

"What's wrong?" I asked.

"I was running along the Pawcattawaye River when I saw something floating in the water. Looked like a mannequin. But it wasn't." He twisted his neck in Mindy's direction. "A body." He paused and looked directly at Pix. "The cameraman."

CHAPTER SIX

I sat in my office and waited. My gut told me it wouldn't be for long. I reached into the beverage fridge near my desk and pulled out a bottled water. My eyes flicked around the room and settled on the framed photographs decorating the walls of the small but efficient workplace. They depicted scenes I'd shot of Bayleys Landings. Some displayed historical views like the Old Railroad Hotel and the African American Melodist church constructed in 1890. Others showed scenes of everyday life— Simon hanging a painting in the gallery, Dolly pouring tea in her shop, a couple looking at antiques through a store window.

I glanced at the framed photo near the corner of my desk. Duncan. The solid black old Tom belonging to my aunt. During those dark days, she tried to hide it, but I knew Aunt Marianne missed her sister with the same intensity that I mourned my parents' death. Her only goal had been to be there for me, and even if I tried, I couldn't have found a better surrogate mom. That's when Duncan became my shadow. Snuggling in my lap with his calming purrs and sandpapery kisses on my cheek. Duncan showed me how to smile again. I lifted the photograph and realized since my parents' death, there'd always been cats in my life. Even during my undergrad years with the clowder of feral kitties, I tended.

My sight wandered to the opposite wall and the photos of my purrs. The little furballs have the option of hanging out in the office or upstairs in the apartment since the door to the connecting staircase is always open. Most times, they show up wherever I am. I glanced around the room and wasn't surprised they'd joined me. Caspurr, my blue-eyed white domestic short-hair, lay curled up, asleep on the oak file cabinet next to my waning African violet. Jaspurr, likewise, slept on one of the two guest chairs flanking my desk. But Coppurr paced.

Even though he's Jaspurr's littermate, the two of them couldn't be more different.

Jaspurr, with his flowing, fluffy fur and bright wide eyes, knows he's beautiful and works it to full advantage at the local cat shows. He woos the judges by playing with their streamers, scratching the jute covered post, and facing the audience with an openly amused expression. He purrs and always makes sure to snuggle against the judge before being returned to his ring cage. Coppurr, on the other hand, is opinionated and demanding. He knows which judges he likes, and woe to the judges he doesn't—Coppurr screams his disapproval so emphatically the whole show hall can hear him. However, when he likes a judge, his sleek, muscled body extends artistically, so he can show off his perfect bulls-eye markings designating him a classic tabby.

Both cats are fiery red with white and have lime green eyes though Coppurr's almond-shaped ones always seem to be half-closed as if scrutinizing the situation to the nth degree. And that's what he was doing now. He crossed the floor, paused, lifted his head, and looked at me.

"Do you agree?" I eyed the cat with a nod. "The cameraman didn't fall into the river."

Coppurr concurred with a deep, gravelly purr.

"Especially since after saying goodnight to Pix, he headed for the inn. A good mile away from the river and in the opposite direction."

The purr grew louder.

"Foul play then."

Coppurr leaped into my lap. His little pink tongue tickled my cheek. I stroked his short, soft fur and smiled.

My office door swung open. In a blink of an eye, all three cats congregated at the feet of the visitor. My purrs are always the welcoming committee, no matter who walks through the door.

I didn't rise but leaned back in my swivel chair and folded my arms. "I had a feeling you'd show up sooner or later."

"Instead of a word of welcome, I get a pronouncement? What the hell happened to hello, how you doing?"

I pressed my lips together and silently counted to ten. Daniel James Daily, the county's chief homicide detective, has a way of making my blood boil. Fireworks exploded the instant we met two months ago when my missing person's case turned into a near homicide. From his perspective, I was off the case, but I was adamant I wasn't going anywhere. In the end, I guess it turned out a draw. I had located the victim, and he'd found the would-be killer.

He flashed a perfect smile. I forced myself not to respond as I casually took in his usual impeccable appearance. Dressed in Italian leather loafers, razor-sharp creased khakis, a navy sports jacket, and a pink collarless shirt, he looked like a throwback to the eighties TV hit *Miami Vice*. Except he didn't look dated or clichéd, instead he looked hot. Damn hot.

"Hello, Daniel James."

"Rebecca." He took a step closer to the desk, pulled a chair back half a foot, and eased into it. "Hmmm. You know, I have no problem with you calling me DJ."

I raised the water bottle from my desk, twisted off the top, and took a sip. "I assume this visit concerns the death of—"

"Dominick Rizzo. Hurrah Channel's cameraman assigned to *Lingerie Exposed*. I'm questioning all individuals involved with the filming of the show. I was surprised to learn you were a guest."

I pressed my lips tight.

"Funny, I never imagined you an aficionada of frilly, silky, sexy lingerie. I kinda pegged you for an admirer of the more sensible—utilitarian underwear—long johns, for example. Take your sidekick, Pix. It's obvious where her interests lie since she peddles the stuff. And that's exactly what I would expect from a sexy piece of eye candy like her." A smile touched his face for a split second before he looked at me straight in the eyes. "Do you prefer thongs or panties?"

Daily never allowed political correctness to inhibit his comments. Had gotten him into hot water more than a few times at the station. But from what I'd gathered, he'd only suffered the occasional slap on the wrist, the result of the "good old boy" system being ingrained in the county's police department.

I hated that his snide comments had a way of raising my blood pressure as my cheeks heated up. I took a deep gulp of air. "What I wear under my clothes is my business."

"A bit touchy, aren't we?"

Determined not to play into his razzing, I sat up straighter and folded my hands. "I saw Mr. Rizzo during the filming. Didn't talk to him except when I told him to get that camera away from me. Unfortunately, he didn't."

"What about Pix?"

"What about her?"

"She and Rizzo had a thing going on?"

"Really?" I shook my head. "They only met yesterday. Went to dinner. That's all."

He pulled a pad from his jacket pocket and flipped it open. "Tiber Bistro at half-past seven," he read. "No nightcap, I take it."

"A last-minute decision had been made to continue the filming this morning. I assume you already know that."

He raised his eyes from the pad. They targeted on me.

I grabbed my water and took a deep swallow.

"I've already spoken with a Dolly Evans," he said. "A bit peeved about not being able to air her, um, negative opinion about Treasure's Trove of Lingerie to all the world. She'd need the cameraman for that. So, she's an easy scratch off the list."

"List? You mean the cameraman's death *is* a homicide?"

Daily didn't answer. Instead, he pressed his thumb into the dimple creasing his chin. "What about the chocolatier? Chuck Stetson." He dropped his hand and glanced at the pad.

"He discovered the body."

He gave me a look like how stupid do you think I am.

"Did Stetson have a beef with Mr. Rizzo?"

I wondered where he was going with this. "No."

"Look, it doesn't take a genius to figure out Stetson has a thing for Pix. There was a time, not too long ago, when you couldn't open the B.L. Gazette without reading an article about the confrontation brewing over Treasure's Trove. And there'd always be that one paragraph loaded with supportive arguments from Stetson as to why Main Street needed a lingerie shop. I thought it kinda weird that a guy would put himself on the line for something as frivolous as lingerie. Butthat was before I met Treasure Winslow."

"It's nothing like that," I lied, believing it was none of his business who Chuck liked or didn't like. "Chuck has a well-developed sense of fair play. He thinks everyone, including Pix, should have the opportunity to fulfill their dreams."

I noticed Caspurr staring at the detective. With every fiber in my body, I wished he'd jump into Daniel James Daily's lap. Then as if the cat and I had communicated telepathically, Caspurr did just that. After kneading his paws into Daily's lap for a full minute, he brushed his sturdy body against the detective. I fought the smile that wanted to form.

He scratched Caspurr on his head and under his chin. Even from my place on the other side of the desk, I could hear Caspurr's joyful purr.

"He's a big cat," Daily said. "What's he about twenty pounds?"

I nodded. "Caspurr's a champion show cat. But he's retired for the time being."

"He's impressive. And those blue eyes are something else. Is he deaf?"

"When I found him, he had a little smudge on the back of his head between his ears.

Turned out it wasn't a streak of oil, as I suspected, but a few black hairs."

"Ah. So, he's one of the lucky thirty percent that can hear. Guess the black hairs disappeared by the time he became an adult."

"Most people don't know that about white blue-eyed cats."

He shrugged and continued running his fingers through Caspurr's thick fur.

Who would've believed that Daily would be a cat lover, I thought with a shake of my head, duly stupefied. *Sort of out of character with his macho persona.*

"That's all I need for now," he said.

His words shook away my musings. Then I noticed his lip curl.

"Oh, by the way, how's the P.I. business? Any earth-shattering embezzlement cases I should know about?"

I bit the inside of my cheek to stop saying something I'd probably regret.

He winked, stood, and placed Caspurr gently onto the floor.

Before he turned for the door, I said, "Better take a look at your jacket." Caspurr was in the throes of losing his winter coat, and, to my pleasure, he'd deposited a fair amount of white strands crisscrossing Daily's indigo-colored jacket. That'll take him down a peg or two. From the first day we met, it was obvious that his appearance catered to his vanity. A most unattractive trait.

I couldn't help but smile as he hastened to the door.

CHAPTER SEVEN

A s soon as Daily left, I offered the cats a few morsels of their favorite treats and grabbed my keys. I hurried out of the office, made a right at the corner, and walked the half-block to the Prescott Painting and Sculpture Gallery, more commonly known as the PPS Gallery. The gallery's proprietor and art enthusiast, Simon Prescott, inherited the business four years ago when his uncle died unexpectedly from a brain aneurysm. I'd never met the uncle, but from what I'd gleaned from local gossip, he'd embodied the stereotypical qualities deemed essential for an artist; moody and temperamental, torn with angst and foreboding. Besides the abstract expressionism and minimalist paintings he favored, he'd loved cigars. It hadn't been unusual for a haze of smoke and the pungent aroma of tobacco to greet customers entering the gallery. Probably wasn't too good for business.

Prescott Sr. had been the gallery's third owner since its opening in 1922 as the Forum Salon. The original establishment had showcased American Impressionism and works of natural realism and beauty, which came to be known as the Pawcattaways River School of Painting. With the current management now under the leadership of the younger Prescott, the initial flavor of the work displayed was present once again.

Apparently, the two Prescotts didn't have much in common except for a deep devotion to art. Recently, I'd seen a photograph of the uncle in an exhibition catalog from the late 1990s, and he reminded me of Picasso (of whom he was an ardent admirer). But Simon, tall and lanky, had a quick smile which emerged mostly hidden behind a voluminous mustache and a matching ginger beard. His everyday dress consisted of faded jeans and a tee shirt usually emblazoned with the name of a heavy metal band. During opening receptions, he gussied up by donning a tooled leather vest. Down to earth and friendly, Simon knew his stuff, and fortunately for me, he really liked my work.

I glanced at the gallery's expansive window. One of my paintings displayed there along with others by various artists was missing. I crossed my fingers, hoping that meant good news. After all, it was one of my better landscapes depicting sunlit foliage and flecks of light shimmering on the Pawcattawaye. It had taken more hours to finish than I wanted to remember, but the bucolic scene deserved the extra effort. First, I'd made some plein air studies, including several thumbnail sketches and a couple of small paintings while studying the view from my easel under the shade cast from a group of trees along the river.

Referring to the preliminary works, I completed the final piece in my so-called studio. Catty-corner to my office it had been originally used for storage. The best thing about the minuscule studio was its gigantic window that allowed streams of natural light to flood the small space.

My set-up was a struggling artist's dream by being so close to a natural setting with its abundance of trees, wildlife, and the wide Pawcattawaye. The river, located on the far side of the elevated railroad that crossed Main Street, was less than a ten-minute walk from my apartment. I loved the peaceful location—until the cameraman wound up floating face-down in the river's green, roiling water.

I took a deep breath and bounded into the gallery.

Simon stood facing the back wall with his hands balled against his waist in front of a canvas set in an ornate gilded frame.

"My painting?" I broke the silence, and he turned.

"Sold about an hour ago."

I wanted to shout yippee, but instead, I nodded and offered a demure smile.

"Meant to call you right away but with all the excitement." He shrugged. "There hasn't been a murder here since well, since this place was the old Forum Salon."

I scrunched my forehead, unaware of a roaring twenties murder or really any other murder taking place in Bayleys Landing. Before I could ask for details, he continued talking.

"It happened in 1927 during the height of prohibition. A bootlegger was gunned down by a disgruntled client—one Alfred Greene—the owner of a speakeasy that used to be in the basement of what's now the Emperor's Brewing Company."

"Whoa. I had no idea. It seems almost every day, I learn a bit more about Bayleys Landing's colorful past."

"My uncle told me all kinds of stories about the town. The old railroad depot, the long-defunct opera house, and, of course, the ghosts which include the cheating bootlegger."

How many ghosts supposedly roam around here, I wondered, losing track of what Simon was saying. I refocused, trying to pick up the thread.

"When I was a kid, I could hardly wait for our annual visit from our farm in New Hampshire. My parents would drop me off at the gallery, and they'd spend the weekend at the Candlestick Inn. Uncle Freddie taught me a lot about the local history—and art, of course."

"Then he left the gallery to you?"

He nodded and brushed his fingertips through his luxuriant beard. "I heard the victim was Pix's boyfriend."

"Seriously?" I rolled my eyes. "Pix met Nick Rizzo yesterday at the filming. You were there, weren't you?"

"I figured with the shoot at Pix's shop, there wouldn't be much business. Besides, Mondays are always slow anyway, with most of the shops closed on Main Street. And actually, I wanted to give Izabelle the day off."

Izabelle Cohen, Simon's assistant, would've been invisible but for the colorful chunky jewelry, she was fond of wearing. Nice, but shy as a dormouse, she possessed a love of art and stayed current with the ever-changing trends in the art world.

"Guess I was wrong," he said. "Heard there were crowds we only see at Christmas time."

"Well, summer's right around the corner," I offered brightly. Besides the holidays, the long, humid days of summer drew hefty crowds to Bayleys Landing.

"If Pix met the cameraman yesterday, why did they have dinner together?"

"You know Pix. Nick was a handsome guy. I'd chalk the dinner up to mutual attraction. The perplexing thing is that she left him at the upper parking lot—she couldn't park in her usual spot because the road was closed to traffic—and he took off for the Candlestick. Then this morning, Chuck found Nick's body in the river."

He stroked his beard again and squinted his left eye. "Interesting turn of events for a town seemingly stuck in its past. Might even pull us into the chaos of the twenty-first century. Not so sure I'd like that, though."

"The past is what makes this place special."

"And a bit mysterious."

"Hopefully, Detective Daily will solve this crime pronto," I said.

"DJ's handling the murder?"

I nodded. "You know him?"

"Sorta. Take it from me, DJ's no open book. He's tightlipped about his work and his personal stuff. During football season, we meet over at the Emperor's to watch the Ravens and have a couple of beers. Sometimes he drops by the gallery, and we shoot the breeze. But it's obvious, his work is his life. He'll nab the Pawcattawaye River Killer, no sweat."

"Pawcattawaye River Killer?"

"Yup. That's the way the newscasters are referring to him. PRK for short." He flicked a ginger lock of hair off his forehead. "Must've been quite a shock for Pix. How's she holding up?"

"I'm not sure. Got a text when she left the police station. She decided not to open the store today."

"Not a suspect then?" He pursed his lips.

"Suspect?" I crinkled my nose thinking it a weird question.

He abruptly turned and gestured to two of my paintings hanging on the opposite wall. "The guy who purchased your painting liked these too. Might buy them. Said he'd be back later in the week."

"Yes." I pumped my fist. "Who is he?"

"Name's Geoffrey Taylor."

"Any relation to the Taylors of Bayleys Landing?"

He threw his palms upward. "I didn't ask. He lives in Bethesda. Works in D. C. A lawyer."

"This Mr. Taylor may be an answer to my prayers. Maybe he's a collector. Wouldn't that be fantastic?" I paused a moment to suppress my excitement. If I could scrounge up a benefactor or two, I definitely could close up the detective agency. Things usually didn't work out that way, but at least he'd bought one of my paintings. "When Geoffrey Taylor stops back, *please* tell him he's welcome to stop by my studio. I have several finished paintings and a couple I'm still working on." I'd done the math in my head. Minus the gallery's commission, I'd clear twelve hundred dollars for the painting. I wanted to nurture this lawyer's interest in my work. If I'm lucky—and that's a big if—Mr. Taylor could turn out to be the first serious collector of my work. A smile tugged at the corners of my lips.

"Becca."

I shook the delicious thought from my mind and refocused on Simon.

"You think it'd be okay if I dropped by Pix's place? Just to double-check."

"That's sweet of you. But I'm heading over there like in five minutes." I turned to leave but twisted my neck to glance in his direction. "I'll be sure to give her your regards."

CHAPTER EIGHT

Unlike me, Pix doesn't live above her place of business. She has a gorgeous, sprawling house ten minutes outside of town but, in reality, it seems like a world away with wide-spaced yards, tree-shaded streets, and recent constructions. In contrast, Bayleys Landing endures like an ancient crone, caught in a time warp, festooned with drab blue-gray granite buildings that offer a severe, stately mien. Thankfully, its austereness is offset by stained glass windows, potted plants, crisp herringbone brick sidewalks, and colorful, inviting wares filling wavy glass storefronts. Often as I walk amid the labyrinth of twisted lanes and alleyways, the unknown histories of nameless generations who've lived along its main thoroughfare for over two centuries pervade my thoughts. What stories those ancient blocks of granite could tell.

What I do know is that Bayleys Landing, like Rome itself, was founded on seven hills. Due to professed, though exaggerated similarities, the city fathers employed ancient Latin names for various landmarks. The original owner of the PPS Gallery had chosen the center of ancient Roman life for the designation of his art salon and the creek running beneath the structures lining Main Street was named after the Eternal City's life-sustaining artery of water. Sanctuary Lane leads uphill to St. Paul's Church, and it's curious that the apostle to the gentiles, who is believed to have been executed on Rome's Vatican Hill, became the church's namesake. The Winged Victory Pub, Bacchus Wines, Venus Spa, and the Capitoline Restaurant are a few of the modern businesses that kept to the practice of using classical monikers. The Appian Way, a winding road, meanders off lower Main Street to the original courthouse, now an archeological museum stocked with remnants from the town's history. When I visit the museum, I'm drawn to the room that houses a multitude of artifacts from the heyday of the industrial revolution. The mushrooming of Bayley Landing's mills and factories had spurred the rise of American manufacturing, the seed of which first spurted and flourished in this now quaint town nestled in the Patapsco Valley.

I steered my twelve-year-old Honda Civic off the National Pike and tapped the brake as I negotiated the snaky road that led to Pix's house. A showplace with vaulted ceilings, hardwood floors, and a newly renovated gourmet kitchen. All appliances were swapped out for energy-efficient ones and the solar panels used for heating and cooling the house had been affixed to the roof of Pix's empty six-stall horse stable courtesy of EnviroTech, her dad's company.

Pix certainly doesn't need all the space the forty-two hundred square foot house provides. But her dad, Peter, had bought the residence thinking its ten acres of fields and wooded scenery would remind Pix of her idyllic summers at the Harmony Vista commune. According to Pix, Peter's life at the commune had been the closest thing to this side of heaven. And she certainly didn't want to hurt his feelings by turning her nose up at his lavish gift.

I know what she really wants. A luxurious condo in Baltimore overlooking the harbor. While in college, she'd fallen in love with the city and longed to live there again. I didn't get it. Sure, Pix likes the city's quirky neighborhoods with unique shops and craft breweries, ethnic festivals, restaurants, and world-class art museums—her favorite being the American Visionary Art Museum—which I've got to admit is pretty amazing. But

Baltimore is ranked like the third most dangerous city in the country with streets that look like war zones. I'm sure Pix never treaded into those parts of the city. Could be all those boring summers at Harmony Vista with its isolation that influenced her preference for city living.

Outside of the beltway, suburban neighborhoods and small towns offer a laid- back vibe. How could she prefer Baltimore to the lush, wooded countryside surrounding her house that stands adjacent to a horse farm, has a stream, a meadow, a fenced paddock, not to mention the pool, hot tub, and cabana? The whole package presents a grand, if not, pretentious offering of a country manor. Or a starter castle.

Perhaps, Pix is just a city girl at heart.

I shrugged, pulled into the long driveway, and alighted from the car. A spurt of water tinkled from the marble fountain topped with a classical, half-human-half goat faun. The stone statuary reminded me of the famed villa in Pompeii. Seems even here, a trace of the early settlers' fascination with Rome lingers.

I rang the bell, and its musical chimes filled my ears. I tapped my foot as I waited before ringing the bell again. The intercom clicked on. "Yes?"

"It's me."

"I'll be down in a sec."

I continued tapping my foot and Pix's second turned into two, then three minutes. I sighed and shifted my sight to the fountain. A robin, settled on its curved lip, flapped its wings enjoying the spray cast from the spouting water. The door finally opened.

Pix looked terrible. Her red-rimmed and puffy eyes told me, she'd been crying. She was taking Rizzo's death hard. Perhaps too hard for someone she'd known for only a few hours.

I stepped inside. "How are you holding up?"

She shrugged. I wanted to order her to buck up. To grab her by the shoulders and shake her out of this daze of questionable misery. Instead, I crossed the enormous foyer and followed Pix into her favorite room, a study off the main hall. Though it wasn't cold outside, in the mid-sixties, she had a blaze roaring in the stacked travertine fireplace. I slipped out of my woolen cardigan and tossed it onto a sleek, armless, white leather chair.

"Who would do such a horrible thing?" Her moist eyes pleaded.

I shook my head.

"Some kind of monster." Her shoulders shook as the waterworks started up for, I guessed, the umpteenth time.

I opened my arms. She fell inside them as her tears turned into raking sobs.

"The police will get to the bottom of this," I said.

Pix pulled away, tugged a tissue free from her jeans back pocket, and blew her nose. She crossed the room and tossed the soggy Kleenex into a wastebasket. She repeated the process with the tissues twice before facing me. "Don't even mention the police. Your friend, Daily, grilled me like a suspect."

"We're really not friends," I muttered, then cleared my throat. "Look, he's only doing his job. You want them to catch whoever did this, right?"

"Of course, I do." She nodded. "But why, Becca? Why would someone want to kill Nick? I can't wrap that around my brain. He wasn't your average, run-of-the-mill type of guy." She sat on the edge of the white leather sofa facing the fireplace. "He did normal stuff like play on a softball team and worked out though he did have one of those celebrity trainers. In his spare time, Nick volunteered at an animal shelter for non-adoptable cats with serious medical conditions. He played with the poor kitties, gave them meds, shots, set up IVs, and offered them love. Giving their little lives joy and meaning."

I couldn't help but start liking the poor, murdered guy.

Pix sighed and glanced at the amber flames. "Oh yeah, I was impressed by how he doted on his little niece. Took her roller skating, worked with her on her soccer skills, and encouraged her —she loves to draw cartoons." She twisted and looked at me. "Even showed me her photo he keeps in his wallet. Nick Rizzo was who he seemed to be, an all-around nice guy."

"On a first date, people don't reveal everything about

themselves, especially if they're involved with something unsavory or illegal." I felt compelled to say the words though, at this point, I didn't mean them. I wanted to keep my opinion close to my vest, hoping Pix might offer more information about the slain cameraman.

She shot me one of those looks. The ones that convey I've lost my mind.

"Okay, maybe you're right. Nick Rizzo equals golden boy. I've been thinking, his death could've been the result of a robbery gone wrong." I didn't believe my suggestion, but I had to tell Pix something to appease her.

She gazed straight ahead at the crackling fire. "I know this is going to sound crazy, but I may know what happened."

"What?" I hurried to the couch and sat next to her.

"During dinner, I had this creepy feeling someone was watching me. I didn't say anything about it to Nick, 'cause I didn't want him to think I was paranoid. But then I saw *him*. I glanced out the window, and he was there."

"Chuck?"

"Not Chuck. Robert Sullivan."

"Don't tell me. The ghost is jealous."

"He must be. I think . . . he killed Nick."

"You didn't tell Daily that?"

"Of course not. He'd think I'm nuts."

"Look, Pix, ghosts don't fall in love, and they don't get jealous. Nick was killed by a living, breathing human being."

"You don't know that. Robert Sullivan could've done it."

For a split second, I inwardly fumed at her mother, Brenda. She was the one who planted the seeds for kooky ideas to sprout in Pix's mind with her devotion to off-beat ideologies. Since I wasn't getting anywhere with her, I'd have to try another approach.

"For the sake of argument, let's say this ghost is a killer. If that's the case, why hasn't anyone else who's stuck on you fallen victim to Robert Sullivan's machinations?"

"Maybe because Nick is the first man I've shown an interest in."

"Be for real. If it's male, you're interested. Or at least, you do a good job of giving the guy the impression that you're fascinated, entranced, and captivated by his every word."

"I do not."

I raised my eyebrows. "No use denying it."

"Who are all these men that I'm supposedly enthralled by?"

"Well . . ." I took a deep breath. "There's Chuck, of course. The guys who work at the Hot and Chilly Bean, Antony at the bookstore, Toy store Tommy, Ben and the rest of the crew at the Crab Kettle, Simon, and . . . and even old Willoughby Weygant."

"Now you're being ridiculous. Woody Weygant?" Pix rolled her flashing eyes. "You know the people who work on Main Street are a close-it group. We're friends. That's all."

"I wouldn't include Dolly Evans in that company."

"True. Some of the women are . . . are . . ." Pix shrugged.

"Not captivated by your charm? But there is someone who really is. Chuck."

"Maybe Chuck is too good for someone like me."

"What do you mean?"

She opened her mouth to answer, but then pressed her lips into a tight line.

"You're not giving yourself enough credit," I said. "You're a bright, savvy businesswoman who's warm and friendly and possesses a big, generous heart."

Pix's eyes widened a second, but instead of commenting, she shifted her gaze to the pristine white carpet.

"Anyway," I said. "I've never known you to have an inferiority complex. I think you're scared."

She frowned. "I am. Scared to death of whoever killed Nick."

"Don't pin this murder on the ghostly Robert Sullivan just yet. We'll know more tomorrow when the autopsy is completed. Once I know how Nick died, then I can—"

"You'll do that for me?"

"Do what?"

"Find out who murdered Nick."

"Detective Daily is—"

"No, Becca. I want you to uncover who did this to Nick. Ghost or not."

"What?"

"You found that kidnapped woman when the police didn't have a clue."

I knew that would come back to bite me one day. I'd accepted the accolades with a nod and a big smile, but the truth of the matter is I'd stumbled into the heroic act. I'd been jogging and heard muted cries coming from an abandoned house slated to be demolished. Sounded like a cat trapped inside the ramshackle building. Determined to free the wayward kitty, I kicked in one of the cracked basement windows. More than a bit shocked, I came face to face with my missing person case. The poor woman, bound to a chair, had been able to emit squeaking noises through her cloth gag.

Just a chance of dumb luck. I'm a licensed investigator but my forte is infidelity cases.

I'm good at following people. But finding a murderer . . . ah, no.

"Will you, Becca? Please."

I recognized the spark of hope that had chased the tears from Pix's eyes. How could I say no?

"Daily will probably lock up the murderer before you know it. But I'll do whatever I can to help."

"He won't even think of checking out Robert Sullivan."

I nodded.

"Start there."

I nodded again, chewing the corner of my lip.

CHAPTER NINE

B ack in my office, I decided to do a little research on Robert
Sullivan. Googling his name didn't do much because there's
a whole lot of Robert Sullivans out there. After looking up every
conceivable site, including a detailed history of Bayleys Landing
during the Civil War years, I couldn't find a blessed word about
the ghost who walks or, should I say, floats along the brick
sidewalks of our popular thoroughfare.

Not willing to give up yet, I got the bright idea to take a quick
jog to the Archeological Museum and see if Willoughby Weygant
was to be found inside one of its four rooms. Everyone calls him
Woody, not the sensible shortening of his name to Will or even
Willy. Rumor has it that as a small child, he was fascinated with
wood and would imitate his father chopping the stuff hours on
end. His mother began to call him my "little woodsman" which
evolved into his present-day moniker. Of course, I reminded
myself, finding out anything from Woody depended on which of
his alter egos he'd assumed for the day.

I still don't know what to make of Woody. The first time I
bumped into him outside of the PPS Gallery, I thought he was
one of those historians who reenact crucial battles in American

KAREN LEIGH CHARLES

history. That was until I started talking to him. Then I feared him to be an escapee from the psych ward of the local hospital. Once I got to know him a little, I realized he truly believes a grave cosmic error occurred, and his true identity belongs to a past era. Which bygone age is the question. Dressed in a woolen red overcoat and britches with a tricorn hat snugly covering his mostly bald pate, he is a loyal subject of King George. Spats, beaver coat, and elegant ivory cigarette holder Woody is certain to enlighten us with the going-on of local bootleggers and Chicago gangsters. And then, there's his cobalt blue Union uniform with lieutenant strips and brass buttons. I sent up a quick prayer that's who he was today. Not the dustbowl farmer, gold rush prospector, Jamestown survivor, or one of a plethora of other characters.

I hurriedly slipped into my sweats and tied my running shoes. It was nearing four o'clock, and I wanted to reach the museum before closing. I dashed out the door so focused on my goal that I failed to offer a word of farewell to the purrs.

It took close to ten minutes to reach the boxy granite building with deep windows and a stately entrance. The museum's rooms are designated by different historical periods; Early Settlement, Industrial Revolution, Civil War, and Twentieth Century.

I pulled the massive door open and slipped inside. With fingers crossed, I hurried toward the rail-thin, raven-haired Jane Parks, president of the Bayleys Landing Historical Society, as she busied herself with restocking the picture-postcard rack.

"Jane."

She turned. A storm brewed on her deeply lined face.

"Is Woody around?"

She pulled in the corners of her mouth, and her lips thinned. "I knew your friend's shop would bring nothing but trouble. And now a murder. There hasn't been a murder here since—"

"1927," I said, moving closer to her. "It isn't the first murder in Bayleys Landing and probably won't be the last. I get it, you're upset," I said, looking around the empty lobby, "but Pix had nothing to do with it. So don't place blame where it doesn't belong."

"It's a blemish tarnishing our luminous history. This scandal would have been avoided if that lingerie shop," Jane said, lowering her voice to a whisper, "if only the Merchant Association hadn't approved Treasure Winslow's application. Then those horrid television people never would have landed here."

She lifted her chin and thrust it out though I noticed her eyes looked wet.

"Bayleys Landing is two hundred and fifty years old. I doubt this incident will even be remembered within a few years," I said.

"It might be remembered as the catalyst that triggered our plunge into perdition. Rising crime lurks all around us and is moving closer. So far, Providence had allowed Bayleys Landing to remain a refuge from that ugliness. What if our beloved town turns into another Baltimore?" The color drained from her face.

The Parks' ancestors had been one of the town's founding families. Jane apparently took the murder as a personal affront and was blowing it out of proportion. "Baltimore, really Jane?"

"It's not impossible."

"Nick Rizzo's murder won't change our peaceful hamlet."

"Obviously, you're not taking me seriously."

"Of course, I am." I tried to think fast. Like a flash, it came to me. "You do know that Rizzo's body was found in the Pawcattawaye River."

She nodded, narrowing her eyes.

"I'm not one hundred percent, but I think the body was floating on the far side of the river, placing it in Baltimore County. The murder could've actually happened in Othello, not Bayleys Landing."

Jane pursed her lips.

"I'll check out the specifics with Detective Daily. But for now, have no worries since the murder may not have happened here at all."

"Really, Becca?" She grabbed my hand.

"Wouldn't be surprised." I nodded, trying to extricate my extremity from her vise-like grip. "It's plausible."

She released my hand. I wiggled my fingers a few times in an attempt to resume the blood flow to my freed appendage. "Even so, Bayleys Landing has survived much worst—war, depressions, deadly floods, destruction—and has always bounced back better, stronger. This time won't be any different." Though the town means everything to the sixty-some-year-old spinster, I never would have imagined the murder of Nick Rizzo could cause her to have a meltdown.

"Of course. I don't know why I felt so anxious. For a while, I even feared for my own life. Irrational, I know, but the media is always inundated with such horrible news. I lost a bit of perspective," she said with a tilt of her head. "Not like me at all." She exhaled deeply. "Anyway, it'll be a colorful addition to the ongoing history I'm writing about Bayleys Landing. Did I tell you a local publisher has shown an interest in my book?"

I offered her a tiny smile. "Um, Woody is he—"

"I have to get to work right away." Jane freed a pencil, I hadn't noticed, from her puffy hairdo. She turned but then looked over her shoulder. "He's in room three. Civil War."

I pumped the air with my fist as I dashed down the hallway leading to the room. As I stepped inside, I noticed it was empty save for Woody. His back faced me, but it was evident he was the Union soldier today. For a split-second, I recalled the time I ran into him at the Emperor's Brewing Company. I almost didn't recognize him. He'd leaned against the counter, beer in hand, dressed in a plaid flannel shirt and jeans, cheering on the Raven's football team.

I cleared my throat. "Lieutenant Weygant."

He spun around in crisp military fashion. "Good afternoon, Miss Flynn." He tipped his slouch hat with its gold braiding, US insignia, and jaunty feather. After a gallant flourish of his arm, he bowed. "Lovely day for a stroll."

With his arm still mid-air, he offered it, but I shook my head. "I need some information and hoped you could help."

"It'd be my pleasure, Miss."

"Robert Sullivan."

"Ah." Woody rocked on the balls of his feet a couple of times.

"Most folks thought he was a yellow-bellied coward, but that wasn't the case."

I moved closer and pulled the pad and pen free from my hoodie's kangaroo pocket. I flipped through a few pages, not removing my eyes from him.

"Truth be, Robert Sullivan was a man deeply in love." He shook his head. "That, Miss Flynn, was his downfall."

I jotted the word love with a question mark.

"He was a dashing young man, a corporal in 69th Irish Brigade out of New York."

I scribbled down the information fearing Woody would talk too fast, yet I dared not ask him to slow down.

"Keep in mind that a multitude of young Irishmen arrived here during the Civil War—didn't care which side they fought on —only wanted to learn how to be soldiers."

I looked up from my pad, certain that a quizzical look claimed my face.

"They had one aim, Miss. To learn the art of warfare in order to free their homeland from the tyranny of the British. Robert Sullivan was one of those men."

"He was planning on going back to Ireland to fight the English?"

"Precisely."

"Well then, how did he wind up being shot to death in Bayleys Landing?"

"He made the fateful decision during the Battle of Fredericksburg. On that blood-soaked field of Virginia, the war cries of *vaugh a ballaugh* slashed the chilly December air. Amid the deafening explosions of cannon fire and the charging Confederacy, the "Fighting 69" infantry didn't have a prayer." A faraway look filled Woody's eyes. "The regiment had been sixteen hundred strong. They'd given their all, but when the air stilled and the smoke cleared, only two hundred and fifty-six war-weary men survived."

So caught up in his story, I'd stopped taking notes. I glanced at the page and then refocused on Woody.

"He'd been one of the lucky ones. It was after the battle that he'd walked away from his regiment. Robert Sullivan hadn't deserted because he was a coward." Woody moved next to a display cabinet and glanced inside. I waited patiently, hoping he had more to say. He grasped the hilt of his sword and turned toward me. "Sullivan's brother had met up with the "Fighting 69" as the battle was winding down. What should've been a happy reunion quickly turned sour. Robert's wife had given birth to a healthy boy, but she wasn't thriving. The doctor had all but given up hope. Infection. Bridget Sullivan was surely dying." He looked at the scuffed wooden floor as if studying the rough, splintered boards. "That was the true reason Sullivan went AWOL. A fool's mission since his wife had probably already succumbed before he made it to the Maryland line. He was hunted down, arrested, and boarded on a train to Bayleys Landing for his court-marshal hearing. I assume you know the rest of the story."

The tale of Robert Sullivan had taken on an unexpected twist. "He never saw his wife or newborn son?"

Woody shook his head. "I have something you're sure to find interesting." He crossed the room and pulled open a drawer from the built-in along the windowless wall decorated with maps and sepia photographs of bearded soldiers and battlefields. When he returned, he'd donned white cotton gloves and held a creased, yellowed sheet of paper. "Robert's brother had given him a letter from Bridget. He'd kept it folded in his breast pocket next to his heart. Look here."

I moved closer and noticed a ragged edge tinged with a deep brown stain.

"When Sullivan broke free of his captor's grip, the bullet fired to stop him struck directly in his heart. Nicked the edge of this letter. That's his blood." His finger brushed the darkened edge.

I chewed my lip, moving closer, and noticed the small, tight handwriting. I squinted, trying to make out the words, but unexpectedly Woody began reading. His usual booming voice dropped to a soft whisper. "*My darling. I pray our dear Lord continues to protect you and that I may once again gaze upon your countenance. I long to see your face, to hear the sound of your sweet voice, and feel your tender touch. I fear my days are coming to an end, and my deepest desire will remain unanswered. Please remain strong for me and our son. know that I will love you throughout all of eternity.*"

I waited a moment as Woody brushed his fingers across his closed eyelids. "How tragic," I murmured. "He was killed trying to make his way back to his dying wife."

Without a word, he placed the letter back into the drawer.

I headed to the door but stopped, turned, and faced him. "Do you believe that Robert Sullivan's ghost is roaming along Main Street?"

"Of course, he is, Miss. No doubt about it."

CHAPTER TEN

The startling facts surrounding Robert Sullivan occupied my thoughts as I trudged down the winding street back to my office. The perplexing thought plaguing me was that if the Civil War corporal was so madly in love with his wife, why didn't his ghost head straightaway for New York? Now I'm as bad as Pix, I chided myself, imagining the ghost of Robert Sullivan real.

I twisted the knob, pulled my office door open, and gingerly stepped inside, trying to avoid treading on any of my three kitties blocking the doorway. Once inside, they circled around my feet. Their little cries, I suspected, were not of welcome but rather a scolding for neglecting them. "Poor little purrs," I said soothingly.

I scooped up Coppurr, and the other two followed on my heels up the stairs and into the apartment. The instant I dropped onto the couch, Coppurr snuggled into my lap, Caspurr curled around the nape of my neck, and Jaspurr attempted to sit on my head. I disentangled him from my hair and placed him against my chest. Their rhythmic, whirring purrs filled my ears and lulled me into a much-needed state of relaxation. My eyelids closed, and as I started to drift into slumber, my cell phone sounded. I willed for the cheery ringtone to end. The four of us were comfortable, and I didn't want to be disturbed. That was until I remembered Simon. He might be calling with news from the collector interested in my paintings. With the slightest shift of my hand, I inched toward my pocket and the jangling phone. The movement proved to be too much, and the cats scurried across the room. I glanced at the screen and seeing Chuck's handsome face displayed there, I couldn't help but smile.

"Hey, Chuck. What's up?"

"You're not going to believe this."

I couldn't place the emotion lacing his voice. Disgust? Anger? Astonishment?

"DJ has been grilling me because they found my footprints at the crime scene."

"Of course they did. You found the body." I wanted to wring Daniel James Daily's neck.

"Do you know a lawyer that can get me outta this jam?"

"They're arresting you?"

"DJ is trying to pin the cameraman's murder on me. According to him, I was jealous because Pix went out to dinner with him. I'd like to know how he came up with that half-assed motive. What a load of crap."

Chuck was royally pissed-off and for a good reason. His interrogation told me that Daily hadn't waited for the Medical Examiner's report, which wouldn't be available until tomorrow. But had decided to forge on assuming Rizzo's death *was* the result of foul play.

"Forget about Daily. He's an idiot. Anyway, you've got nothing to worry about. You've got an air-tight alibi. Remember, you were with me."

"I told DJ that. Said he'd have to check it out."

"When he does, I'll set him straight." I imagined my hands around Daily's neck. "Are you at the police station?"

"The Chocolate Box. DJ and another detective stopped by here. I closed the shop and took them upstairs to the office. They compared my running shoes to a plaster cast and asked me a lot of questions. About five minutes ago they took my shoes and left. The ones I've been training in for the Boston Marathon."

A new surge of irritation filled his voice. I had to say something to calm him down.

"Even though he's a jerk, Daily is a good detective." The words almost choked me. "You won't be a suspect for long." I glanced at my watch. It was nearly six. "Why don't you close the "Box" early and stop by here for dinner? Afterward, we can go to the Emperor's for a beer and watch the ballgame."

"Thanks, Becca, but I told Pix I'd pick up some Chinese and stop by her place after work. She's still upset over the cameraman's death. It's the least I can do."

"Right."

"After all, there's nothing like a tragedy to bring people closer together. Might be a turning point for Pix and me." He paused. "But that's probably wishful thinking." A second later, he bade me a good evening and cut the connection.

I tapped the phone against my chin, surprised Chuck would take advantage of such a dreadful situation. Then that old adage came to mind; all's fair in love and war. Still musing, I jumped when I heard an insistent rapping.

I hurried to the door, pulled it open, and then wanted to slam it shut.

"Good evening, Rebecca." Daily flashed his brilliant smile.

"Detective." I noticed he wasn't wearing the navy blazer where earlier Caspurr had deposited a wealth of cat hair.

"I have a few questions about the Rizzo case. Didn't think you'd mind—"

"Of course not." I attempted a smile. "Come in." I opened the door wider. Inside my living room, I got a better view of him and noticed he must've changed into his off-hours clothes. You'd think a guy dressed in a tee shirt and jeans would look relaxed. DJ Daily looked like a model for a print ad—I'm certain his ensemble hadn't come from the local Wal-Mart—probably handmade Italian imports.

"Chuck Stetson said you're his alibi. True?"

Daily didn't wait for an answer but instead walked around my small living area. He stopped in front of one of my landscape paintings that filled the space between two narrow windows and studied it for a minute then turned and faced me. "Well?"

"Chuck arrived here promptly at seven pm. We had dinner and watched the Orioles game on T.V."

"What time did he leave?"

I squinched up my face trying to remember the exact time. Apparently, I was taking too long.

"I don't mean to be indelicate," he snickered, "but did Stetson spend the night here with you?"

My blood began to boil. "He left after the eleven o'clock news."

"Then he was here the whole time. Seven until eleven-thirty." He looked me directly in the eyes.

"Yeah. But . . ." I couldn't believe I'd forgotten. During the seventh-inning stretch, Chuck had slipped out to grab a tin of my favorite dark chocolate-covered pretzels stuffed with peanut butter from his shop. The O's were creaming the Yankees, and I was in a festive mood. It had taken him longer than I'd expected, and he returned to my place at the start of the ninth inning. "He left for a few minutes to get some chocolates from his shop."

Daily's eyebrows shot up. "What time was that?"

"Around eight-forty-five."

He pursed his lips.

"Chuck wasn't gone long. Ten-fifteen minutes."

"How long do you think it takes to stab someone to death?"

CHAPTER ELEVEN

Neither my morning run nor cuddling with the purrs had been able to chase away the gripping sense of foreboding causing a tangle of thoughts to clamber for prominence in my tired brain. Worst of all, I couldn't shake the notion that I had betrayed Chuck. Down to the last fiber of my being, I believed he would never hurt anyone. Especially a dinner date that Pix had no intention of ever seeing again because Nick Rizzo lived clear across the country. Knowing Pix the way I do, a long-distance romance wouldn't hold her attention. After all, an overabundance of fawning men already surrounded her, ready and willing to answer her every beck and call. The implication that Chuck could be a murder suspect was preposterous. *Why couldn't Daily see that?*

If only I hadn't had a craving for those decadently delicious pretzels. Then Chuck would've been with me the entire evening, and his alibi irrefutable.

The only case, and I use that term lightly, to take my mind off of the murdered cameraman was that of Pix's ghost. I paced across my office, hoping to burn off an abundance of nervous energy. I hadn't the slightest intention of setting up a "ghost stakeout" and was too antsy to even think about painting. I turned and walked the length of the office again. Caspurr busied himself with his daily ablutions as his tongue darted and probed every inch of a front paw. The other two cats hadn't made an appearance, and I guessed they were napping in the slices of sunshine that filtered through the apartment windows. I stroked Caspurr's favorite spot, at the bridge of his nose, before heading once again to the room's opposite wall. Mid-step, the phone rang.

"Flynn Investigations and Photography," I said, praying it to be an actual client.

"Hey, Becca."

I recognized Simon's voice—a cross between maple syrup and straight Kentucky bourbon—smooth and smoky.

"Rumors are flying like lightning in a bottle. Is it true that Chuck is a murder suspect?"

I ignored commenting on his mixed metaphor and took a deep breath. "Murder investigations are complicated. But no, he isn't a suspect, only a person of interest because he found the body. Typical police procedure." I wanted to put an end to idle gossip about Chuck's role in the inquiry.

"That's a relief. I'm generally a good judge of character and consider Chuck a buddy. The real reason I called is to let you know that Geoffrey Taylor's going to be at the gallery around one today. He's looking forward to meeting you. I'm pretty sure he wants to purchase your two other paintings."

"That's the best news I've heard for days," I almost squealed. The tension gripping the base of my neck began to relax as I rolled my shoulders. "I'll be at the gallery. Thanks, Simon."

I cut the connection and headed to the staircase leading to the apartment, eager for this meeting and determined to make a good impression. If this Geoffrey Taylor decided to purchase the paintings, I'd pocket a small fortune.

Unlike my practical parents, Aunt Marianne urged me to pursue a career in painting since she marveled at my talent. Though I wanted to embrace that plan completely, I hesitated, not wanting to be the proverbial starving artist. I enrolled in the art teaching program at college. But my teaching career ended the first time I faced a classroom of twenty-seven fifth graders. They chewed me up and spit me out. So much for being an art educator.

I guess it boiled down to watching all those old TV reruns —*Magnum PI, Rockford Files*, and *Charlie's Angels*—that sparked my imagination and led me to my present occupation. Unfortunately, my job paled in comparison to my fictional counterparts.

Maybe the time is right for me to go for it. Forget the P.I. business and pursue my dream of being a full-time artist. I pulled my favorite sweater, soft cashmere tinted a warm peach, over my head and slipped into a black pencil skirt. Perhaps I'd been selling myself short. After all, I am a member of several prestigious art organizations with several paintings juried into national shows.

After running a brush through my shoulder-length hair and adding a smattering of lip gloss, I took a look at myself in one of my few antiques, a free-standing mahogany mirror dating to the 1930s. Pleased with my reflection, I headed to the gallery.

I arrived at the Prescott Painting and Sculpture Gallery precisely at twelve-forty-five. A trickle of people milled around the two large connecting rooms. I spied a couple, hand in hand, in front of one of my landscapes. I strolled in their direction, hoping to hear their comments. As I sidled next to them, Simon emerged from the lower level where he housed his framing shop. He held a package wrapped in butcher paper neatly tied with a string. The couple hurried in his direction, eager to take possession of their purchase.

I noticed a new painting on display. After a few minutes of intense study, I decided I didn't like it at all.

I felt a tap on my shoulder, spun around, and faced Simon.

"I'm a little nervous about meeting Mr. Taylor."

"No worries. He's an aficionado of fine art. And it's clear he has great taste, especially since he's interested in your paintings."

Though Simon's words should have been reassuring, I folded my arms and tapped foot.

"How's Pix?"

"Okay, I guess." I glanced at the entrance hoping yet fearing

71

to see the person who might launch my painting career. "Chuck checked on her last night."

"Chuck?"

"Uh-huh."

"He spent the night with her?"

I faced him and shrugged. "She's taking Nick's death hard. I think the more people supporting her, the quicker she'll bounce back to her old self. I'm planning to have her sleep-over with me tonight. The last thing she needs is to be in that big house all alone."

Simon combed his long, artistic fingers through his ginger beard. "My thoughts exactly. I'm taking her out to dinner, and hopefully, she won't have to spend the night with you." He offered me a quick wink.

"Simon."

I turned my head and saw, who I imagined, was Geoffrey Taylor heading toward us. Sprinting, more like it. Tall and slender in a blue pin-striped suit that fit like a glove, dark eyes shone behind tortoise framed glasses, and short silvery hair framed his intense though rather handsome face.

"Is this Rebecca?" He thrust out his hand.

I took it, and mine disappeared within his warm grasp. "Becca," I said.

"It's a pleasure to meet you. I'm a big fan of traditional landscape painting, and when I saw yours, well, there's an emotional quality there I find most appealing. Plus, your technical skill is amazing."

I managed a quick thank you before Simon herded us to the spot where one of my paintings hung. I focused on Geoffrey Taylor. His eyes flitted as if trying to memorize every detail of the stormy sky and raging river.

"I must have this one and..." He spun around. "That one too." Geoffrey crossed the gallery and stopped at my other painting, a sunset with a crimson-tinged sky.

I couldn't believe my luck. This man, crazy about my work, seemed to have appeared right out of my dreams. I cleared my

throat and found my voice. "It's always . . . exciting . . . to meet . .
. an admirer," I sputtered. Something about the man made me
tongue-tied.

"Becca has several paintings in her studio. Perhaps you'd like
to plan a visit there?" Simon asked wide-eyed.

"I would. The next couple of weeks are rough for me. I'm
preparing for a major trial in D. C. but some time . . ." He
whipped out his cell phone and scrolled down the screen. "In mid-
May—the 17th—if that works for you."

I didn't have to check my calendar. Any day an interested
collector wants to visit my studio is damn fine with me. I nodded.

"May 17th," he said, tapping the phone's screen, "at one?" He
raised his eyebrows.

"That'll be fine. Great, actually."

"My assistant will wrap up the paintings for you. If you'd like
to come this way," Simon motioned to his Queen Anne-styled
desk where he handled all of his transactions. "I'm always pleased
when someone discovers an artist he's head over heels with." He
glanced at me over his shoulder and beamed a smile that
reminded me of the Cheshire Cat.

CHAPTER TWELVE

The morning crowd had thinned out as I sipped the house blend at the Hot and Chilly Bean. Pix was late as usual, so I decided to do a bit of research. I scrolled down the listings on my phone's screen that mentioned Geoffrey Taylor. There wasn't a whole lot, but I did discover the name of the prestigious law firm where he worked in Washington, D. C. But as to any personal information, I'd come up blank. I jumped when Pix pulled out the chair opposite me.

"Beautiful day, isn't it?" She placed her coffee on the table and sat down.

The tightness around her jaw had vanished, her eyes shone, and a smile played at the corners of her mouth. *This is the Pixie Winslow I'm used to. Not the teary-eyed, stressed-out version.*

"Indeed it is." I swiped the phone's screen and dropped it into my fanny pack.

Ralphie, one of the baristas, deposited two apple fritters in front of us. "Straight out of the oven. Just the way you like."

He glanced at Pix with a worshipful look on his face. I rolled my eyes.

"Anything else I can get you?"

"We're fine, Ralphie," I said. It was apparent he wanted to linger in Pix's presence, but instead, dutifully made it back behind the bar.

"I'm glad to see you're in a better mood today." I lifted the pastry. Its aroma had my mouth watering. "I'm surprised you turned down my offer of a sleepover." I couldn't hold off another second. I took a generous bite of the confection.

"I appreciate how you've been watching over me like a mother hen." Pix sipped her coffee. "But so much has happened in one short night. All because of Chuck."

Not able to speak with my mouth full of delicious, sugary dough I raised my eyebrows.

"Chuck telephoned after I got home from having dinner with Simon. He insisted on stopping over. Since we'd had such a great time the night before, I agreed. Then it happened and everything changed."

I swallowed and took a gulp of coffee. "Changed?"

"You know how close Chuck and I are. I've always considered him as someone who had my back, whom I could depend on, and most importantly trust."

I nodded.

"Last night, over a chilled glass of champagne and chocolate-covered strawberries Chuck opened his heart to me. He shared a bunch of experiences ranging from the time he was a kid to his last love affair that didn't work out. His memories allowed me to see his vulnerable side and I was touched by the depth of his emotions. His eyes even teared up a couple of times." Pix lifted her apple fritter but placed it back on the plate. "Right when he said he'd better be going, I remembered the fortune cookies we hadn't eaten from the take-out we had the night before. Chuck read his fortune first. It said true happiness is within his grasp. Then I read mine." She slipped her hand into the back pocket of her trendy jeans and withdrew the tiny strip of paper. "The love you seek is facing you."

She handed me the slip. I glanced at it and handed it back. "So?"

MURDER IN PLEIN AIR

"Don't you get it? Chuck and me. We're destined to be together."

"You determined this from a fortune cookie?" I squinted at her.

"Don't be silly. This," she said, raising the fortune, "showed me what I've taken for granted. Chuck is smart, kind, caring, thoughtful. He makes me laugh. And if you haven't noticed, he's a bonafide hottie."

Everything she said was true. For an instant, a twinge of jealousy touched me, but then I realized this is what I'd wanted for Pix all along.

"So, you're exclusive."

"Exclusive," she said with a nod. "Isn't that just—amazing?"

"What's amazing?" Simon pulled out the chair next to me and sat down. "Oh, you must be talking about Becca's good news."

Pix tilted her head. "Good news?"

"Didn't she tell you?" Simon said. "She snagged a client who might turn out to be a genuine, honest to God patron. Could launch her art career."

I couldn't stop the smile from spreading across my face. "I might be replacing my shingle from P.I. to Artist."

Pix reached across the table and grasped my hand. She squeezed it as a generous smile claimed her face. "So both of us have fantastic news."

"You have news? You didn't tell me last night." He rested his elbows on the table and tented his fingers.

"It happened suddenly, like a flash of lightning, but it's the best thing ever," Pix said.

A dreamy look filled her dark eyes.

"The suspense is killing me." His face brightened and he snapped his fingers. "You snagged the bid for that antique sleeping bonnet from the online auction."

Pix shook her head. "Chuck and I are dating. Actually, we're a couple."

He lifted his coffee and took a sip. "That news is gonna break a lot of hearts around here.

Mine included. But I couldn't be happier for you two. Does Ralphie know yet?" He thrust his chin in the barman's direction. "When I ordered my coffee, he could barely tear his eyes off of you."

A trace of pink touch Pix's cheeks.

"You two are the first to know," Pix said. "I'm going to stop by the Chocolate Box before opening up Treasure's Trove." She slid her untouched pastry in front of Simon. "I'm too excited to eat." She grabbed her take-out cup, jumped up, and stepped next to him. "I just love your red hair," she said running her fingertips through it, "and your matching beard." She bent down and kissed his fuzzy cheek. Straightening up, she flashed him a warm smile and headed for the door.

"Hey, wait up. I'll walk with you to Chuck's," I said.

After a quick farewell to Simon, I caught up to Pix, linked arms with her, and exited the coffee shop.

THE INSTANT we stepped into the Chocolate Box I knew something was up. Daily faced Chuck and spoke in a hushed tone.

"What's going on?" I said.

Both men whipped her heads in our direction.

Chuck opened his mouth but before he could utter a word Daily said, "Police business."

Pix moved next to Chuck. "If it affects Chuck, it's my business too."

Daily pursed his lips and looked from the lovebirds to me. "Something going on here, I don't know about?"

"We're dating." Pix said.

Chuck's lips thinned as he pressed them into a tight line.

"Really, now." Daily folded his arms. "This a new development?"

She nodded. "That doesn't mean I'm any less interested in finding out who killed Nick."

"That's exactly what I'm aiming on doing," Daily said.

"Any leads?" I asked. "Because I'm thinking . . ."

Daily eyed me. "If I'm ever that desperate that I need your help, I'm really in trouble." He turned his attention back to Chuck.

"I've told you everything I know, DJ. Talking to another detective, at the station, isn't going to change anything."

"You can't believe Chuck had something to do with Nick's death." Pix stepped closer to the detective. "You have a lot of nerve, DJ Daily, accusing Chuck of what? Murdering Nick?" Her voice rose as her eyes flashed daggers. With an awkward motion, she raised her balled hand, brought it toward her face, as if she was going to bang her forehead out of frustration.

Chuck grabbed Pix's arm. "He's only doing his job. The police want a DNA sample and a polygraph test."

"You're kidding." I tapped my foot in an attempt to contain my anger. "For real? A lie detector test?"

Chuck wrapped his arms around Pix's shoulder and my waist. "I think you two should get to work," he said, ushering us to the door. "I'll call you later." He bent over and kissed Pix's forehead.

Once outside, I took a few deep breaths trying to calm my racing heart. "Daily is such a jerk. Dragging Chuck to the police station for a polygraph will be nothing but a waste of time. Time he could be using to find the actual killer."

"I'm okay with it," Pix said.

"It didn't look that way to me." I motioned toward the Chocolate Box.

"Maybe I was a bit emotional—"

"I thought you were going to slug Daily."

She shrugged. "Like Chuck said, DJ is only doing his job. Anyway, a lie detector will definitely rule out Chuck from being a suspect."

"Not really. The findings will be inadmissible in a court of law. To nab the actual killer, Daily will have to search for witnesses and collect physical evidence. He won't get a collar by jumping to conclusions." I glanced at Pix. Worry lines had again sprung to her face. "But Daily is going to be disappointed big time when he discovers Chuck had nothing to do with the murder. He'll scratch Chuck's name off the suspect list and that will leave him with a big nothing."

"You like him, don't you."

"Who?" I faced Pix.

"Who do you think? DJ."

"What?"

"I could feel it inside the Chocolate Box," she said. "Bolts of highly charged electricity bouncing between you two."

"What are you talking about? You did hear him insult me."

She brushed her hand as if sweeping away my comment. "I think maybe you two are burying your passion for each other. False pride shouldn't keep you from embracing your true feelings."

"Okay, Pix. These are my heartfelt true feelings," I said, making air quotes, "about Daily. I can't stand that irritating, vain, pompous, know-it-all detective."

She sighed. "I want you to have what I've found with Chuck."

We stopped in front of the entrance of Treasure's Trove of Lingerie.

"I know you do," I said. "But honestly Pix, I'm not going to find a morsel of happiness with that over-blown, egomaniac. He's a self-centered idiot."

She slipped her key into the lock and opened the door. Looking over her shoulder she said, "I believe a line from Will Shakespeare says it all, 'The lady doth protest too much, methinks.'"

With that Pix entered the store and left me wondering why in heaven's name would I ever be romantically interested in Daniel James Daily. The only pleasure I could imagine involving Daily was if I'd beat him at his own game. A slow smile crept across my face. That's it, I decided. Not only will I clear Chuck's name, but I'm going to find the culprit that murdered Nick Rizzo if it's the last thing I do.

The only problem—how?

CHAPTER THIRTEEN

I headed toward my office but paused at the window of the Prescott Painting and Sculpture Gallery. Simon was displaying some new paintings. I was taken aback that the painting I'd seen earlier and decisively didn't like stood in the place of honor, front, and center. Mystified, I tried to comprehend why he'd chosen to showcase it as an example of the fine art found inside the gallery. A large landscape, it contrasted sharply with the others around it, since all details of nature had been stripped away, leaving swatches of garish colors which were neither natural nor representational. I wondered if Uncle Freddie had whispered into Simon's ear and pontificated upon the wonders of minimalist paintings. I shook my head, surprised at how easily I'd fallen into accepting the idea of ghostly apparitions.

Simon tapped on the window and motioned me inside.

After a quick greeting, I said, "What's with the abstract landscape?"

"You don't like it?"

I shook my head. "I thought you love realistic paintings, not blobs of color."

"I do. But I've concluded that to grow the business, I have to offer a variety of artistic styles. There's a lot of different tastes out there." he said with a shrug. "I don't want to fall into the same trap as Uncle Freddie by limiting my stock to only one type of painting and sculpture." He pointed to a mangled piece of steel twisted into God knows what.

"Hmm, I see."

"If anyone would understand, I expect it to be you. After all, you attended one of the best art schools in the nation and were exposed to different types of visual expression."

And rejected most of them, I thought. Not that I didn't see merit in the work. In fact, I was fascinated by the scope and imagination of my classmates. But representational art spoke the loudest to me. I thought Simon felt the same way.

But I guess all of us have to make sacrifices for our businesses. Pix with her assortment of racy lingerie, and now Simon accepting abstractionism, minimalism, cubism, modernism, post-modernism, expressionism, impressionism, and whatever other kind of ism out there.

"I understand," I said. "It's probably a smart move. After all, variety is the spice of life, or so I've been told."

I turned to leave, but before reaching the door, Simon called, and I faced him.

"What's your take on Pix and Chuck getting together? Do you think the murder has anything to do with it?"

"Maybe indirectly." I shrugged. "The unexpected death of Nick might've shown Pix how fleeting life can be. Gave her a much-needed push to realize that Chuck is a great catch."

"But now that he's a murder suspect, you'd think—"

"Person of interest," I corrected him. "Anyway, Daily is only following procedure. Once they examine the DNA evidence, Chuck will be ruled out for good."

"Don't they need the murder weapon for fingerprints and DNA?"

"For all we know, they have it. Probably a knife."

"Oh, yeah." He swiped a lock of hair off his forehead. "I heard on the news the cameraman was stabbed to death."

"Any kind of blade could've killed Nick; box cutter, scissors, even an Exacto knife. If they haven't recovered the weapon, forensics has developed ways to analyze extraneous data like hair and fibers, that kind of thing."

"However they do it, I hope they catch the guy soon," he said, reaching for an impressionistic seascape painting propped against the wall. "A killer on the loose is bad for business. The crowd at the Emperor's has been like half the normal size."

"I'm not surprised. It's not helping that Daily is walking around like a peacock, thinking he's got the murder investigation all tied up. Normally, I'd be pleased as punch to see him knocked down a notch or two. But not this time. Our town is known for antiques and ghosts, not murders. And I want to keep it that way."

"We all do. But what can you do about it?"

"I'm going to do my damnedest to figure out why Nick Rizzo was murdered and bring the suspect—"

"Hold up a second. You're a P.I., not a cop. How in God's name are you going to solve a murder?"

I shrugged.

"It's going to take more than wishful thinking." He placed the landscape into the display window. "You should let DJ handle the investigation, after all, he's the professional." Simon took a quick glance at me over his shoulder. "You'd be better off finishing those paintings languishing in your studio."

"You're right. But I can't shake the idea that the killer is close by. Maybe someone obsessed with Pix. Or a person who hates Treasure's Trove of Lingerie."

He turned away from the window display and shot me a quizzical look.

"You believe in ghosts, right?"

"Yeah?" Simon narrowed his eyes.

"Do you think Robert Sullivan could be behind the murder?"

He shook his head. "Look, Becca. I think all this talk about the

83

murder is getting to you. Ghost can't kill people. On top of that, I really doubt that lingerie is a motive for murder. Go home. Relax. Paint."

He'd offered me the best advice I'd heard in days.

CHAPTER FOURTEEN

After spending most of the day shooting photographs for this year's designer house, Coventry, a wave of exhaustion hit me as I stepped into the apartment. The historical society's board of directors will review the photos and decide which ones to use for promoting the event. Next to the annual gala held at one of the county's most swanky country clubs, the designer house is the society's biggest fundraisers. The proceeds literally keep the archeological museum running.

I always enjoy traipsing through the historical houses chosen for a complete make-over at the hands of local designers. Being a traditional type of gal, some of their re-envisions have left me quite literally speechless. Nevertheless, I was tickled pink that I was hired to photograph the current one. Granted the privilege of being one of the first to be inside the transformed house, I traveled from room to room, clicking away and humming a soft tune of my own invention.

In the formal living room, I'd squatted in an attempt to capture the best angle to showcase the two-hundred-year-old fireplace as Jane Parks whispered that we were in the most haunted room in the house. Oh great, I thought with a roll of my eyes. Apparently, the original owner of Coventry had died suspiciously—the circumstances remain shrouded in mystery—in that room. The present-day owners reported that it wasn't unusual for them to wake up and find their furniture rearranged.

"Might cause some trouble when the house opens up to the public," I scoffed.

"That's why your photographs of this room are vital," Jane said. "That way we'll have a visual to direct us on how to replace the furniture according to the designer's exact specifications."

The memory from the photoshoot caused me to roll my eyes again. "Am I the only one who doesn't buy into this ghost stuff, hook, line, and sinker?" I questioned the purrs as I gingerly stepped between them and made my way to the kitchen area. I was starved, but as was my habit, the kitties always ate first. I reached into a cabinet and grabbed a couple cans of Fancy Feast. They waited brushing against my legs, except Jaspurr, who jumped onto the countertop when I flipped open a can of white meat chicken. I grabbed him by his mid-section and gingerly landed the cat onto the floor. Amid their insistent cries for me to hurry, I scooped out the mixture of gravy and chicken flakes and filled their bowls. They bolted to their individual food trays and gobbled down their dinner as if they hadn't eaten for days as I refilled their water fountain.

With their tummies full, I yanked open the fridge and pulled out the Pyrex baking dish with enough left-over lasagna for a decent dinner. I reached for the dial to pre-heat the oven when a sharp rap on the door startled me.

"Becca!"

Recognizing Pix's voice, I raced through my living space and jerked the door open. "What's wrong?"

"Everything." She stormed into the apartment and faced me. "Chuck failed the polygraph. The only reason they haven't arrested him is that they're waiting for the DNA results. That might take weeks. You've got to do something."

I dropped on the edge of the sofa and looked at her through questioning eyes.

"I'm Chuck's girlfriend, so DJ won't listen to me. But he respects—likes you."

"How'd you come up with that?"

She shook her head. "Please, talk to him. Persuade DJ to look for another suspect."

For an instant, I wondered if Chuck had something to do with Nick's death. Though I willed to expunge the idea from my mind, the possibility lingered. "Be real, Pix, Daily wouldn't give me the time of day. He knows we're all friends. Anyway . . . Hey, where's Chuck?"

"He left his lawyer's office about ten minutes ago. Said he's going to meet us here."

"Okay. How 'bout some dinner?" I walked to the kitchen, shut off the over, and returned the lasagna into the fridge.

"I'm too sick with worry to think about food."

"You'll be no good to Chuck if you don't take care of yourself." I didn't wait for a reply. "Stay here. I'll run over to the Crab Kettle and pick up some crab cake sandwiches, fries, and coleslaw."

She dropped onto my well-worn recliner. Coppurr jumped into her lap, and Pix absently stroked the top of his head. He craned his neck in my direction and let out a deep mew.

"Even Coppurr wants you to eat. He'll keep you company until I get back. So will the other two." I noticed Jaspurr eyeing Pix and Caspurr's elegant stride in her direction. Without giving her a chance to voice opposition, I slipped out of the apartment.

The Crab Kettle, located two short blocks west of my apartment, was always packed, especially during the dinner hours. The crew working the take-out counter were known not only for their courtesy, but for their speed and generous portions. I jogged the first block but slowed as I spied Woody, surprisingly dressed as himself, in a long-sleeved plaid shirt and gray flannelled slacks, loitering at the adjacent corner. I hurried toward him as I crossed the street.

"Miss Flynn," he said with a half-bow.

"Hey, Woody." I nodded, then stepped past him.

87

"I heard the detectives haven't found the murder weapon used to kill the television cameraman."

I stopped and did an about-face.

"They haven't given up the search," Woody continued. "In fact, the police believe it to be a small-bladed knife." He stroked his fleshy jaw.

I wrinkled my brow. "How do you know that?"

He shrugged as a wry smile crossed his jowly cheeks. "I've got my connections."

One of Woody's alter egos was a 1930s detective, an Elliot Ness type, with a loose-fitting suit, wide tie, and a flannel fedora with its brim set low on his forehead. His wealth of knowledge regarding the dawning of forensics during the 1930s was startling, though not completely surprising since his understanding of all the time periods he found himself living vicariously resulted through painstaking research.

"Pix thinks the ghost of Robert Sullivan killed Nick Rizzo."

"Ah, Miss Winslow."

I couldn't help but notice the dreamy expression claiming his face.

"I believe she's mistaken." He expelled the look of awe from his countenance. "What motive would entice Corporal Sullivan to commit such a savage act? Not to mention, my dear, a bayonet would certainly produce a deeper wound then say . . . a paring knife."

I puffed out a mouthful of air. "What possible reason would instigate the cold-blooded murder of a cameraman who'd only been in Bayleys Landing for barely a day?"

"Jealousy, of course."

I drew my brows together.

He withdrew the fat cigar from his shirt pocket and stuck it into the corner of his mouth. I stood dumbfounded as a transformation washed over him. His posture became ramrod straight, his eyes narrowed, and his voice rang abrasively sharp.

"Listen, sister. A dame like Pix Winslow could drive a saint to commit murder. All she's got to do is crook her little finger, and she's got guys falling silly all over themselves." He paused a second as his teeth sunk into the tightly wrapped Havana. "Now, my theory is some bozo got the hots for her real bad. Wants to can the competition if you get my drift. So, he offs the 'shooter'." He paused a second, probably noticing my confusion. "Offs the cameraman and pins the crime on the most obvious love-struck schmuck."

I reached into my purse and freed my notepad. I wanted to get this down because even though it sounded crazy, it made sense.

"Who do you think did it?" The words sounded raspy to my ears.

He withdrew the cigar and held it horizontally as if studying the unlit stogy. "Well, that's the kicker, sweetheart. My gut's telling me it ain't one of them lovesick puppies that follow on her heels. Gotta be someone beyond reproach. Respectable. Take a copper, for example. It may seem like we're immune to the weaker sex, but that ain't entirely true." He snapped his stubby fingers. "There's that soppy fella—"

"Woody!"

A woman's sharp voice cutting through the air caused his persona to vanish. His eyes lit up when they fell on her barreling form. I narrowed mine and pressed my lips together, spying Dolly Evans. She flounced toward us dressed in a frilly pink number that looked circa 1960. On her head sat a matching pillbox hat while a boat of a handbag swung in her white-gloved hand. She abruptly stopped, two feet away from us.

"Oh, Rebecca," Dolly said. "I didn't notice you standing there."

"Miss Flynn and I were having a little pow-wow about this mysterious murder," Woody said.

"From what I understand, Chuck Stetson did it. He was jealous of the cameraman." The trace of a smile vacated Dolly's thin lips as she tore her eyes away from Woody. "Hasn't that Treasure Winslow caused enough trouble around here?" She thrust her chin in my direction. "Mindy Marks is in town after being summoned by the police. But the good news, like I'm known to say—there's always a silver lining— is that we're finally going to wrap up our interview. Tonight. Mindy assured me that this time, they've procured a more reliable cameraman. One that won't lose his head—or life—over that lingerie floozy."

"Pix is in no mood to be grilled by the likes of Mindy Marks."

She ignored my comment with a toss of her head. It made her hat bounce landing it a bit lopsided atop her silvery, over-permed hair.

"Finally, the truth about her tacky business will be revealed." I heard the glee tinkling in Dolly's voice. "Then it'll be easier for the Board to revoke her business license." She bore into my eyes. "Her father's big bucks aren't going to be able to bribe anyone this time." Dolly swung around and grabbed Woody's arm. "Come on dear, we don't want to be late for our six o'clock reservation at the Capitoline Restaurant."

I didn't move for a couple seconds as Dolly's words sunk into my brain. Pix's father, no, that can't be right. Peter wouldn't have paid off members of the Merchant Association to ensure enough yay votes to set up her shop. He's a suave, upright businessman. I swallowed hard. For a moment, thoughts swirled through my mind—Pix, the only child of a billionaire, spoiled, her every whim delivered on a silver platter. I took a deep breath. *NoNoNoNoNo.* Every fiber in my being objected. But a fact lingered that I didn't want to face. *Peter always comes through for Pix.* A pessimistic knot twisted my stomach. Hadn't he told me the last time I visited Pix' parents that he'd do whatever it takes to make his little girl happy. I shook my head, trying to make my doubts take flight.

I took a deep breath keeping my sight targeted on Dolly, arm in arm, with Woody as they headed toward the restaurant. *I don't know if she's the one who started that malicious lie, but it's certainly in line with her subtle mode of stirring up trouble.*

I took a few quick steps and noticed the pad still in my hand. With a quick glance at my scribbled notes, I closed it and tossed the pad back into my bag. I hurried as my stomach screamed for food. But two storefronts away from the Crab Kettle, I froze.

"Can't be—can it?" I pulled out the notebook and flipped through the pages. My eyes fell on the sentences. *The killer. Above reproach. Respectable. Cop?*

Chuck's railroading was starting to make sense. Especially if Daniel James Daily killed the cameraman.

CHAPTER FIFTEEN

When I made it back into my apartment, Chuck and Pix sat nestled on the sofa with their hands entwined. Jaspurr had snuggled into Chuck's lap while Caspurr made himself comfortable, sound asleep, wedged against Pix. Coppurr sat on the floor with his keen eyes focused on the two of them.

"Hungry?" I held up the paper bag. The aroma of sweet crab and Old Bay Seasoning wafted in the air.

Chuck jumped up and took the bag from my hand. "Being grilled at the police station made me lose my appetite."

Even so, the stressful ordeal of being accused of murder hadn't tarnished his chivalrous manners. He walked to my tiny dinette table and started emptying the bag.

"You girls enjoy dinner. I'm going for a run. Try to clear my mind."

I whipped out my notepad. "I'd like your take on this." I glanced from Chuck to Pix. Desolation and despair covered their faces. Well, maybe I was overanalyzing, but they did seem tense and strained, with Pix chewing her lip like a piece of bubble gum and Chuck frowning. "I bumped into Woody on my way to the

Crab Kettle. And he," I said, flipping through the pad's pages, "thinks a jealous cop is responsible for Nick's death".

Chuck's jaw tightened a moment before he shook his head. "Don't tell me. One of his split personalities told you that. Get real, Becca."

"Hold up a sec." Pix sprung up from the couch. "Woody and DJ are friends. And DJ is investigating the case, after all. Maybe he shared some inside information with Woody."

"DJ and Woody are pals?" Chuck's eyebrows shot up.

"Haven't you ever noticed those two drinking beers and shooting the breeze on karaoke nights at the Winged Victory?" Pix said, brushing his arm.

"Nope." He shrugged. "I guess I only had eyes for you."

Pix kissed his cheek.

I found the touching scene a bit nauseating. Especially when Chuck pulled Pix close and kissed her hard on the lips. I stepped next to the table, snatched a fry, and popped it into my mouth. "Okay, you two, there'll be plenty of time for that later. First, we've got to figure out who is the lovesick puppy in blue and if he's smitten enough to take out the competition."

Chuck crossed his arms and eyed me. "You really think a cop is behind the cameraman's death?"

I shrugged. "It's possible."

"I don't know any cops," Pix said, "well, except for Officer Zimmer. Fred makes a habit of stopping by Treasure's Trove to check the store and make sure everything is okay. He thinks the hostility surrounding the opening of my shop was unfair." She pursed her lips. "Anyway, he says I remind him of his daughter so, it's obvious he doesn't have romantic feelings for me."

"I wasn't thinking of Officer Zimmer but more along the lines of . . . of . . . of Daniel James Daily."

"What?" Pix and Chuck exclaimed simultaneously.

"It makes perfect sense." I glanced between the two of them as the reaction I'd expected took hold. Chuck shook his head, and Pix flung out her arms in disbelief. "Hey guys, hear me out, at least."

Coppurr circled around us, his mewing growing louder. Insistent. As if telling them to listen to what I had to say. I picked him up and pressed the cat against my chest like a shield that would deflect their objections.

"Daily thinks you're a piece of eye candy," I said, looking at Pix. "He acts aloof, but the truth is he's not infatuated with me, as you suspect, but with you. Big time. Then there's the way he's railroading Chuck. I think he wants to pin the murder on you," I said, waving my hand in his direction, "so that Pix will be at such loose ends that she'll turn to Daily for support. Which would only be natural since he is the lead investigator." I inhaled sharply, ready to reveal the *pièce de résistance*. "He'd worm himself into Pix's affection by lying about how hard he's trying to clear you of the murder, that is until you wind up in a jail cell doing twenty-five to life."

"Just because I suggested that you and DJ share some romantic attraction for each other," Pix said, widening her eyes, "you come up with this cockamamie theory?" She shook her head. "Did Woody say the officer was DJ?"

"Not exactly. Just that a cop could've been responsible."

"So, there isn't any evidence?" Pix said.

"Not yet but . . ."

Coppurr jumped out of my arms, landed on the floor, and brushed against Pix's leg. Traitor, I thought.

"Whoa. Hold on a minute, Pix. Becca might be on to something." Chuck shrugged. "I'm gonna mull over your idea during my run." He offered me a nod, kissed Pix's cheek, and headed out of the apartment.

Once the door shut, Pix said, "I'm glad Chuck runs. It helps relieve the stress he's been under. He has his heart set on participating in next month's race. It's a qualifier for the Boston Marathon." She pulled out a dinette chair and sunk into it. "He's been training since this past January and runs three times a week, racking up about thirty-five miles in total."

"He is serious."

"But ever since Nick's murder, he's lost his incentive and has only been doing short runs."

I pulled open the fridge and yanked out a bottle of Sicilian Nero d' Avola. I'd bought the wine yesterday as a way to celebrate my recent good fortune in selling three paintings. I poured two glasses and handed one to Pix. She sipped the red liquid as I finished setting the table. I dropped into the chair opposite her, grabbed a fry, pleased that it was still warm.

"Something's bothering me." Pix sat the wineglass down next to her plate.

I swallowed a bite of my crab cake sandwich. "Oh?"

"If Chuck is innocent, how in God's name did he fail the polygraph?"

"A polygraph isn't a Pinocchio meter. The results are based on autonomic arousals." I noticed Pix frown. "Changes in the heart or respiratory rates, for example. But really, it's not that unusual for an innocent person to fail a lie detector test. Sometimes just the anxiety surrounding the prospect of failing the test can produce a deceptive reading. But in Chuck's case, I imagine all it took was the indignation of being accused of the murder to spin his autonomic system haywire."

I noticed the tightness along her jawline soften. Though I didn't want to stress her out again so soon, I couldn't shake the thought that she'd agreed to the interview with Mindy Marks. "I ran into Dolly on my way to the Crab Kettle."

"I'm surprised you still have an appetite."

I picked up a fry and pointed it at her. "She told me Mindy Marks is back in town." I popped the crispy potato into my mouth.

"She is?" Pix freed her cellphone from her back pocket. "I haven't been checking my texts. This thing with Chuck . . ." She scrolled down the screen. "Here it is. Oh, wow. She wants to do the interview tonight at the Tea Pot Shoppe. Nine o'clock."

"You're in no frame of mind to face that pariah. Tell her no."

"Then she'll think I have something to hide," Pix said. "Like my father bribed the Merchant Association or something equally crazy."

"I heard something about that."

Pix rolled her eyes. "That proves it. I have no choice." Her thumbs danced on the phone's keyboard. "You will be there for moral support?"

"Of course. But there's a bit of investigating I need to do first. I'll meet you there at half-past eight."

"Does this investigating of yours have to do with DJ?"

"You bet it does."

CHAPTER SIXTEEN

I paced the length of my one-room apartment. Coppurr followed close on my heels while Jaspurr, asleep on the sofa, displayed the epitome of cuteness laying on his back with his white paws curled against his furry chest, as Caspurr eyed the pantry in hopes of a treat.

Now that I had telephoned Daily with the pretext that I had a lead, I worried I'd been impulsive. As usual, I hadn't quite thought the idea through since I'd happily jumped to the conclusion that he could be Nick's killer. The probable reason—I liked the idea of the arrogant, self-centered detective driven in a fit of jealousy to murder. Even if I didn't have a lick of evidence. All I had was my gut instinct and the musing of an eccentric gentleman who lived in a fantasy world. And Woody hadn't even fingered Daily. How could I've been so stupid?

I stopped walking and rubbed my throbbing temples. My dinner felt like a rock in the pit of my stomach. Of course, Daily had shown interest when I'd contacted him. He'd insisted that since he was down the street finishing dinner at the Capitoline Restaurant, he could swing by my apartment to discuss the matter. Stupidly, I'd agreed. But what if I was right and Daily had murdered Nick . . . The last thing in the world I'd want is a killer inside my home.

What did I know about Daily anyway? Except that he's a pompous SOB, and though I didn't want to admit it, even to myself, a pretty good detective. I first met him, I closed my eyes, trying to remember. "February. That's right. It was Valentine's Day," I mumbled. And from the onset, he was disagreeable—crabby really. I'd chalked it up to the fact that I'd stolen some of his glory by locating the missing woman. Daily was interviewed on the news as some kind of hero for foiling the murder attempt and nabbing the perpetrator, which only intensified his already enormous ego. The news reporter barely mentions my part in saving the victim's life. A mother of three young children and the perp's wife.

The sound of a sharp rap filled the apartment. The cats flew to the door, even Jaspurr, who'd been suddenly awakened, no doubt, from a happy cat dream. I sucked in a deep breath, shooed the purrs away, and opened the door. Daily stood there with an egotistical smirk on his all too handsome face.

I didn't give him a chance to speak. "Look, I'm sorry you came over here for nothing. I was mistaken." I started to close the door.

"Hold up."

Daily stepped past me and entered the apartment. The cats hovered around his feet. He reached toward Caspurr and patted my kitty's snow-white head. Straightening, he eyed me for a second before folding his arms. "Now, what exactly was this lead you thought you had?"

I shook my head.

He plopped down on the couch across from my thirteen-inch T.V. screen. "You're telling me, you've got nothing Miss Private Investigator?" A smile played at the corners of his mouth. "Just as I expected. So, this was only a ruse to get me over here. I kinda guessed you wanted to pick my brains about the case." He paused a second, then looked me straight in the eyes. "Unless," he said with a shrug, "I think you're fascinated, no—scratch that—I think you've developed an inexplicable obsession with me."

My jaw dropped as I sputtered a denial. My reaction made him laugh.

That was it. I'd had enough. Never had I met a more infuriating man. A rush of anger zoomed through me that not only made me see red, it released my tied-up tongue. "I think you're over the moon infatuated with Pix. You're the one who's crazed with jealously."

He frowned.

I bit my tongue, but it was too late.

He stood. The wild expression on his face scared me. I moved backward and banged into the wall.

I pressed my lips together as a slew of emotions took over, from embarrassment to strong-willed pride. A streak of determination strengthened me. I refused to allow Daily the chance to accuse me of jumping to half-baked assumptions. After all, he'd be only too eager to crow that I base my investigations on hunches, or worse yet, emotions. I grit my teeth waiting for him to say something.

"Do you actually think I was behind Rizzo's death?"

"Well," I said with a shrug. "It's evident that you have a thing for Pix and your treatment of Chuck has been over the top."

"Over the top?" His forehead wrinkled. "I'm treating him no different than any person of interest. And when it comes to Treasure Winslow, I believe she has enough starry-eyed men bonkers over her. But I do think it's kinda interesting that the minute the cameraman is out of the picture, she and Stetson became a couple."

I exhaled a puff of air. "All that means is Pix finally came to her senses. Realized what a great guy Chuck is. Anyway, Pix never pays much attention to the adulation she receives from those starry-eyed men." I made air quotes.

Daily sucked in his bottom lip. "That may be. But I believe one of those guys is responsible for Rizzo's death. And Stetson has been her champion since the minute she set foot into Bayleys Landing with her plan for that outlandish lingerie shop."

"Just because he supported Pix—"

"Look, Rebecca, don't ever diminish the power of jealousy and what it's capable of."

"Which brings me back to you. I don't think it's a coincidence that you always seem to show up on karaoke night at the Winged Victory exactly when Pix and Chuck take center stage. You'd have to be blind not to see how close those two are, and it's not surprising that now they're a couple. Perhaps landing Chuck in jail is your way to eliminate the competition. That way, the field would be open for you to swoop in and make a play for her."

"Don't be ridiculous."

"I'm serious."

"I'm married."

"Married?" The breath died in the back of my throat. How stupid could I be? He's never worn a ring, so I assumed he was single. Wrong assumption, big time, I thought with my cheeks burning.

"At least, that's how I feel."

I frowned. He'd lost me.

"My wife died two years ago. Amy was an exceptional athlete and was training for a half Ironman competition. She was struck while running on Route 99, and the driver didn't bother to stop. Left her to die in the gutter."

I wanted to say something, but words escaped me. I rested my hand on his arm.

"She was my world." He focused on my ancient hardwood floor. "It may sound strange that even though she's gone, I can't let go of her or my marriage."

"I'm so sorry," I said, finding my voice. "I had no idea."

"Every scumbag I arrest is a vindication for me. One day, I pray to God, I'll be able to lock up that bastard who stole Amy's life." He sighed, then shook his head. "I gotta go."

"Wait." I didn't know where that came from, but I couldn't bear to see him like this—bereaved, desolate, anguished—broken.

I wanted the Daniel James Daily I knew to resurface; the one I could spar with, compete against, dislike.

"I'm gonna head to the animal shelter where I volunteer. I help walk the dogs. It's been good therapy for me."

Daily volunteers at a shelter? There's a lot I don't know about him. Especially why he revealed his heartbreak to me.

He moved toward the door, but Coppurr stopped in front of him. With one smooth motion, he lifted the cat and cradled the kitty in his arms.

"The cats don't get a whole lot of company," I said. "Why don't you stay a few minutes and play with them?"

He glanced at his watch and nodded. "Your cats are great. Rescues?" He carried Coppurr, whose gravelly purr intensified as Daily scratched the cat under his chin. He reclaimed his spot on the sofa and started rubbing Coppurr's belly.

"Coppurr and Jaspurr were adopted from Animal Control, and I found Caspurr collapsed in terrible condition smack in the middle of Main Street."

"It's terrific that you've made such a great home for them."

Did I hear that right? Daily offered me a compliment?

"Would you like a drink?"

"A beer would work."

I moved to the kitchen area and yanked open the refrigerator in search of a couple leftover bottles of Natty Boh. Chuck had brought the beer to go with our steamed crabs while watching an Orioles game. One of our weekly rituals that would probably end since Pix didn't drink beer, pick crabs, or watch baseball. I grabbed a bottle, opened it, not bothering to look at the puzzle inside the cap, and poured the amber liquid into a glass.

I noticed that Coppurr had vacated Daily's arms and had snuggled next to him. I handed him the beer. He raised it to his lips and swallowed. Instead of placing the glass on the nearby coaster, he looked at the foamy liquid. "You know," he said, "Pix Winslow is the polar opposite of my wife, but you . . ." He glanced away from the beer and targeted his sight on me. "You remind me a lot of Amy. She liked to paint, too. I've seen your stuff over at the Prescott Gallery. You're really good."

I nodded, wondering when he would add a snide comment.

"I think you should can the P.I. work and concentrate on your art. Because really, Rebecca, you basically stink at investigations."

"Ah." A reappearance of the Daniel James Daily I knew. "A D.C. lawyer has shown interest in my paintings. If I find a few more like him, I just might do that."

He absently ran his fingers through Coppurr's fur as he took a long draught of beer. "That sounds like a plan. That way there wouldn't be any conflicts with us getting to know each other better."

I raised my eyebrows, realizing a mystified look must've claimed my face. *Is he suggesting what I think he's suggesting? That we become friends? Me, friends with the most irritating, arrogant, and conceited man I know? God, please, no.*

I ignored his comment. "That may not be for some time yet. I don't relish the idea of being a starving artist."

"So why the hell hasn't your friend Pix stepped up to the plate. She's loaded, isn't she?"

Pix had offered to financially help me out on more than one occasion, but I'd flatly refused.

I cherish the bond between us and don't want money to jeopardize our friendship. Ever.

"I don't use my friends that way." The words sounded curt to my ears, but I wanted him to understand Pix's money wasn't an option.

"I hear you, but . . ." He shrugged.

I glanced at my watch. Eight forty-five. Pix is going to be wondering where I am, I thought, puzzled about how I'd lost track of the time.

"Speaking of Pix, I was supposed to meet her fifteen minutes ago at the Tea Pot Shoppe. Mindy Marks," I paused a sec noticing him roll his eyes when I mentioned her name, "she's interviewing Pix and Dolly in hopes of getting to the bottom of the conflict over Treasure's Trove of Lingerie."

"I'd bet my last dollar sparks are gonna fly."

"I believe that's what Mindy is betting on."

My cellphone sounded. I grabbed it from the end table and swiped the screen. "It's Pix." At first, the words I read didn't register. But then I felt my knees go weak, and I dropped onto the edge of the couch.

"Something's wrong?" Daily said.

His face had tensed as if he was ready to spring into action.

"Come on. Chuck's in the hospital. Someone tried to kill him."

CHAPTER SEVENTEEN

I took up Daily's offer to drive me to the Baltimore trauma center believing we'd get there quicker with his police car lights flashing. Even with siren and lights, the ride seemed interminable. I willed my heart to stop pounding, took several deep breaths, and offered up a quick prayer knowing that if I didn't pull myself together, I'd be useless to Pix. What she needed now was a pillar of strength, not a weak-kneed nervous Nellie.

Daily turned into the lot and parked next to the entrance reserved for police vehicles. I jumped out of the car before he'd turned off the ignition, flew through the automatic glass doors, and sprinted to the registration counter. I craned my neck, trying to locate Pix somewhere within the first floor waiting room. The touch on my shoulder made me jump.

"I'll check up on Stetson," Daily said with his fingers lingering on my back. "Pix needs you."

I nodded, answered the receptionist's questions, and pressed the visitor's pass onto my shirt.

Before removing his hand, he patted me a couple of times. His touch left me with a surprising burst of encouragement as I moved into the waiting room. It took a minute to locate Pix standing against a far wall with her eyes shut and arms folded across her chest. She was dressed in a smartly cut suit with her hair pulled up into a knot. Tendrils had escaped and cascaded around her face. She must've been at the Tea Pot Shoppe for the interview when the news reached her about Chuck. Across from her stood a matronly-looking woman. I couldn't see her face but she seemed familiar.

Unsure of how to comfort Pix, I headed toward my devastated friend. I stopped a few steps away, not wanting to jolt Pix from what I imagined would be tense, scary thoughts. I whispered her name. She flashed her eyes open and fell into my arms. I held her for a few seconds until she pulled away, unable to mask the desperation from her face.

"Why is this happening?" Pix's voice cracked. "Someone hates me so much that he's killing my friends?"

"You mean Chuck has . . . has —"

"We're waiting for an update."

I turned toward the familiar voice and did a double take seeing Dolly Evans. I stared at her with, I'm sure, a look of disbelief on my face.

"Treasure was at "The Shoppe" when the call came from the hospital," Dolly said. "She was in such a state I wouldn't dare allow her to drive. Well, anyway, I wanted to make sure she arrived safely. Now that you're here, I'll be on my way." Dolly stepped closer to Pix. "Keep in mind what I told you. You have to have faith."

To my shock, she squeezed Pix's arm and kissed her flushed cheek.

"Thank you," Pix said. "When we know something, I'll contact you."

Dolly nodded and headed for the exit.

I took Pix's arm, a bit perplexed over the exchanged I'd just witnessed, and led her to a couple of newly vacated chairs. I was anxious to know how Chuck was fairing but decided to stay quiet until Pix felt up to talking. It didn't take long.

"Chuck's in surgery." She took a deep breath. "He'd been

stabbed. A man walking along the Pawcattawaye pulled him out of the water. I don't know the details except he resuscitated Chuck and saved his life."

"Thank God for the good Samaritan." I grabbed her hand and squeezed it.

Pix stared straight ahead. "I'm nothing but a curse. I'm going to move away from Bayleys Landing before all my friends wind up dead. I'm worried, especially for you." She faced me, and I saw tears well in her red-rimmed eyes.

"Shhh," I said, rubbing her hand. "You are not a jinx. And you know me, I can take care of myself." I shot her a reassuring smile. "The important thing now is to focus on Chuck. Would you like to visit the chapel?"

Pix nodded as I caught a glimpse of Daily headed our way. He wasn't alone. Mindy Marks stood at his side.

Daily rushed ahead of the lingerie host, stopped in front of us, and focused on Pix. "Look, I'm really sorry."

"Have you heard anything," Pix squeaked the words out, standing up.

"Chuck is still in surgery." Daily stepped closer. "I swear to you; we're gonna catch this piece of crap and lock him up so he'll never see the light of day again."

"I just want Chuck to survive," Pix said. Her shoulders started to shake, so I stood and slipped my arm around her waist.

Mindy Marks faced us. I could tell by the way her eyes twinkled that she was enjoying the unfolding scene.

"Treasure . . . Pix . . . don't worry about the interview," Mindy said. "I've talked to my producer and have made plans to stay in Bayleys Landing a few more days."

The nerve of her. But being a typical reporter, I assumed that like a mouse on a wheel, she'd be in perpetual search for a juicy story. Mindy sure wasn't finding anything newsworthy to report from *Lingerie Exposed*, that is, until now. After all, what had started out as a fluff piece about a lingerie shop had morphed into a murder mystery. I feared she'd milk the tragedy for all it's worth regardless of the pain it brought to Pix. *Well, Mindy Marks, you sure aren't welcomed here.*

"I'll text you later so we can reschedule," Mindy said. "Hopefully, everything will turn out okay for your friend so we can get back to business." Her words trailed off as a young woman dressed in scrubs stopped in front of us. Pix slipped out of my grasp only to wrap her arms around her chest.

Mindy bumped into me, nearly pushing me over, in her quest to move closer to the nurse. I'd had enough. Before I could make a move, I noticed she'd slipped out her cellphone and was aiming the screen at the nurse. No one else seemed to realize that Mindy was filming the exchange, so I stepped in front and blocked her view. I swore under my breath that I'd do my damnedest to prevent Mindy Mark from making a circus out of Pix's distress.

"You better put that away before I put it away for you," I hissed, facing her.

She glared at me but dropped the phone into her oversized handbag.

I missed whatever the nurse had said but did notice Daily hand her his card. He started to walk away.

"Please, DJ," Pix said. "Come with us."

He rejoined our little group.

A good move, I thought. If the news turned out to be devastating, at least Daily could provide Pix with a measure of physical support. She didn't share the same hostile feelings I harbored toward the detective.

As we followed the nurse to the surgery waiting room, I heard the sound of heels clicking behind me. I glanced over my shoulder. Mindy was once again fiddling with her phone, but this time she was looking at the screen. For goodness sakes, I thought, that woman isn't going to worm her way into our private affairs. "Pix," I said. "I have to check something. I'll meet up with you in a couple of minutes."

Pix didn't comment, but her hollow eyes said more than words ever could.

I spun around and faced Mindy. "Where do you think you're going?"

She looked up from the phone. "Where do you think?" Mindy took a sideward step.

Even though I could feel the blood pumping through my veins, I decided to swallow my emotions and try a rational approach. "Mindy, please, have some respect for Pix's feelings."

"I don't deal in feelings. This is a news story. My story. I have an obligation to get the facts."

I've never before had such a strong urge to slug someone, but instead of belting her one, I sucked in a mouthful of air.

"Now, get out of my way." Mindy's eyes narrowed with determination as she sashayed past me.

I noticed a hospital attendant rolling a bed down the corridor. I waved my arms, attempting to get his attention. His eyes remained focused on the cot. "Call security," I yelled, pointing at Mindy. Utter confusion filled his face.

"Becca?"

A voice sounded behind me. Startled to hear my name, I swung around. Simon jogged toward me. Still a few feet away, he said, "How's Chuck?"

"Get her," I said in response and started rushing toward Mindy, who'd quickened her pace.

For a second, I believed Simon thought I'd lost my marbles until he sped past me. Then I noticed the orderly had abandoned his task and was in hot pursuit of the rogue reporter.

It took the two of them only seconds to grasp Mindy by the arms. Relief flowed through me as I joined them. I itched to flash her a victor's smile instead, I faced Mindy with my best deadpan expression. Her eyes bulged, and her cheeks flushed an angry red.

"Let go of me. I'm a television reporter for a national show." Indignation filled her voice. "I have the right—"

"Reporters aren't allowed to interview patients," the attendant said. "Hospital policy. You'll have to go through a patient representative."

"That would be me," I said. "And at this time, I have no comment."

"Well, I . . ." Mindy huffed. She spun around on her stilettos and stomped away, muttering under her breath.

"Thanks," I said to the attendant.

"Hey, no problem. Glad to help." He headed toward the abandoned bed.

I grabbed Simon's arm. "Come on. Pix needs us."

CHAPTER EIGHTEEN

S imon and I arrived at the surgery waiting room too late to hear the doctor's update. But I feared the worst since Pix sat with her hands covering her face. Before I could reach her, Daily grabbed my arm and steered me out of the small waiting area. The pounding of my heart intensified as I steeled myself for bad news.

"Chuck made it through surgery."

I exhaled. It wasn't until hearing Daily's words that I realized I'd been holding my breath. "That's a relief." I turned back to the waiting room.

"However . . ."

I stopped walking and faced him.

"The good news is that the knife missed his heart. But there are some internal injuries. A perforated diaphragm, three lacerations on the surface of the liver, and a cut to the stomach. The doc said it may be touch and go, but if he makes it through the night . . ."

A wave of dizziness hit me as my knees went weak. Daily grabbed my arms and saved me from hitting the floor. He pulled me close. I wanted to break away but couldn't. His arms offered much-needed comfort, as he gently stroked my back.

"You okay?" He whispered into my ear.

I pulled away, and he released me.

"The doc gave me the green light," Daily said, "so I'm gonna see if Stetson can provide any pertinent info."

"I'll go with you."

He shook his head. "Police business."

"But Chuck needs to see a friend's face—" I began to protest until he cut me off.

"Pix needs you now more than ever."

I knew he was right, but what harm could it do if I tagged along? Then I'd be able to give Pix a first-hand report on Chuck's well-being. I tried another tactic. "Seeing you might worsen his condition." After all, Daily had been doing his best to alter Chuck's future by having him slapped with a twenty-five to life prison sentence. "Let me question him."

He touched my shoulder. "I'll find out when Stetson will be allowed visitors." With that, he left me standing alone.

I took a couple of deep breaths before entering the waiting room. Simon had an arm around Pix's shoulders, and the color had returned to her face. He whispered in her ear, and she smiled.

Thank God for Simon. He's helping her to relax. I planted a smile on my face and joined them.

"Simon told me how you two put Mindy Marks in her place," Pix said. "But why was she hanging around the hospital? Chuck doesn't mean anything to her."

"I suppose Mindy thinks she's got her claws on a hot story since two guys interested in the same woman wound up in the Pawcattawaye River. I wouldn't be surprised if she makes you out as a black widow or some other sort of idiocy."

"I should've known that she's fishing for a story," Pix said. "Mindy put on a good front pretending she cares about Nick and Chuck, but all she really wants is to stir up trouble. The woman has no morals." Pix took a sip from a coffee cup. "Take that interview between Dolly and me. Mindy's one and only objective

—to restart the controversy surrounding my shop. But it won't do her any good. On the way to the hospital, Dolly told me she's having second thoughts about the interview. She's probably going to back out, leaving Mindy with a big, fat zero."

I nodded absently. Pix had hit upon something that hadn't crossed my mind. *Was it only a story Mindy was after or was it more?*

"Becca?" Pix's voice thwarted the kernel of an idea taking root in my brain. "Where's DJ?"

"The doctor OK'd him to ask Chuck some questions."

"You mean Chuck's awake?" She flew from her seat but stopped in the middle of the room. "Why haven't they taken me to him?" She flung her arm wildly at the door.

Simon eased her back into a chair. "The police are always the first ones to see a crime victim. They need to gather as much relevant information as soon as possible. You want the person responsible for hurting Chuck to be found, don't you?"

She worried her lip with a forefinger. "Of course, I do. But what I really need now is to see my sweet man's face. To hear his voice. To know he's okay."

I glanced at Simon. His shoulders stooped as he hung his head. Poor guy. He hasn't gotten over his infatuation with Pix. But then again, most of the Main Street guys are probably jealous that Chuck won the prize of dating Pixie Winslow.

"That may not happen for hours yet." He looked at Pix. "You hungry? Why don't we head to the food court and grab a bite to eat?"

Pix stood and rolled her shoulders. "Sounds good. But first, I want to stop by the chapel and pray for Chuck's full recovery."

Simon narrowed his eyes. "Food will do you a lot better than prayers."

The nurse from earlier stepped into the room. "Mr. Stetson has asked for you. Please come this way." She motioned toward the door.

"That's great," I said, linking Pix's arm with mine.

"I'm sorry," the nurse said. "Only one visitor for now. Tomorrow—"

"No problem," I said. "Give Chuck our love."

"I don't know what I'd do without you. Thanks, Becca," Pix said before racing from the room.

I faced Simon. "How 'bout we head to the eateries?"

He checked his watch. "It's getting kind of late. I still have to finish framing a watercolor. Can I take a rain check?"

"Of course," I said, a bit confused since it was his suggestion after all. "Have you seen Detective Daily? He was my ride but—"

"No worries. I'll give you a lift." Simon moved next to me. "Today, a customer asked about you. Wanted to see your plein air paintings."

I grabbed his arm as we exited the waiting room. "Tell me more." Talking about my paintings was the diversion I needed, or else I'd worry myself sick over who wanted to murder Chuck. And how I was going to find his would-be killer.

CHAPTER NINETEEN

I raced up the outside metal staircase leading to my apartment, suppressing a yawn. No doubt about it, I'd fall sound asleep the minute I crashed on the couch. I didn't even have the strength or desire to pull down the Murphy bed.

I turned the key to unlock the door, and greetings from the purrs filtered into the night air. Not happy salutations, but complaints scolding me for leaving them alone for hours. I stepped inside, and they scurried around my feet. To make amends, I ran my fingertips through their silky fur and cooed reassurances of my devotion. After a few minutes, they apparently forgave me, and took off chasing each other from one end of the apartment to the other.

I stretched out on the couch and closed my eyes. I'd almost drifted off when a weight settled on my chest. Not having to flick my eyes open, I knew the heft belonged to my snowy white cat, Caspurr. With a sigh, I scooted against the back of the couch and stroked his dense fur. Way too tired to think straight, I focused on the purring cat. Out of nowhere, a sense of peacefulness gifted by the cat's humming gave way to a troublesome recollection. The gleeful expression I glimpsed on Mindy Marks' face at the hospital, while Pix was lost in the throes of a major breakdown. Regardless that Mindy's job was to report "news" on the lingerie front, the drama in the emergency room had nothing to do with her. I stroked Caspurr a couple times, but then, with a start, I jumped up. The kitty landed unfazed on the floor. "Maybe the murderous attacks do connect to Mindy Marks. But how?" Now I was the one roving from one end of the apartment to the other, as the cats, still as statues, eyed my movements.

Except for the fact that Mindy was irritating as the day was long, I knew next to nothing about her. I rushed to the wide wooden shelf that graced the wall near my dinette and grabbed my laptop. I placed it on the kitchen table, fired it up, and tapped my foot, waiting for the darned thing to turn on. There has to be oodles of info—some true and some not—about the lingerie host.

My fingers flew across the keyboard as I googled Mindy's name. I was a bit shocked to discover the many pages of stuff written about her. The first site I checked was Wikipedia which listed the basics—hometown, father's profession (physician), education, work history, personal life. Turns out, Mindy started her career working for a news station in Elkins, West Virginia. Quite a ways from the bright lights of Hollywood.

I scanned the page and stopped at the heading: Controversy. The breath caught in the base of my throat as the words revealed that Mindy's husband had died under suspicious circumstances— he'd drowned in their in-ground swimming pool. She'd been considered a suspect until the autopsy revealed that his blood alcohol was .30, high enough, I'm sure, to make an elephant a bit tipsy. The coroner declared his death accidental, so that left Mindy off the hook.

Reenergized, I padded to the refrigerator and pulled out a can of diet cola, flipped the tab, and took a long draught. Though the Elkins police found Mindy to be innocent, the fact that Nick and Chuck wound up in the Pawcattawaye River had me grasping at some kind of direct link. I blew out a stream of air as I inched down the Google listings. I stopped at an entry posted by *Razzmatazz*, the Hollywood gossip show. I clicked it and sat back as a smiling Mindy filled the screen. The overly made-up interviewer shot Mindy a toothy smile as she inquired about the lingerie host's love life. Batting her impossibly long eyelashes, Mindy spilled the beans, which was apparently a surprise by gauging the host's expression. Mindy and David Regan, the director of her new series, *Lingerie Exposed* were dating.

"Mindy and the director?" My eyes popped wide open. I hadn't been around those two for any length of time, but they certainly didn't seem like a couple. Professional, yes.

But that was about all I could come up with since they didn't even seem a bit friendly.

"Hmm. Maybe there's a reason for that." I glanced away from the computer and noticed Coppurr looking up at me. "What do you think?"

Coppurr offered a tiny meow.

"Are you thinking what I'm thinking?"

Coppurr's mew resounded louder.

"A messy break-up full of accusations and incriminations?"

Coppurr jumped onto the table and hopped into my lap. His gravelly purr filled my ears.

"Let me see." I pulled my attention away from the cat happily kneading in my lap. "If Mindy is who I think she is . . ." I typed the words, "Facebook Mindy Marks" into the search engine. A second later, I was scrolling through her social media page. I'm not surprised, I thought, that she shares the most inconsequential minutia with the whole world. "Lucky for me," I said with a nod. I stopped at a photo of Mindy with the director. The caption stated: *Me and David in happier times.* I checked the entry date. Just about two months ago. I took a quick sip of soda and almost choked. The next posting was of Mindy and Nick Rizzo. *Me and my new guy. Isn't he adorable, not to mention, sexy?*

I jumped up—sending poor Coppurr to the floor—and paced the width of my narrow apartment. Mindy and Nick—a couple? Her overreaction to Pix's date with Nick started to make sense.

Coppurr had jumped back into the chair, curled into a fluffy ball, and had fallen asleep. I gingerly lifted the cat, set him onto his cat bed, and reclaimed my place. I scrolled down Mindy's timeline, not sure what I was looking for—but then I saw it. Mindy, with a smug expression plastered on her perfect face, had her hand on Chuck's arm—an uncomfortable-looking Chuck. I glanced at the caption. "Maybe he's more than just a fan." I checked the stats—4.2k likes, 437 comments. I glanced at the first remark: *What a hottie! Is he your new love?* Mindy's response set my teeth on edge. I stood and walked to the kitchen window. Looking outside, I saw a veil of blackness akin to the darkness that clouded my brain.

I'm too tired to think. I rubbed my temples as Mindy's response ran through my brain. *If he knows what's good for him.* She'd punctuated the sentence with a smiley face.

Her late husband, Nick, and Chuck found in bodies of water. Two dead. One clinging to life. Could she be dealing out deadly revenge to men who . . . What? Dumped her? Blew her off?

I glanced at the clock hanging on the wall above the sink and stifled a yawn. 1:45. Too late to try to make sense of this. Tomorrow, I thought with a shake of my head, tomorrow all the pieces will fall into place. At least, I hoped so. I ambled over to the wall and pulled down my Murphy bed.

CHAPTER TWENTY

The sound of my cellphone's ringtone woke me. "Hello." I managed to whisper as I looked at the clock on the combination nightstand/bookcase next to my bed. 6:30.

"Did I wake you?"

Pix.

I rolled onto my back. Jaspurr, stretched out at the foot of the bed, didn't stir. The phone hadn't interrupted his sleep.

"I was planning on getting up. In a couple of hours." The fuzzy fog of sleepiness began to vanish. "How's Chuck?"

"I'm worried about him. He's in a lot of pain and—"

"That's to be expected. But he'll improve day by day. You'll see." I was dying to ask if Chuck had said anything about the attack but decided to let her bring it up. Instead, I said that I'd stop by the hospital later.

"I know you're right, but I can't help but worry," Pix said.

"Chuck is a fighter. He's not going to let a few stab wounds stop him, especially since he's dating the girl of his dreams. Which means you're all the motivation he needs to recover."

"I plan to be with him every step of the way."

"I'll be right behind you."

"You've always been there for me. Thanks, Becca," her voice cracked. Pix paused a second before continuing. "I called my parents from the hospital last night. I didn't want them to find out what's been happening through a skewed news report by Mindy Marks."

"Smart move on your part."

"Except now they insist on flying here to offer support. The last thing I need is for Peter to confront Mindy and Brenda to hover over me like I'm a ten-year-old. They think it's their mission in life to shield me from even the tiniest sign of trouble. I get it. But they fail to grasp the fact that I *am* capable of solving my own problems."

"Of course you are." I tried to sound confident. But I couldn't shake Dolly's insinuation that Peter had bribed some of the shopkeepers into supporting Pix's side in the battle for the lingerie shop to become a business on Main Street.

"Peter did say he has business here so it wouldn't be an imposition, but—"

"Business?" I sat up in the bed. "What kind of business would Peter have in Bayleys Landing?"

"The renewable energy market is hot everywhere. He was a pioneer in the field back in the 1970s, so I wouldn't be surprised if he's meeting with clients—government officials, local utility companies, contractors."

"Hmm." I kicked the sheet off and slipped my feet over the edge of the mattress. "It'll be lovely to see your parents again. You think they need some artwork for that new house of theirs?"

"I wouldn't know. They have every single painting I ever made hanging on their walls. Yours would be a great improvement." Pix sighed. "With Peter occupied with his business dealings, Brenda will take over my kitchen and toss out just about everything in my fridge. For the next week or so, I'll be drinking gallons of herbal tea and chowing down on tofu, figs, goat cheese, and dandelion greens."

"Hey, not to worry. I'll smuggle you away for a quick lunch at Pantheon Pizza so you can get your junk-food fix."

She sighed again. This time louder. "I explained to them that I'll probably be spending all my time at the hospital. Oh, Becca. Who would want to kill Chuck . . . and Nick?"

I wasn't ready to share my hunch. But I did want to assuage her anxiety, if only a smidgen. "I did a little digging last night, and I think I might've come up with a suspect."

"Really?" A trace of hope sounded in her voice.

"When I'm certain, I'll let you know."

"It's Robert Sullivan, isn't it? The Civil War ghost is jealous. How did you figure it out?"

I wanted to shout some sense into Pix, but I didn't. She was stressed out, frightened, and probably exhausted. How could she be expected to think clearly since twisted threads of dread held her mind prisoner?

"I guarantee you, it isn't a ghost, but a living, breathing, spiteful, hate-filled human being responsible for these crimes."

"Come on, Becca. Spill it. I need to know."

"I don't want to get your hopes up. I could be dead wrong."

"You still don't suspect DJ?"

"DJ." I chewed my lip, remembering the solace I felt nestled within his embrace. "I've scratched Daily off my list. So, no, I don't suspect him."

"Well, good," Pix said. "But I wouldn't flat-out reject Robert Sullivan. It drives me crazy seeing him every day camped outside of my shop window. To me, he seems like the ideal perp." She paused a sec. "I'm heading out to the hospital after I stop by the Hot and Chilly Bean.

Hopefully, a good jolt of caffeine will calm my nerves."

"I'll meet you at the hospital in a couple of hours. There's something I want to run by Daily first."

"About your suspect?"

"Uh-huh. What I've got is circumstantial, even though it is pretty powerful. Now, I've got to talk Daily into realizing it's the best lead so far."

"Knowing that someone's gonna be arrested and that my

friends are out of harm's way will lift the weight-of-the-world off my shoulders. Just tell me who it is already. Please."

"I promise. You won't be in the dark for long. That's if Daily—"

"Oh, alright. I'll keep my fingers crossed that you're right. See you later."

I looked into the darkened screen of my cellphone for a second. The idea of going back to sleep was now down the tubes.

CHAPTER TWENTY-ONE

After leaving a message on Daily's voicemail, assuring him that this time I had an actual lead in the case, I decided to head to the hospital. I breezed down the staircase, exited through my office, and breathed in the freshness of the day. My step was light, and the tension binding my shoulders had all but disappeared, probably because I was onto something substantial regarding the mysterious attacks.

I pulled open the driver side door of my Honda. But then, an idea seemingly out of the blue hit me. My jaw dropped. *Could it be?* I leaned against my burgundy sedan with arms crossed. Maybe it isn't Mindy who has an ax to grind. The director. David Regan. Could he be the one who can't accept rejection—rejection from Mindy Marks? It's possible, I frowned, remembering that both attacks happened when Mindy and the entire crew was in town.

I eased into my car but didn't turn the ignition. Instead, I closed my eyes and tried to slow down my brain. After a couple of seconds, I pulled out my notepad and started a list.

ATTACK #1 Monday, April 2

Murder of NICK RIZZO

- Mindy and Nick dating
- Nick dumps Mindy while in Bayleys Landing?
- Mindy furious that Nick asked Pix out for dinner
- David Regan—if he didn't know about the breakup
  —still jealous/angry that Mindy dumped him
  for Nick
- Regan does away with Nick believing he could resume
  his relationship with Mindy?

Attack #2 Friday, April, 7

CHUCK STETSON

- Present at filming for *Lingerie Exposed*.
- Mindy romantically interested (?) in Chuck re:
  Facebook post
- Mindy flirting with Chuck—maybe a means to incite
  Regan
- Regan attempts to kill Chuck because he's blinded by
  jealousy?

I LOOKED at the words scrawled on the page. The motive seemed thin. Then I remembered a comment Daily had made about the power of jealousy. They didn't call it the green-eyed monster for nothing.

But, regardless, Mindy stood directly in the center of the mystery, whether she was the mastermind or the catalyst for the attacks. I wished to high heaven that Pix had never agreed to do the segment for *Lingerie Exposed*. I shook my head, realizing I sounded like Jane Parks. Maybe Chuck will be able to shed some light, I hoped, backing out of my parking pad.

Luckily, the traffic was light for a Saturday morning, and I'd made it to the hospital in record time. After checking in, I headed to Chuck's room. He'd been transferred out of the trauma center and was settled in the step-down unit. A cop guarding the door nodded after checking the hospital tag stuck onto my hoodie. Poised in the threshold, I took in the room. Pix pressed against the bed holding Chuck's hand. He appeared despondent, hooked up to an I.V. and a monitor that flashed out his vital signs. His skin, depleted of its healthy glow, looked leathery, stretched taut across his cheekbones. Father McCarthy, with his arms folded and lips pursed as if deep in prayer, stood near the window. The priest's face brightened as he glanced in my direction.

"Father." I acknowledged him with a nod as I stepped closer to the bed. "Chuck," I said under my breath. "How are you holding up?" I moved to the bedside opposite Pix.

Instead of speaking, Chuck's eyes locked with mine. He didn't have to say a word. His desire for me to uncover the scofflaw who'd attempted to kill him passed between us telepathically. At least, that's what I thought. His drooping eyelids closed.

I spoke softly next to his ear. "Don't worry. I promise I'll find this—"

"This . . . this . . . fiend who didn't get away with murder." A malicious tone filled Pix's voice. "At least this will prove to DJ that you're innocent." She brushed a wavy lock of hair off Chuck's brow. "What kind of detective is he anyway? He needs to have his head examined for even thinking that you had something to do with Nick's death."

Father McCarthy moved next to Pix and rested a hand on her shoulder. "Perhaps we should leave and give Chuck some time to rest."

In peace. I finished the priest's sentence in my head. Pix apparently hadn't noticed the way Chuck winced when she'd brought up the comment about Daily. This certainly wasn't the time to grill him about the attack.

"You've been up all night. You'll be no good to Chuck if you don't take care of yourself." Father McCarthy took Pix's hand and squeezed it.

"Thank you, Father, for the prayers and anointing Chuck with the sacramental oil." Pix said. "I guess a few hours of sleep couldn't hurt." She looked at me.

I nodded, seconding Father McCarthy's suggestion.

"I've hired a private nursing agency so Chuck's every need will be attended to 24/7." Pix said.

"Great. So go home and get some sleep." I paused a second. "There's a cop outside the door. Daily is behind that, I presume."

She nodded. "An added layer of protection in case . . ."

The thought that someone might enter Chuck's room to finish what he started sent an icy chill through me.

"I'll walk you girls out to your cars," Father McCarthy said, glancing at his watch.

"You go ahead," Pix said. "I'm going to stay here until the nurse arrives. She's due here any minute."

After telling Pix I'd touch base with her later, Father McCarthy and I left her with a slumbering Chuck. We headed toward the elevator, but instead of pressing the down button, I motioned to a sitting area nestled within a small alcove. I wanted to know if Chuck had shared any information about what'd transpired at the river.

I cleared my throat, taking a moment to center my thoughts. Father McCarthy dropped his loosely folded hands into his lap and focused on me. Before I managed to utter a word, he asked how I was dealing with the situation.

"I've been racking my brain trying to understand why someone would attack Chuck. I have a few ideas, but I was wondering, did he mention anything to you about what happened?"

"In his state, I thought it better not to press for any specifics."

I chewed my bottom lip, accepting the inevitable. The good Father didn't have anything to share.

"He was, however, adamant that he wants to thank the person

who saved his life. I reassured him, when he was up to it, that could easily be arranged."

"Wait. What? You know who saved Chuck's life." I leaned over the armrest in his direction. "Who?"

Father McCarthy settled back into his chair and closed his eyes. The priest isn't a spring chicken, but he's not that old he'd drop off in the middle of a conversation. No. He was wrestling with his conscience. Trying to decide what or how much to tell me.

"Chris Tucker fished Chuck out of the Pawcattawaye River."

"Chris Tucker." The name didn't ring a bell.

"I had the opportunity to get to know him this past winter at the church's cold weather shelter."

I frowned. "You mean he's—"

"Homeless." Father McCarthy shook his snowy white head. "He's part of a small group of people who live down by the river. Chris is a veteran. Saw combat in Iraq and Afghanistan. He was wounded trying to save a buddy who eventually died. When he came home, he was diagnosed with PTSD, but instead of getting medical help, he turned to the bottle." He let out a deep sigh. "Chris stopped by the rectory to talk to me last night. His instincts had taken over when he saw Chuck's nearly lifeless body. But afterward, flashbacks from the war just about overwhelmed him. He said he needed a drink, but he really wanted to talk to someone who wouldn't judge him."

I closed my eyes remembering the times I'd see scruffy, unkempt men walking along Main Street. I'd looked the other way. Tried to put distance between me and them fast. Now, I felt ashamed. One of those poor souls had saved Chuck's life.

I opened my eyes and searched Father McCarthy's kind face. "Did he witness Chuck being assaulted?"

He stroked his strong jaw. "I'm not sure. When he arrived at the rectory, Chris was sweating, shaking. Anxiety had a powerful grip on him. So we talked about his time as a soldier way into the night. Thank God, he fell asleep, but he'd left the rectory before I rose to say early Mass."

"Do you know where he's camping?"

He nodded. "I drop by there quite often with food and supplies. About a quarter of a mile before the State Park boundary. But Becca, it's too dangerous of a place for you to be traipsing around. Because of my interaction through the shelter, I've forged relationships with these people, albeit mainly superficial ones. I have the privilege to offer them spiritual and physical assistance, which for the most part, they accept. It has been a blessing in my life." A sad smile crossed his face. "According to Chris, he gave a statement to the uniformed officers at the scene last night."

I nodded absently, trying to reign in the thoughts tumbling through my mind. Of one thing, I was a hundred percent certain, I had to get to that encampment and talk to Chris Tucker.

A shadow crossed my face, and I turned my attention away from the priest. Pix stood across from us. She rubbed her eyes with her fingertips.

"I just remembered," Pix said, stifling a yawn. "I don't have a way home. Dolly Evans drove me here last night. Could I hitch a ride with you?"

"Sure, no problem," I said. "Except I have an errand to run and—"

"Concerning who attacked Chuck?"

"Well," I said, glancing at Father McCarthy."

"Rebecca, I strongly suggest you don't—"

"No worries, Father. Say a prayer for me. Okay?" I jumped out of my seat and took a few steps toward the elevator. I looked over my shoulder, and eyeing the good Father said, "Thanks for giving Pix a lift home."

CHAPTER TWENTY-TWO

The banks of the Pawcattawaye were not unfamiliar to me. Between cases, I'd head to the river, locate a spot and settle in the shade cast from clusters of trees. There I'd set up my French easel and fashion small *plein air* sketches. The quick studies served as references. In my closet studio, I'd rework my ideas into finished paintings. The three oils that Geoffrey Taylor had purchased had evolved in that fashion.

An image of the distinguished lawyer flitted through my mind as I focused on the ground making sure not to trip over a tangle of vines or the interwoven network of exposed tree roots. I couldn't help but smile, remembering our one and only meeting in the PPS Gallery. There was something about that man that piqued my interest.

I paused at a nodding cluster of lavender bell-shaped flowers. Their sweet fragrance filled the air, and for a second, the freshness of the spring day made me forget my mission of locating the homeless camp. I snapped a tiny bunch free from a leafy branch and brought the delicate flowers close to my face. They felt like velvet against my cheek. I leaned back against the coarse trunk of a soaring tree and closed my eyes.

"Geoffrey Taylor," I murmured. He's the kind of man I've dreamed of—an art lover, professional, polished, and polite. The polar opposite of Daniel James Daily. Then why in God's name can't I forget the warmth of Daily's touch and being held in his arms? It was like I'd found a safe harbor, a peaceful refuge . . . a sweet haven.

I flashed my eyes open, sensing movement. My muscles tensed as I moved closer to the dirt path that followed the river's bank and spied one of the homeless men. Though he looked ancient, he probably wasn't older than forty, his long greasy hair streaked with gray, as well as his unkempt beard. Overdressed for such a warm day, I imagined he'd be sweating, clad in a flannel shirt, covered by a pullover sweater, topped with a splotchy and dusty olive green zip-up jacket.

I threw the bluebells to the ground and reached into my pocket. My fingers curled around a plastic bottle of pepper spray. Our eyes locked for a moment before he offered a nod and stepped past me.

"Hold up a sec," I called to the back of the receding figure.

He slowed but didn't stop walking as he glanced over his shoulder.

I raced toward him.

"Do you know a man named Chris Tucker?"

He turned, facing me, with his arms crossed.

"I'm a friend of the man whose life he saved. And a P.I. investigating the case. I only want to ask him a few questions. So if you know where I can locate him, I'd—"

"I'm Chris Tucker." He dropped his arms.

"You?" I said under my breath. I didn't have any idea what I expected the homeless veteran to look like, but I'd guessed, he'd be solid and virile. The slogan "once a Marine always a Marine" flitted through my brain—not the image of a broken-down specimen of a man. But now, the dark spots on his jacket made sense. Blood. Chuck's blood.

"Hi." I thrust my hand in his direction.

He didn't reach for it. "What do you want to know?"

132

"Well, first off, I want to thank you. Chuck is a dear friend and—"

"Whatever."

"Did you witness the attack?"

He stared at me with a blank face.

"Look, let me buy you lunch. How 'bout the Capitoline Restaurant?" I blurted out the invitation without thinking. The Capitoline is an upscale restaurant. It was obvious to both of us that Tucker lacked the appropriate attire.

"I have somewhere to go so . . ." He shot me a lopsided grin. "I'll have to turn down your gracious invite."

"Certainly, you have time for a cup of coffee?"

He pressed his lips together as if considering my offer.

"Okay." He continued walking.

His rapid gait had me nearly jogging to keep up with him. I wanted to engage Tucker in conversation but had no idea what to say. Finally, I muttered something about the weather. He reacted like he hadn't heard me, looking straight ahead. The remainder of the walk continued in silence. Relief washed over me when we reached the Hot and Chilly Bean. I only hoped that a hot brew would loosen his tongue and give me something—anything—even the smallest kernel of a clue regarding the attack on Chuck's life.

The coffee shop stood nearly empty since it was that off-time of day, after the breakfast rush but before the lunchtime crowd. I motioned Tucker toward a table in the back of the room and stepped next to the counter. A quizzical look crossed Ralphie's face. "Two house blends."

"He's a friend of yours?" Ralphie tossed his head in Tucker's direction.

Though his incredulity was justified, a spark of anger caused me to snap, "He's a down on his luck veteran. A hero. Was injured trying to save another soldier's life. And the man who pulled Chuck out of the Pawcattawaye."

He raised his palms in a surrender gesture.

"Sorry, Ralphie. I'm a bit on edge."

He offered an understanding nod.

"Along with the coffee—" I looked into the long glass case packed with designer sandwiches and desserts. "Two chicken salads on whole wheat and five chocolate chip cookies." I handed him the credit card that earlier I'd stuck into the back pocket of my jeans along with a couple of dollar bills, signed the receipt, and slipped the card away.

As Ralphie busied himself with the order, I glanced at Tucker, reading a newspaper left behind on the table. In less time than I'd expected, Ralphie had filled the order. On the tray, he'd added an additional sandwich—a ham and cheese—that could've been mistaken for a Dagwood, crafted with three slices of Deli bread, lettuce, tomato, peppers, onion, pepperoni, and even a couple slices of turkey. I widened my eyes questioningly.

"A small token of thanks for his service," Ralphie said before turning away.

With a tiny smile, I walked the length of the narrow room. I placed the tray on the table and sat down opposite Tucker.

"I thought you might be hungry since it's almost lunchtime. The ham and cheese is a thank you for your service from the barista."

Tucker took a long sip of coffee and looked me square in the face. "To answer your question, I didn't see anything."

My heart sank.

Tucker lifted the chicken salad and took several bites. He chewed slowly, not taking his eyes off of me. He washed the food down with a long draught of coffee. "I found your friend nearly drowned. Gave him mouth to mouth. Relieved when he came to."

I nodded, urging him to continue.

"Initially, I didn't know what to think. Maybe he'd tripped over some rocks and landed in the river. Then I saw the stab wounds. My first assumption. Suicide."

"It wasn't that," I said under my breath.

"Yeah. You're right. Once he came around, he started talking. Said he knew who tried to kill him."

"Wait. What?" I leaned halfway over the table.

"Said he knew who knifed him."

"Who?"

"Look, the guy was gonna bleed out. I couldn't waste a second trying to decipher what the hell he was mumbling about. But the name sounded like Min." He took another bite from his sandwich.

"Min. Mindy? Chuck said, Mindy?"

His brow bunched up, causing deep lines to cross his forehead.

I was right. Mindy Marks is behind the attacks. First, she kills her husband, then Nick, but didn't quite get it right with Chuck. Who would've thought—a lingerie host serial killer?

"I think a woman attacked Chuck."

He squinted at me. "A woman? Hmm. It's possible, I guess. But unlikely," he said, blotting his lips with a paper napkin emblazoned with the coffee shop logo.

"Why?" I said the word like an accusation. I cleared my throat, determined to temper my voice. "Women do commit murder." I paused a second and looked into his eyes. They were blue—a very light blue—like a summer's sky. "Why do you think a man did it?" Tucker must've witnessed a lot of killing in the Middle East. I wanted to know the reason he doubted a woman could've attacked Chuck.

"Your friend, um, Chuck is a big dude. Six-three. Six-four. And from what I could tell in top physical condition—wasn't an ounce of fat on him—plus, I noticed his hands. They were cut. He put up a fight. A guy like that would've easily whipped the ass of any female."

Especially a ninety-five-pound lingerie reporter. But Chuck, a throwback to the age of chivalry, would never lay a hand on a lady even if one was wielding a knife. So, I decided there's no reason to dismiss my theory. *Besides, she could've been with her henchman. Most likely her ex, David Regan.*

"I'd bet my last nickel the assailment is a guy. Named Min," Tucker said, lifting the remains of his chicken salad sandwich.

"Min." I took a sip of coffee. I do a lot of shopping in greater Bayleys Landing along the five-mile stretch of the Korean Way, named for over a hundred Korean-owned businesses located there. That's why I easily recognized Min as a Korean name. Only two of the businesses are located on Main Street—a dress shop owned by a mother and daughter and a restaurant, Seoul Sushi and BBQ, and to my knowledge, neither owner have the surname Min.

"You're sure it was Min?" *Not David or Dave or maybe Regan.* I took a slow swallow from my cup. Something began to click. I tried to unravel the thoughts flying through my brain. Tucker's voice scattered them like dried leaves on a city sidewalk.

"Yeah. I'm sure, but for some reason think otherwise." His shoulders slumped as he dropped his head and stood.

He thinks I don't believe him. "Look, I don't doubt that Chuck said Min. It's just I don't know anyone with that name."

"Perhaps you don't know all of your friend's enemies." He reclaimed his seat. "Whoever this Min character is, he must be a Kali."

"A what?" I frowned.

"A master of death. In other words, a cut and thrust expert."

I bit the corner of my lip. *I doubted Mindy Marks was a master of anything except for getting her own way. Maybe Regan knows his way around knives.*

"Ask your friend. He's sure to know."

"Right. I will."

Tucker finished his sandwich and picked up one of the cookies.

"Let me get you a box for that." I pointed at the leftover sandwiches and cookies on the tray. "I'm not hungry." I shot up and hurried to the counter to get a couple of take-out boxes for a homeless hero twice over.

CHAPTER TWENTY-THREE

Arriving at the hospital, I checked my cellphone. I hadn't heard from Daily and hoped he'd texted while I was driving. I glanced at the screen. Nothing.

I marched to the elevator, trying to work off my irritation. Daily is such a narrow-minded, egotistical jerk. He probably ignored my message because he doesn't believe I'm capable of piecing together a viable theory for these attacks. He makes me so mad, I steamed.

But, as I stepped into the elevator, the memory of being in his arms almost melted my anger. *Almost.* The thing that infuriated me the most was that last night Chuck probably told Daily who had attacked him. And Daily hadn't bothered to share that vital piece of info with me. If that's the case, I thought, stepping out of the elevator, then the perp could already be in jail. I chewed my bottom lip. Sure would explain why Daily had blown me off.

With the air knocked out of my sails, I trudged toward Chuck's room. I'd desperately wanted to uncover the miscreant who'd wreaked havoc on the town because of the anguish he'd caused Pix. A paralyzing dread consumed her the last few days causing Pix to believe somehow she'd been the reason for Nick's death and Chuck's attack. But now," I thought brightening, "she can relax. The malevolent threat has been thwarted. We can all slip back into a semblance of normalcy. A sense of lightness filled me as if a twenty-pound weight had slipped off my shoulders. I increased my pace, relieved I could visit Chuck not as an investigator but as a friend.

I turned a corner and stopped in my tracks. A cop stood outside Chuck's room. That's strange, I thought, wrinkling my brow. If Daily arrested the perp, why does Chuck need protection? I hurried down the hall, ready to find out.

"Hi," I said with a smile.

The officer nodded.

"Any news on an arrest?"

Instead of answering, he looked at the hospital sticker on my sweater. Chuck's room number was printed on it, verifying that I had permission to enter.

"You can go in," he said.

"Thanks," I murmured.

Still confused, I entered the room with soft, tentative steps. If Chuck was asleep, I didn't want to disturb him. But I found him wide awake, sitting up in the bed. It took only a second to see that he was alone.

"Becca." He smiled.

"Hey, Chuck." I rushed to his bedside and kissed his cheek. "How are you feeling?"

"Sore as hell. But a lot better. Nothing's definite yet, but the word is I may be discharged early next week."

A bit of color had returned to his face. "Oh, that's wonderful." I sent up a prayer of thanks. My friend was not quite out of the woods, but a visible path ran through it. That happy feeling evaporated too quickly. I tapped my foot, not knowing how to broach the subject of the attack and its perpetrator.

"You just missed Pix. Her parents arrived in town, and she wanted to meet them at the airport," Chuck said.

I nodded.

"You know them, don't you?"

"Pix's parents? Yeah, they're great."

"That's good to know. From what Pix has told me, they seem a bit . . . um . . . unusual."

"Well, that's one way of putting it. Her mom, Brenda, is kind of a free spirit, but you couldn't find a sweeter, kinder person if you tried. And Peter is really insightful, the way he managed to be a frontrunner in the environmental revolution."

"That's the problem."

"Problem?"

"Let's face it, what do I have to offer Pix? I'm only a chocolatier." Before I could answer, he continued. "It's a good thing I've made solid investments from my modeling days."

"Huh?" *Good Lord. Chuck was an underwear model?*

"In college, I started modeling, you know, for some pocket money. But then, I jumped into it full-time. Print ads, commercials, that kind of stuff."

"Why have you kept it secret?" Had I'd seen Chuck's face on the cover of *GQ* and not made the connection, I wondered, or pictured inside the *Land's End* and the *L.L.Bean* catalogs?

"What kinda guy wants to admit to making a living off his looks? It's embarrassing. But I was going to tell Pix. Because this weekend, I was scheduled to fly to New York for a shoot. I still do it part-time. That's why my staff at the Chocolate Box is exceptional. I depend on them to keep the shop running smoothly while I'm gone. But it's usually only a couple of times a month." His lips slammed tight as he stiffened in the bed.

"I'll get a nurse." I headed toward the door.

He exhaled loudly. "I'm okay. Could you hand me . . ." He pointed to a covered water cup with a plastic straw sticking through the top.

I grabbed the container and gave it to him.

After a long swallow, he looked at me. "I hate being in the hospital. I feel so damn helpless. The doctor said it may take up to six weeks until I'm fully healed. I can scratch the Boston Marathon off my list."

"Must be disappointing but thank God you're alive."

"Of course, You're right. I could've ended up like Rizzo. Thanks for reminding me what an idiot I can be, sometimes."

"Hey, no problem." I shot him a bright smile. "Anyway, I think the hospital is the best place for you, at least, for the time being."

"Because there's a cop outside the door." His eyelids started to droop. Common sense told me he'd been given powerful painkillers that caused drowsiness. I couldn't let him nod off before asking him the million-dollar question.

"I met the man who saved your life."

"You did?" Chuck's sleepy eyes widened. "That's great. The first thing I'm gonna do, after being sprung from here, is to thank him. Big time. He'll have a lifetime pass for free candy from my shop."

"Chris Tucker is a hero."

"Chris Tucker?" Chuck yawned. "Hmmm. I don't think I know him. But he's probably stopped by the Chocolate Box a time or two. Once I see him, I'll recognize him."

"Maybe." I paused a second. "Chris said once you came around, you mentioned something about knowing the person who attacked you."

Chuck closed his eyes. "Like I told Daily, I have no memory of the attack at all. Let alone who knifed me."

He doesn't remember?

"Maybe if you tried relaxing and—"

Chuck flashed his eyes open. "I've been racking my brain, but nothing. I recall you bringing in dinner from the Crab Kettle, leaving your place for a run, but after that—" He shrugged. "The doctor assured me that temporary amnesia is not uncommon in my situation."

"I don't know if this will help or not, but Chris Tucker said you named the attacker. Min."

"Min? Min." He rubbed the center of his forehead. "Why would the owner of Seoul Sushi and BBQ would want to kill me."

"The owner?"

"Min-Jun Min." He paused a second. "I eat there quite a bit, but his kids basically run the place. I've never actually seen him there but spoke to him at a couple Merchant Association meetings. Like me, he supported Pix in opening up her shop on Main Street. He thinks most of the local businesses are too stogy. Believed the lingerie shop would bring in a younger, more hip clientele. That Treasure's Trove would be like a breath of fresh air."

My stomach flipped. *Don't tell me Mr. Min-Jun Min also has the hots for Pix?*

CHAPTER TWENTY-FOUR

The dinner hour was fast approaching when I returned to the apartment. The purrs, as usual, greeted me at the door. Instead of looking at me with soulful eyes, their little voices fussily mewed while Jaspurr climbed up my leg as the other two bounced around me. I wanted to scoop up the cats and cuddle them until their throaty rumbles of contented purrs filled my ears. However, I suspected their ostentatious welcome wasn't due so much because they missed me as to the fact that they're hungry. Well, the purrs are always hungry, but when I glanced at my watch, it became evident that I'd missed their usual dinnertime by a full half-hour.

"Okay, okay, guys. Hold your horses." I crossed the apartment and stopped at the pantry where I store their cat food. I pulled out a couple cans of Fancy Feast, flipped the tops, and scooped out the whitefish pâté. Before I had a chance to place the bowls at each one's assigned eating area, my phone sounded.

"One minute, guys, it's probably Pix," I said, pulling the phone free from my back pocket.

"Hello."

"Becca?" Expecting Pix's voice, I was startled by the male voice I didn't recognize.

"Yes?"

"Geoffrey Taylor."

"Oh, Mr. Taylor." I glanced at the cats. With mounting frustration over not being immediately fed, Caspurr leaped on top of Jaspurr. The smaller cat squeaked out strangled cries and wriggled in an attempt to free himself from beneath Caspurr's considerable girth. A mouthful of red fur hung from between Caspurr's lips. "Please, hold on for one sec." I put the phone down, pulled out as much fur from Caspurr's mouth as possible, and landed the food bowls on their trays.

I picked up the phone. "Mr. Taylor—"

"Please, call me Geoff." He didn't wait for a response. "I know we set a date in May for me to visit your studio, but I'm in Baltimore and hoped you'd be free to give me the tour. I know it's short notice, and I understand—"

"I'd love to," I said, cutting him off. In my book, when it came to Geoffrey Taylor, my time was his time. After all, how many struggling artists are on the verge of having a patron? "Except..." A fleeting image of Daily fluttered through my mind. But he might've already arrested the culprit.

"If this is a bad time—"

"No. It's perfect." I gave him my address.

"Great. I'll see you in about forty minutes."

I tapped the screen ending the call, took a couple of deep breaths to steady my nerves, and hurried to my clothes closet. I scanned the garments hanging there with a frown. I have three categories of clothing: painting clothes (paint smeared and speckled), work clothes (mostly casual mixed with some trendy pieces), and church clothes (generally conservatively leaning). I thumbed through my work clothes and stopped at a white long-sleeved silk blouse. I pulled it from the hanger with a pair of tailored black slacks. I'd top it with my favorite green wool blazer.

It took only twenty minutes to pull myself together. After a final look in my free-standing mirror, I hurried to my studio. I flipped through a stack of finished paintings leaning against a wall and selected three I believed were my best. Nobody had seen them yet—not even Simon—since I wanted to be sure they were perfect before schlepping them to the gallery. I hung them on the wall opposite the window. As I studied them, the sound of the door buzzer made me jump.

I raced from the studio, through my office, to the door. After a deep breath, I flung it open. "Come in," I said, "I hope the traffic wasn't too horrible."

"Pretty smooth for this time of day."

I took a second to look him over, not surprised that his attire reflected his professionalism. His tailored white shirt sported a striped blue tie tucked neatly behind a gray pinstriped vest matching his suit coat. He wasn't wearing his horn-rimmed eyeglasses, and I noticed his eyes were dark and warm.

"The studio is right this way." I flung out my arm in the direction of my painting area.

"I had no idea that you're a private investigator and a photographer. I'm impressed."

He had read my shingle. I felt my cheeks warm.

"You're a young lady of many talents."

I half-shrugged, feeling a bit embarrassed. "I want to warn you. My studio is a converted closet." I moved to the opened door.

"It's not the workspace that matters, but the work," he said, following behind me.

I wondered if he always knew the right thing to say. But then I remembered he's a lawyer and spent most of his life gauging his words to be persuasive. I stepped inside the studio, snapped on my true-light LED floor lamp, and gestured to the paintings on the wall.

Geoff stood silent, staring at my work with his arms crossed.

The seconds seemed to drag. His upcoming appraisal, good or bad, had my nerves tingling. I had to break the silence. "This one," I said, stepping next to one of the two landscapes, "is of the Pawcattawaye River beyond the old mill."

He placed a finger over his lips.

Okay. I'll shut up.

I looked at my watch and followed the secondhand jump around its face. His voice made me start.

"I'll take them."

Had I heard him right?

"The landscapes are lovely—one can get lost in them—the light, calm atmosphere, realistic details." He stepped closer to the third painting. "This still-life is remarkable. The shine of the satin, the texture of the glass, it's as if I could almost lift the objects off the canvas." He reached inside his suit coat and pulled out a checkbook. "How much do I owe you?"

"I . . . I really don't know. They're so new, I hadn't thought about prices."

"How about fifteen hundred for the landscapes and twenty-five hundred for the still-life? That makes it an even four thousand."

I couldn't keep my jaw from dropping but promptly closed my mouth. I hoped he hadn't noticed. "Sounds about right," I managed.

He opened the checkbook, scribbled, tore the slip free, and handed it to me.

"Thanks very much. I really appreciate your interest in my paintings."

"I've been searching for an upcoming artist to invest in. I believe you're the one I've been hoping to find."

"I'm honored. Truly, I am."

"Just keep doing what you're doing."

"I will. Yes. Yes, of course. Thank you." I was babbling but couldn't help myself.

"Are you hungry?"

"Hungry?" I hadn't really thought about food. "A little."

"Good. I'd love to take you to dinner. To celebrate. Any good restaurants around here?"

"The Tiber Bistro is nice."

"I'll pick up the paintings after dinner." He offered his arm, and I took it.

A few minutes later, we sat at a table nestled in front of one of the two bay windows facing Main Street.

"Let's order a feast," Geoff said. "We'll start with champagne. How does lobster sound?"

"Wonderful." No client had ever treated me like this, I thought, closing the menu. *Maybe he wants to be more than a client.* I immediately shut down that thought believing it to be wishful thinking. *But, good Lord, he must be a very successful attorney to afford thousands for paintings and at least another hundred for lobster dinners.*

"How about shrimp cocktails for appetizers? And some steamed mussels with garlic butter?"

I nodded.

"Oh," he said, looking up from his menu. "They have surf and turf. Do you eat beef?"

I nodded again. I didn't want to dampen his spirits by explaining that beef didn't really agree with me.

"Let's see," he continued, "baked potatoes, corn on the cob, and broccoli soufflé."

"Fine." I wondered who was going to eat all of the food he planned to order.

Bonnie, a long-time waitress, approached us. "Hiya, Becca."

"Hey," I said with a nod. "This is Geoff."

"Pleasure to meet you. Are you ready to order, or do you need a few more minutes?"

Geoff rambled off the long list of food. As Bonnie left our table, Geoff's cellphone sounded. He whipped it free from his inside jacket pocket and glanced at the screen. "Excuse me. I have to take this call." He ambled toward the bar area.

A wine steward approached with the champagne on ice and two chilled glasses. He deftly poured the sparkling liquid into the glasses.

The second after the sommelier departed, Bonnie returned to the table. "Who is Geoff?" she said, leaning close to my ear. "And what army is he planning on feeding?"

I shook my head with a smile. "He's interested in my paintings. He's already bought six of them."

"You go, girl. That's great." She smiled. "I'll be right back with the appetizers."

Finally alone for a moment, I leaned back in the chair, allowing the amazing news to sink in. I had an honest-to-God patron. Maybe I could chuck the P.I. business and focus on art. A knock on the window started me. I glanced over my shoulder. Daily.

A second later, he hovered over me. "Sorry I haven't gotten back to you. I've been swamped."

"Have you made an arrest?"

Daily shook his head, pulled out a chair, and sat.

"I want to discuss that lead of yours." His eyes fell to the bottle and glasses. "Oh. You and Pix having dinner?"

"Well, actually, no."

I hadn't noticed Geoff had returned until he touched my shoulder. "Daniel James Daily, this is Geoffrey Taylor."

Daily jumped up and took Geoff's outstretched hand. "Glad to meet you. By the way, it's DJ." He turned to me. "Look, let's discuss that bit of business tomorrow."

"You're welcomed to join us," Geoff said. "I might've gone overboard with the food. food. Since we're celebrating, the more, the merrier, as they say."

"Celebrating? Thanks, but no. Nice meeting you." With that, Daily turned and exited the restaurant.

Geoff reclaimed his chair. "Now, where were we? Ah, the champagne." He lifted his glass. "A toast. To our new partnership."

I clinked his glass with mine, not believing my incredibly good fortune.

CHAPTER TWENTY-FIVE

I woke up, still in a happy daze, assuring myself that Geoffrey Taylor had indeed written me a check for four thousand dollars. And that he was going to support my painting career. I wanted to stay in bed and savor my blessings. A low rumble of laughter took hold and bubbled through my lips as I recalled the look on Daily's face when Geoff returned to the table. Daily thinks I'm nothing more than a doddering hawkshaw but, I showed him all right, me being wined and dined by a suave . . . dashing . . . handsome gentleman.

As quickly as it started, the laughter ended. *I can't be falling for Geoff.* I cringed with the very idea. My track record with relationships was dismal, and that's putting it mildly. But he isn't anything like those losers. "Nevertheless, I swear, I'm not going to do anything to muck up this collaboration. It will be strictly business, but Daily doesn't need to know that."

Caspurr jumped on the bed, padded across the mattress, and landed on my chest. He didn't make a sound, but his questioning blue eyes bore into mine.

"You want breakfast."

He started his chirpy chatter as if agreeing with me. The

twitters and tweets increased in volume as I jumped out of bed and slipped into my terrycloth robe. By the time I reached the pantry, all three kitties circled around me in unbridled anticipation. I hurried the process of filling their bowls and contentedly watched as they gobbled their breakfast, knowing that once their tummies were full, they'd fall into the first of many catnaps throughout the day.

I wanted nothing more than to change into sweats and enjoy a good, long run, but resigned myself to more pressing matters. Maybe this afternoon, I hoped, as I dropped two slices of wheat bread into the toaster and put the kettle on. I glanced at the wall clock and took a double take. It was nearing ten. No wonder the cats chowed down in record time. I gathered their empty bowls and placed them in the sink.

After gulping down breakfast, I showered and dressed. The first stop on my day's schedule was noon Mass at St. Paul's and then a visit to the Seoul Sushi and BBQ. Even though I was itching to call Pix to see how she was faring with her parents, I decided against it. Since there'd been no word from her, I went with the old adage, 'no news is good news' and left it at that.

I checked my work messages which boasted junk emails except for one from Geoff. I skimmed through his words, afraid that once he got the paintings home, he realized he'd made a mistake. I breathed an audible sigh of relief after his words sunk in. He loved the new additions to his collection. I reread the message, this time relishing his words of admiration and thanks for a lovely evening. I clicked the save icon, refilled the purrs' water fountain, and raced out the door.

After Mass, I waited for the throng of people to pass through the wide, green wooden doors attached to the church's austere, granite façade. Father McCarthy had already taken off in the direction of the rectory.

"Father," I called.

He turned, and his face lit up. His purple chasuble rippled in the slight wind as we met each other halfway.

"Beautiful Mass." I sensed he knew it wasn't the service I

wanted to discuss. "I talked to Chris Tucker yesterday. He's given me a lead."

The priest pressed his lips together.

"I'm going to check it out later." I slipped the knapsack in my hand over a shoulder. "I was wondering, are there treatment programs available to help people like Chris?"

"Plenty, I imagine. The best bet is to check with the Veterans Administration. But as the tried and true saying goes, 'You can lead a horse to water, but you can't make him drink.'"

"Exactly," I said with a sigh.

"After luncheon with some of the local ministers and rabbis—"

"Very ecumenical, Father."

A smile broke out on his face. "We meet once a month at the Capitoline since we've become dear friends. Sure to be stimulating, as usual." His eyes twinkled. "Afterwards, I'll stop by the hospital to check on Chuck."

I wished him a good lunch and walked down the hill to Main Street to check out my lead.

Seoul Sushi and BBQ, a popular venue for the college crowd, located at the top of Main Street, wasn't far from my office. I'd often wondered if it attracted the ivy leaguers because of the food or because Min-Jun Min's two daughters worked there. So much so that the only way the girls could somewhat socialize with their friends was if they patronized the restaurant. Probably a mixture of the two.

The thought of *Kimbap* and *Gae Maeuntang* made my mouth water. I hadn't had sushi roll and spicy crab and vegetable soup for a couple of weeks. But even with the anticipation of the delectable meal, I didn't rush. In fact, I all but dawdled toward the restaurant trying to devise a strategy of how to approach Min-Jun Min. I gathered he might not take it well that I suspected him of murder. I knew his daughters, but I'd never met Mr. Min. But I probably caught a glimpse of him at the few Merchant Association meetings I'd had the displeasure of attending. The only reason I showed up at those hot-tempered discussions was to support Pix. I trembled with just the mere remembrance.

I reached the restaurant, still not certain of a casual way to question the proprietor. With a shake of my head, I pulled open the door and paused longer than usual in the entrance with its glass-enclosed waterfall. I loved watching the water flow between the two glass slabs. I moved inside. Instead of entering the dining area with its modern industrial décor, I stopped at the slate carry-out counter. I glanced over my shoulder into the dining room. Trendy, I thought, taking in the exposed ceiling with its labyrinth of pipes, wooden tabletops attached to metal legs with matching benches, guard pendant lights, and a reclaimed brick wall. The space was filling up already. *The after-church crowd.*

"Hi, Becca."

I turned toward the voice belonging to Chan-ri, one of the owner's daughters. Belying my nervousness, I shot her a bright smile. "How're you doing?"

"A little uneasy with what's been happening. Any news about Chuck?"

"He's improving. Hopefully, he'll be released from the hospital soon."

She blew out a puff of air. "He's such a great guy. He's made it a habit of giving me a couple pieces of my favorite chocolate every time he stops by the restaurant. Jacked Up." I must've frowned because she continued. "It's a milk chocolate candy with a ganache center infused with Jack Daniels whiskey." She winked as a bright smile crossed her face.

"I'll have to stop by the Chocolate Box and sample one."

"Believe me, you won't be disappointed." She tapped the stack of take-out menus. "Your usual?"

"That'd be great. Um. Is your father around?"

Lines popped up on her forehead.

"I wanted to run something by him that we discussed at the last Merchant Association meeting." I hated lying, particularly right after leaving church, but really, did I have a choice?

152

"I'm afraid that will have to wait. He's visiting family in Seoul."

I pursed my lips. *So, with Min-Jun-Min in Korea, he isn't the Min responsible for attacking Chuck unless* . . . "Gee, I thought it was yesterday when I ran into him," I said, hitching my thumb in the direction of Main Street. "I have the info he wanted." I tapped my knapsack.

"Couldn't have been. He left for Korea two days ago."

"My mistake," I said with a shake of my head. *Chuck was attacked two days ago so Min could've attacked Chuck* . . . I squished up my face.

"You okay?"

I nodded. "I guess you and your sister are holding down the fort."

"Not entirely. Our mom is keeping us on our toes. She didn't go with Dad this time."

"Don't tell me, she's a fussy micromanager?" I kidded. In reality, there wasn't a lovelier lady on all of Main Street than Chin-Sun.

"No, that would be Dad," she said with a shake of her head. "But he's sweet in his own off-beat way. I miss him lots."

Though I barely imagined that the middle-aged husband and father of two would have anything to do with the nefarious activities, I conceded Min still a possible suspect. *Is he off-beat enough to commit murder?*

I missed Chan-ri's response and before I could utter an "excuse me," my cellphone sounded. I pulled it free from the knapsack. Daily. I scanned the text. *Discuss your lead over lunch?*

Ok, I texted back. *Korean Sushi & BBQ.*

See u in 10 minutes. He responded.

I powered off my phone and slipped it away, not wanting any distractions when Daily arrived. I glanced at Chan-ri. She was talking to one of the chefs through a window that separated the kitchen from the guest area. *Placing my order.*

"Chan-ri," I called.

The young woman moved toward me.

"Change of plans. Instead of carry-out, I'll be eating in."

"No problem," she said. "Seat yourself."

I found a table for two nestled inside an alcove at the back of the restaurant. A waitress, I'd never seen before, handed me a menu. "Chan-ri has my order, but I'm waiting for a . . . um . . . an associate. But I would love a glass of white wine. Arneis, if you have it." I needed some fortification before facing Daily. knowing him, he'll probably shoot holes through my possible lead with a wide grin on his face.

With a nod, the waitress left, and I practiced deep breathing.

The wine hadn't even arrived when I spied Daily crossing the dining area. I stood and half-waved. His eyes lit up. A second later, he sat across from me. Never before had I'd seen him dressed so casually in a pale blue, V-necked cotton pullover and jeans. The thought hit me. *It's Sunday. Probably off-duty. So why did he offer to meet me—*

"Nice spot," he said.

"An appropriate table to discuss the ongoing investigation that's caused rampant panic to erupt throughout the town." I made sure to sound professional and hoped my face looked as serious as my words.

"That's a bit melodramatic, Rebecca, even for you."

Before I could respond, the waitress returned with my wine. He looked at her and said, "Coffee and an order of *banban* chicken." He glanced at me. "Have you ordered?"

I nodded as the waitress scurried away.

"You must be some amazing actress," he said, "cause last night I couldn't detect the slightest inkling of distress over your friend Chuck's near murder."

My cheeks started to warm. Even so, I wasn't going to let him get the better of me.

"Thankfully, Chuck is improving. He'll be released in a few days."

"Good." He looked directly into my eyes. It seemed like he was peering into my very soul.

I glanced away and inhaled sharply. "You may have already

checked out what I want to discuss with you." Since he didn't comment, I continued. "I talked with Chris Tucker, the man who saved Chuck's life and . . ." I paused a sec seeing the frown that'd jumped on his face. "Apparently, Chuck knew who had attacked him. But now, he doesn't remember."

He rubbed his stubbly chin with his thumb. "You shouldn't be nosing around those homeless people. It's too dangerous for a girl—"

"Tucker said that the perp's name sounded like Min," I said, "which got me thinking about—"

"Don't tell me," Daily said, "Mr. Min." He waved his arm around as if trying to encompass the now-packed restaurant.

"Not initially. My first thought flew to Mindy Marks."

"Now, how in God's name could a teeny-weeny reporter take on a guy like Stetson?"

"You've interviewed her?"

"Twice. Her alibies checked out."

I noticed the corners of his mouth twitch as if he was trying to suppress a smile.

"You need to recheck her alibies because I think she's capable of murder." I reached into the backpack, which I'd dropped next to me on the wooden bench and grabbed the pages I'd printed from the internet. I handed him the Wikipedia article. "Check out the highlighted area."

He looked at the sheet for a couple of seconds then eyed me. "So? Her drunk husband fell into their pool."

"He died in water. Just like Nick and Chuck almost did."

"Coincidence."

"All right then. Look at this." I handed over Mindy's Facebook posts. This time, he studied the papers longer. When he lifted his head, I could see the wheels turning.

"Marks dated her show's director, then Rizzo, and was interested in Stetson?" He narrowed his eyes. "Really?"

His question sounded like I was the one who'd created the posts and not the queen of lingerie reporting.

"That's right. Mindy apparently has a roving eye. And doesn't take rejection well. She has that trait in common with the director because *Nick* is the one who dumped her." I didn't know, for sure, who did the dumping, but my gut told me it had to be Nick.

He still squinted at me.

"Like you said, Mindy isn't strong enough to attack men more than twice her size, but what if the director, David Regan, wanted Mindy back so badly he'd do anything for her? Evenmurder?"

"That's a stretch."

"You're the one who told me to never underestimate the power of jealousy."

The waitress appeared with our lunch. She placed the dishes on the table and asked if we needed anything else.

"Water with plenty of ice," I said, looking at Daily's plate of half-seasoned and half-plain fried chicken.

Daily attacked the spicy chicken first. "This is my favorite meal here." He glanced at my plate of sushi with a wrinkled nose. "I eat fish but only when it's cooked."

I breathed out a sigh. "It's seaweed."

"Well, whatever." He took another bite of chicken. "Getting back to your theory," he said around a mouthful of *banban*. "Though it is interesting, I think you're way off base."

"Why?"

"Look, Rebecca. You're great when it comes to spying on cheating husbands, but when it comes to actual detective work, you need to leave that to the big guns." He shot her a smile. "I get it. You want to help your friends and put an end to the unhinged panic racing through Bayleys Landing," he said, making air quotes, "but I suggest you stick to painting."

The sarcasm filling his voice made my blood boil. I jumped up, grabbed my knapsack, and stepped away from the table. "I've lost my appetite." With that, I raced to the exit. I heard his laughter rise above the steady hum of voices filling the room.

CHAPTER TWENTY-SIX

S till steaming mad, I turned away from the restaurant. I tried to expunge every vestige of Daily and his overblown ego, but his smug expression lingered in my mind. My quick steps turned into a jog as I trotted along the sidewalk. At this point, I didn't know where to turn for additional evidence than what I'd already dug up. Well, maybe it wasn't evidence, but it was a lead. A damn good one.

For me, not a sliver of doubt remained. But Daily couldn't shake the idea that the assaults sprung from a lovesick Main Street guy. My intuition, paired with research, clearly revealed it wasn't one of those workers, and for heaven's sake, not a Civil War ghost. Mindy, along with the aid of her former lover, stood firmly behind the attacks.

I increased my speed as a fresh blaze of anger buzzed through me. Anger at myself for letting Daily wiggle himself into my good graces. Yes, I told myself, it's a tragedy that his wife was killed but finding consolation in his arms . . . "Never again," I puffed, closing my eyes with a shake of my head.

A couple seconds later, when I flashed them open, I was headed straight for Woody. To avoid a collision that wouldn't be pretty, I swung into a combination sidestep pivot and twisted my back in the process. A shooting pain shot up my spine.

"Whoa. Watch where you're going, young lady." His lips curved into a distaining moue.

Woody's words scolded me. A chewing out I deserved for allowing anger to overcome safety and good sense.

"Sorry, Woody," I said, massaging my back.

"What's got you so fired up?"

I took a good look at him. Dressed in overalls with an old straw hat tucked on his head, I recognized today he was a farmer. But from which century, I had no idea.

"Detective Daily."

He pulled out a corn-cob pipe from his shirt pocket.

"I have a good lead on who's responsible for Chuck's attack and Nick's murder, but Daily is being so stubborn he won't—"

"Hold your horses, gal," he said, looking into the pipe's empty bowl. "We're dang lucky to have a constable that's not swayed by the corrupt arm of local politics. He's straight as an arrow and would rather take a flying leap into the depths of Hades, then take a bribe. Not many towns can boast of that."

I pressed my lips together.

"Besides," he continued, "what's a little lady like you getting riled up over atrocities best left for the law to handle? After all, policing is far beyond the refined, dare I say, dainty nature of the fairer sex. Upholding the law, why, that's the God-given duty of us men." He nodded as if appreciating his own words.

Good grief, I thought as he glanced at the pipe before slipping it into the bib of his overalls.

"Haven't you some embroidery to cross-stitch? Surely, the steady rhythm of the needle will free your troubled mind from such foul matters? Now," he said, reaching for my hand and patting it, "why don't you head to the welcoming hearth of your gracious home."

In one fluid motion, he released my hand and pulled out a pocket watch. "Time's a flying."

Woody shook his head. "Johnny over at Patapsco Grain and

Lumber is loading the wagon." He squinted up at the sky. "Looks like a storm's a-brewing. I need to get home before the heaven's open. Still, it's springtime, and not only is the rain gonna come, bit it's a blessing from above. That it is." He nodded and took a few steps away.

Woody had probably taken a lunch break from the Archeological Museum and didn't want to slip out of character. By his dress and comments, I deduced that today, he must be working in a section of the room dedicated to agrarian life during the latter part of the nineteenth century. It was stocked full of early farm equipment, maps, and photographs. I distinctly remembered one photo, a cabinet card, depicting a couple of men dressed similar to him standing on the front porch of the defunct Patapsco Grain and Lumber General Store. But, like it or not, I was determined to bring old Woody back into the twenty-first century.

"Hold up a minute."

He looked over his shoulder.

"I need to talk to the real you."

He turned around and popped the pipe into his mouth. "Whatever do you mean, Miss?" he said with his teeth holding onto the pipe's shaft.

"Drop the act. Please. This is a life-or-death situation, and I need your help."

Woody sighed, dropped the pipe back into the pocket, and removed the hat. He stood taller, and his eyes narrowed with a hint of misgiving. "What's up, Becca?"

Finally.

"The attacks on the men of Bayleys Landing might continue. A cop is guarding Chuck's hospital room, so he's still in danger. How can we be sure that tomorrow Ralphie or Simon—or even you, won't be floating face down in the Pawcattawaye?"

He stroked his jowly chin and seemed to be contemplating my words, but I didn't give him a chance to respond. "And why in heaven's name did you suggest that a police officer was behind Nick's death?"

He dropped his hand and frowned. "When did I do that?"

"The night Chuck was assaulted. You were that 1930's detective fellow. Don't you remember?"

He shook his head.

Could it be true that Woody doesn't remember when he's living vicariously through his myriad of characters? I tucked that bit of info into the back of my mind. But, at least, now he was himself, alert and engaged.

"You're buddies with Daily. So, I was hoping you'd try to persuade him to consider my theory that Mindy Marks is the mastermind behind the crimes."

"Mindy Marks?"

"The reporter who interviewed Pix."

"Now why—"

"Rejection. Jealousy. I've explained it to Daily."

"Hmm. And I take it, Treasure stands in the eye of the storm."

I nodded. "It seems that guys who have rejected Mindy in favor of Pix wind up in the river. But who's not to say that anyone who is attracted to Pix won't end up murdered."

"Treasure is a beautiful girl . . ." He tented his fingers under his chin. "It seems extreme to commit homicide over hurt feelings."

"Some people's egos are that big."

"No. I think it's something else. Someone else. I don't like to name names but have you or DJ considered that guy who works at Billie's Bagels."

"Who?" I took a step closer to him.

A soft sprinkle started. It left dots of wetness on the brick sidewalk.

"My, my," Woody said. "Here comes the rain. I'd best be moseying on now to the Grain and Lumber. Good day, Miss." After a deep bow, he turned and headed in the direction of the museum.

I ducked into the Crab Kettle, trying to stay dry, wondering if Woody had shared a viable lead. *But Billie's Bagels?* That didn't make a bit of sense. A conversation I'd had with Billie only a few weeks ago rang fresh in my mind. She'd told me about a vow she'd made eleven years earlier when she'd started the business. Billie's Bagels was going to be an all-women enterprise. From the bakers to the counter workers to the delivery drivers. She was pleased as punch that she'd been true to her word.

So who's this guy Woody's talking about?

Probably nothing more than the conjuring of the old fellow's overactive imagination, I decided, working myself to an empty booth as my stomach growled.

CHAPTER TWENTY-SEVEN

I 'd swallowed the last bite of crispy haddock when Simon walked into the seafood eatery. He made a beeline in my direction. My stomach dropped. I had no idea how to break the news to him that I'd sold three paintings to Geoff, and he wasn't going to get his usual fifty percent commission. At first, I'd felt a twinge of guilt, but when I'd held that check with the giant amount written across it, any angst-ridden compunction evaporated.

I swallowed hard. *We're friends. He'd given me the opportunity to publicly showcase my work. He introduced me to Geoff.* A surge of remorse flooded through me. I tucked my head and looked under the blocky table hoping to high heaven he wouldn't see me.

"Lose something?" He plonked into the chair opposite me.

I sat upright. "Ah, just dropped my napkin." I pulled the flimsy paper one off my lap and waved it, in the air, like a flag.

"That storm," he said, hitching his thumb over his shoulder, "came outta nowhere. I hung out at the gallery until it let up, shooting the breeze with Izabelle about the meteoric resurgence of plein air painting. There hasn't been anything like it since the French Impressionists hit their easels." He lifted a menu from the holder behind an arrangement of salt, pepper, Old Bay, and ketchup. "Since plein air is such a flourishing trend and you're great at it, I need more of your work."

I nodded without really listening, concerned about how to make a quick getaway. I wasn't ready to tell him about the paintings Geoff bought.

"I bumped into Pix at the Hot and Chilly Bean."

This got my attention, but I kept my lips tucked together. I still hadn't heard from Pix.

"She was with her mom. Those two could be mistaken for sisters."

Pix and Brenda do share an uncanny resemblance, I thought, dropping the napkin on my empty plate and standing. "But Pix has her father's chocolate brown eyes."

"Of course, she was jumpy. Nervous."

I dropped back into the seat.

"I wanted to wrap her in my arms. Tell her it's gonna be okay," he continued. "But how could I do that after she said Chuck had some kind of relapse?"

"Relapse?"

He shrugged. "They were grabbing coffee before heading to the hospital."

"Why didn't she let me know?" My voice sounded sharp, but I couldn't temper my words with my heart pounding like it was going to heave through my chest. I reached into my backpack and dug around for my cellphone. "Shoot," I whispered. I forgotten I'd turned it off at Seoul Sushi and BBQ.

"I offered to tag along, but she didn't want to impose," he said. "I reluctantly agreed, only because her mother was with her."

I closed my fingers around the phone and freed it from the backpack. I slapped my foot against the tile floor, waiting for the blasted thing to start up. After what seemed like ten minutes, the screen brightened. I had both phone and text messages. I clicked the telephone icon and pressed the device to my ear. Pix sobbed so hard, I could barely make out a word, but I'd heard enough. I stood and plucked a twenty free from my back pocket. There was no time to waste, so instead of waiting for change, I dropped the cash onto the table. "I going to the hospital."

"I'll drive you there." His eyes widened as if pleading. "Pix and Chuck are my friends, too."

I glanced away, not wanting to succumb to the concern filling his ruddy face. "If Chuck's back in the trauma center, they'll be strict about visitors." My temples pounded along with my heart. "I'll call as soon as I know something."

I burst out of the Crab Kettle, rushed down the street, and around the corner to my Honda.

FORTY MINUTES LATER, I headed for Chuck's hospital room. The good news, I kept telling myself, he's still assigned to the step-down unit. I listened to the rhythmic clicks of my cowboy boots striking the tile floor and how the sound kept in time with the beating of my heart. My clothes, damp from the sudden rain shower, felt cool against my skin. As I neared the room, I frowned. The cop on duty wasn't there. What does that mean, I wondered, chewing my lip. I hurried my already quick pace.

I barreled into the room. It looked like the floral department at the grocery store, with fragrant arrangements packing the counters and dresser tops interspersed with get-well cards. Mylar balloons tied to the base of the hospital bed where Chuck lay asleep swayed with the movement of cool air from the overhead vents. Pix and Brenda, seated side by side, talked in hushed whispers. Pix noticed me first and jumped to her feet.

"What happened?" I grabbed her hand and squeezed it.

The private duty nurse entered the room. Pix nodded toward the hallway.

It wasn't until we were in the corridor that I realized Brenda stood beside me. "It's wonderful to see you," I said hurriedly to the woman who never seemed to age, "but I wish it was under other circumstances."

Brenda zeroed in on my eyes. They seemed to penetrate through me as if she could see into my brain. I glanced away.

"You have a bright, brilliant aura. I'm thankful Treasure has a loyal friend like you," Brenda said breathily.

A flush of heat touched my cheeks.

Pix had already moved to an alcove furnished with an arrangement of cushioned chairs. I was surprised that sunlight filtered through the large, adjacent window.

Once seated, Pix looked at me. "You're wet."

"There was a terrific rainstorm and then another downpour when I arrived at the hospital. But," I said, pointing at the window, "it's passed over." I couldn't believe we were talking about the weather until, it dawned that whatever Pix had to share was difficult. Apparently, she wanted a tidbit of chit-chat before delving into Chuck's condition.

"I'd hate for you to catch a cold." Brenda reached into her oversized designer tote bag.

"Here. Take these." She handed me a couple of teabags. "They're great for the immune system."

"I'll make a cup the minute I get home," I assured her and punctuated my statement with a brisk nod.

I turned to Pix and noticed her eyes looked moist. I didn't want to rush her, so I turned to Brenda, hoping she'd take the lead and share the details of Chuck's relapse. But then, Pix spoke up.

"A nurse called this morning when Brenda and I were getting coffee at the Hot and Chilly Bean. She said Chuck had fallen."

My brows knitted together as questions sprung to my tongue. Instead of blabbering, I pressed my lips together and waited for Pix to explain.

"Chuck got out of bed, without supervision, much too fast. A bout of dizziness caused him to lose his balance. He fell into the dresser, bumped into one of the visitor's chairs, and crashed onto the floor." Pix stifled a little cry and wiped her fingertips across her face, drying tears that had seeped onto her cheeks. "The staples popped from his laparotomy—his abdominal incision. The doctor explained they can't close the incision again with staples, so they've covered it with a VAC dressing. That stands for Vacuum-Assisted Closure. It uses a suction pump to remove excess fluid and helps to promote healing."

I didn't dare interrupt but was floored by her fluidity with medical jargon and imagined she'd memorized every word the doctor had told her.

"The scary thing is his liver might be bleeding," Pix continued. "So, his blood count is being checked every six hours. If the liver is bleeding, Chuck will have to have another operation."

Fresh tears sprung to Pix's eyes. Normally, I'd search for a word of comfort or encouragement, but all I could think is why on earth did Chuck jump out of bed? Brenda's cooing filled my ears. She patted Pix's back, assuring her that Chuck would be fine. Better than new. I wasn't so sure. Especially since Daily had pulled the police officer guarding his hospital door.

CHAPTER TWENTY-EIGHT

I t took some doing, but along with Brenda's help, we talked Pix into going home. She looked exhausted with drooping eyelids and dark circles smudging her sallow complexion. Her mother's herbal tea, a good meal, and fifteen hours of sleep would make a world of difference. Pix hesitantly moved toward the elevator after I promised that I'd contact her as soon as Chuck awoke.

After an hour of looking into Chuck's slumbering face, even though the visitor chair was a bit stiff, I found myself dozing off. I fought it several times, willing my eye to flutter open, but lost the battle.

"Becca."

I heard my name. It sounded far away.

"Becca."

This time it rung in my ears. I flashed my eyes open.

"Where's Pix," Chuck said barely louder than a whisper.

"She went home with Brenda for a hearty meal and a nap."

"Good." He started to close his eyes.

"Wait. She wants to talk to you." I grabbed my cellphone off the side table where I'd deposited it exactly for this reason.

"If she's sleeping, I don't want to wake her. She's been here like 24/7." He twisted his neck and looked directly into my eyes. "You're certain her parents are staying with Pix. In her house."

"Of course. They flew out from California specifically to be with her."

"That's a relief. There's nothing like the support of parents when things go haywire."

The breath caught in the back of my throat. *Has anyone contacted Chuck's parents?* I knew he had a younger brother who lived with his folks somewhere in Florida. *Coral Gables, maybe?*

"What about your family?"

He shrugged one shoulder. "I spoke with my dad. Didn't go into much detail. No use upsetting them over . . . this."

"You mean the inconsequential fact that someone tried to murder you?"

He sighed. "I've gotta get out of here."

"I get it. You're going stir-crazy. But that fall only made things worse. I imagine your hospital stay will be extended."

"Dammit," he said, rubbing his temples. "There's no way I'm gonna be discharged with this thing attached to me." He motioned to a bump under his sheet. The vacuum pump. A thick, clear tube snaked out from under the cover and connected to an apparatus seated on a bedside table.

He was bummed out about the setback, so I kept my mouth shut.

"I need to contact Daily," he said, still looking at the lumpy sheet and speaking more to himself than me.

I perked up and leaned forward in the chair. "About what?"

"This." He reached to the nightstand and lifted a card that laid face-down. He handed it to me.

Cute, I thought, glancing at the card's design. A smiley face with the caption: A Big Smile Wishing You Get Well Soon! Why does Chuck want me to see this, I wondered, opening the card. The message scribbled in dark red ink encompassed only a few lines, and the card wasn't signed. I turned to the message and scanned the words written in a mixture of small and capital block letters. I read them again. Out loud.

"You may have survived. Pix won't. Too bad you won't be able to protect her." I stared at the smiley face drawn next to the words and shivered.

I grabbed my cellphone. "I'm calling Daily. He needs to dust this for fingerprints and test it for DNA." I tuned the card over and noticed the card company logo—Four Paws Greetings.

"You think that maniac is so stupid he'd leave evidence?"

I scrolled through my contact list and paused, reaching Daily's info. "Pix needs police protection because this threat is real." I glanced at Chuck. He stared at the ceiling. "So, that's why you jumped out of bed this morning. You wanted to get to Pix. To protect her."

He offered a curt nod. "I want to hire you." His eyes darted to me. "I'll pay any fee to keep Pix safe."

"Don't be silly. She's my best friend, too. You don't have to pay me."

"Okay." He took a deep breath. "Once her parents leave for Harmony Vista, you'll have to persuade Pix to stay with you. I don't want her alone. Her home is in the middle of nowhere—no streetlights—and nothing but woods stretching for miles behind her house. Pix need to be around people. Surrounded by friends."

"That won't be a problem. Especially when I tell her about this." I dropped the card on the side table like it was a snake.

"You can't."

"What?" I frowned.

"I don't want you to breathe a word of this to Pix. She's upset enough about what happened to Nick and me. This would be the breaking point. I'm sure of it."

"You're right," I said. "I'll keep a close watch on her 24/7."

I hadn't the slightest idea of how to keep my promise. She certainly wasn't going to swap living in her mini-mansion for my tiny apartment. This is going to take finesse—and some creative thinking.

"I really screwed things up," Chuck pointed to the VAC devise.

I wiped the concern from my face and attempted a smile.

"Don't worry. Pix will be safe with me. You just focus on getting better." I moved closer to the bed, leaned over, and kissed his cheek.

~

COMPLETELY DRAINED, I pushed through the door leading into my apartment. Though I was bushed, the purrs weren't. They congregated around my feet with their little cat voices squeaking. They didn't have to tell me I was late, and they were starving. But, being fed an hour later, I'd rationalized, wasn't going to harm my little furballs so, I'd made the decision to drop by Pix's house before heading home.

Brenda had answered the door, rushed me inside, and directed me to Pix's favorite room, her study with white furniture and a travertine fireplace. I took in the room with one glance. Pix wasn't there. I dropped into a cushiony armless leather chair.

"Chuck didn't want to disturb Pix if she was sleeping. So, I dropped by to give her an update."

"He's so thoughtful. Peter and I are over the moon that Pix has finally decided to settle down with such a great guy."

"Settle down?" I feared my eyebrows shot up to my hairline.

"Oh, you don't know?" Brenda flipped a lock of gleaming blond hair over her shoulder.

"Since Pix has basically been living in Chuck's hospital room, they've had a lot of time to talk.

Mostly about their feelings and how crazy in love they are. Once Chuck is well enough, they're going to tie the knot. Isn't that wonderful?"

Words escaped me, so I only nodded.

"Oh, dear. You're exhausted. Your aura is fading. Earlier it was a bright, golden yellow, but now it has turned to brownish-yellow ocher."

I ignored her aura comment. "Please, tell Pix that Chuck's feeling better and is planning on a good night's rest."

"I'll tell her the second she wakes up. She'll be so relieved."

Brenda paused a second by looking at the humongous diamond on her ring finger. "Did I happen to mention the wedding is going to take place at Harmony Vista? The exact locale where Peter and I exchanged vows. I'm going to make sure she slips my lucky crystal into her bustier—after all—it's brought Peter and me twenty-two years of wedded bliss."

As if a shiny stone could ensure happiness. I squirmed in my chair. Instead of voicing my opinion, I bit my tongue.

"Though I'm way too young to be a grandmother, Peter was starting to wonder if Pix was ever going to reproduce."

"Reproduce?" I found my voice.

"You know, have a baby."

The notion of Pix being a mother had never entered my mind. The very idea was a bit disconcerting since she didn't seem to possess a smidgen of maternal DNA. Once I asked her why she didn't have a pet, and she'd replied, without blinking an eye, the poor thing would starve to death because she'd probably forget to feed it.

That thought brought me back to my purrs and their demands for dinner. I scooted them out of the way, and within ten minutes, they licked their bowls clean.

I rooted through my backpack and grabbed the information I'd printed out for Daily, my cellphone, and the tea bags Brenda had given me. A cup of tea might be just what I need to calm the unsettling thoughts flashing through my mind. I padded to the refrigerator, pulled out the last bit of leftover lasagna, and placed it in the microwave. I've never before had so much food in the fridge. The doggie bag from last night filled up a whole refrigerator shelf. I decided to eat the oldest bit of leftovers first. I put on the kettle. The oven beeped, and though I was hungry, I couldn't bear the thought of actually eating.

Pix won't survive.

I couldn't chase those chilling words from my mind. With the food still in the microwave, I flopped on the couch, and Jaspurr jumped into my lap. I stroked his cottony fur, trying to make sense of the unnerving threat aimed at my best friend. The more I considered the situation, I realized it wasn't a threat at all, but a promise, and Pix's life hung in the balance.

Even with this new development, I hadn't wavered and remained adamant that Mindy was the mastermind behind the crimes. "Hasn't she hurt Pix enough?"

Jaspurr looked up and rubbed his head against my cheek.

"I guess not. Because now she's demanding Pix's very life. It's hard to believe that someone who seems to have the world by its tail would be consumed by an all-encompassing deep-seated hatred."

Jaspurr's response was the soft fluttering sound of a contented purr.

A sharp rap sounded at the door.

I cradled Jaspurr in my arms, moved toward the sound of another knock, and pulled the door open. Simon faced me.

"Hey, Jaspurr." He patted the cat's head, but Jaspurr wasn't in the mood. She jumped from my arms and ran beneath the couch.

A high-pitched whistle shrieked from the kitchen area. I'd forgotten about the tea pot. I raised a forefinger urging Simon to wait and hurried to remove the kettle from the burner. Over my shoulder, I asked him if he'd like a cup. He'd made himself comfortable on the couch, and Coppurr was looking up at him.

"Sure," he said, bending over to pat Coppurr's head, who scurried away to lie next to Jaspurr.

"Brenda gave me the tea. She promised it would prevent sniffles."

"You're not feeling well."

"Just tired. I have so much on my mind, especially with the new turn of events concerning Chuck."

"How is he?"

"You know Chuck. He's tough." I weighed my words carefully not to give away the slightest hint that Pix was in danger. "Turns out, it was only a small mishap. But you know how emotional Pix can be, sometimes."

"It's nothing serious?"

Afraid I'd flub up, I wanted to steer the conversation away from Chuck. "He'll be back to his old self in no time."

"That's a relief." He took a sip of tea. "Hey, this isn't half bad."

Even though the tea was still fairly hot, I'd guzzled down half the cup not paying attention to the taste.

"With everything that's been going on, I bet you haven't had much time to paint."

This was the other subject I didn't want to talk about. "Honestly, Simon, painting is the last thing on my mind. I'll try to make some sketches next week. Especially since Pix's parents are in town keeping an eye on her."

"How long are they planning to stay?" He raised the mug and took another sip.

"I guess until Chuck is released from the hospital. They've been such a comfort. Especially Brenda. As usual, Peter has been busy with work stuff, but I'm sure Pix is used to that."

He placed the mug on a coaster as Caspurr began to knead in his lap. "How're you doing, big boy?" He scratched the cat's head. "You've gotta have some recently finished paintings in your studio. I'd love to check them out since I'm running low on your stuff."

"Sure," I lied.

He stood, freeing the sofa's corner for Caspurr to curl up against. When I remained seated, he shot me a quizzical glance. "You coming?"

Oh, God, no, I panicked. *Simon wants to go to the studio now.* A rap sounded on the door. *Perfect timing.* I wasn't expecting anyone, but whoever it was, I could just kiss.

I hurried to the door, flung it open, and faced Daily. The kissing idea flew from my mind.

He held a couple of take-out boxes.

"Can I come in?" He shot me a sheepish grin.

"Hey, DJ." Simon moved closer to us. "Oh, damn. Why didn't you tell me you and DJ were having dinner? Look, I'll get out of your hair."

"Umm . . . no . . . no need to leave," I sputtered. "Please, stay."

Simon shook his head. "I'll take a look at those paintings another time. You two enjoy your meal and try not to talk too much shop," he said with a finger wave and slipped through the doorway.

I closed the door behind him and faced Daily.

"Your lunch. You left it behind at the restaurant. Thought you might want it." He handed me the cartons.

"It wasn't necessary for you to—"

"I admit it. I was a jerk. Peace?"

Exhaling loudly, I wondered if this day could get any worse. I took the boxes and motioned to the couch with my chin. "Would you like a cup of herbal tea?"

"Tea?"

I turned away from the stove and looked at him.

"You have anything stronger? We've got something to celebrate."

Leaving the tea pot behind, I moved near him. He had that smug look on his face I despised.

"Celebrate?" I raised my brows.

"Though I didn't get the confession I was after, I made an arrest. Now it's up to the grand jury to indict him and set the judicial wheels in motion."

Daily was talking too much. His words bounced inside my brain.

"I have to hand it to you, Rebecca. You were right. It wasn't one of the Main Street guys."

"Wait. Slow down." I eyed him from across the couch with my arms folded. "Who did you arrest?"

"Don't tell me you haven't figured it out?"

I frowned, wishing he'd answer me instead of playing twenty questions.

"Who had means and motive?"

"Daily." I raised my voice.

"Okay. Okay." He stood and moved closer to me. "Chris Tucker."

I clapped my hand over my mouth.

"Chris Tucker has been arrested for the murder of Dominick Rizzo and the attempted murder of Chuck Stetson."

CHAPTER TWENTY-NINE

"Have you lost your mind," I thundered. Daily showed no expression, and that infuriated me even more.

"I thought you'd be relieved the person who almost murdered your friend is behind bars."

Now it made sense why Chuck wasn't under police protection any longer.

"Look, Daily." I took a step closer to the couch. "You've made a mistake. Chris Tucker didn't murder anyone. He's only a down on his luck veteran, for heaven's sake."

"He was found at the crime site and considering his circumstances—"

"Of course, he was at the scene. He saved Chuck's life." *Why was he being so thickheaded?*

"Or he didn't finish the job before someone else came along."

"Wait. What? Someone else happened on the scene. Who?"

He pressed his lips together.

Thank God, he didn't say that's police business. Then I realized that no response added up to the same result. Nothing.

"So Tucker's violent attacks were motivated by his want of a bit of cash—a credit card—a watch?"

"A damn good motive if you're homeless."

Inwardly I fumed but forced myself to temper my emotions. I had to prove he was wrong, and knowing Daily's ego, that wasn't going to be an easy task. "I've met Tucker, and he's not a thief, let alone a killer."

Daily stared at me blank-faced. But then shook his head. "Correction. He's a trained killer. A Marine with five deployments to Iraq and Afghanistan. And probably an addict. That kind will do just about anything to get money for a fix."

"He may have a drinking problem, but he's not going to kill someone because he needs a cold one."

"Why are you defending the guy?"

I sunk onto the edge of the couch. Coppurr jumped up next to me, keeping his sight fixed on Daily. "Because in my eyes, he's a hero."

"I never took you for a soft touch."

"I'm not. But Tucker and people like him risk their lives for the greater good. Chris Tucker put his life on the line innumerable times, so why would he throw it away on a cheap watch to pawn or a couple of bucks for a bottle of bad whiskey?"

He pursed his lips and sat silent for a few seconds. "PTSD changes people."

I half-nodded. "But tell me this, why would Tucker threaten Pix's life?"

He shot up. "What the hell are you talking about?"

"You haven't spoken to Chuck" I raised my eyebrows. "He received a get well card with a cryptic message." Coppurr snuggled into my lap, and his gravelly purr vibrated a mile a minute. "Something along the line of 'you survived, but Pix won't.'"

He headed for the door.

"Where are you going?"

"To have a little talk with Stetson." He pulled his cellphone free. "By the time I reach the hospital, the CSI team will have arrived." He glanced at me. "I don't want Treasure Winslow to be unchaperoned. Not for one second. Do you understand?"

"You want me—what about police protection?"

"You know the department doesn't provide personal bodyguards. Isn't that more along the lines of your job description?" With that, he hurried out of my apartment.

I stroked Coppurr's soft, fiery-red fur. The kitty craned his neck so he could look into my face. "I guess I don't have a choice."

Coppurr let out a little mew.

"I'll have to tell Pix."

Coppurr's eyes narrowed.

"Chuck doesn't want Pix to know she's the killer's next target." I chewed my lip as indecision tore at my gut. "If I don't break the news to her, Daily will. In his best Neanderthal fashion."

Coppurr started kneading my leg. His claws pricked through my jeans. "Stop," I ordered. I hoped to take him and Jaspurr to the Easter cat show and I'd already scheduled a bath and manicure with their groomer. But Coppurr needed a trim now. I placed him on floor and headed to the cabinet where I keep their grooming supplies but stopped after a few steps. Coppurr treaded on my heels.

"But if I could persuade her to stay here, it'd be a surefire way to get her parents out of her hair. What do you think?" I glanced at Coppurr.

He let out a chippy-churp, and a second later, his throaty purr filled my ears. Forgetting about his nail trim, I hurried to the cabinet and pulled out his favorite treat. The two other purrs came running, not wanting to miss out on the "good" stuff. Each one had their preferred brand of treats so, I pulled out two additional pouches. Their happy crunching filled my ears, as I tapped my foot, hoping I could coax Pix into rooming with me.

I opened the refrigerator, pulled out the Pyrex dish, and placed the lasagna into the microwave oven. In serious need of diversion, I clicked the television. I dropped on the couch, pulled my legs up and pressed a pillow behind my head. At the commercial, I'll open that box of *kimbap*, I decided, realizing I was more than ready to eat. Lasagna and *kimbap* will make a delicious dinner. It was sweet of Daily to bring me my abandoned lunch.

But then I recalled his callousness toward Chris Tucker, and a wave of irritation flew through me.

My cellphone sounded. "Wouldn't you know it," I said, glancing at Caspurr, who was licking his paws clean. "The second I get comfortable." I pressed the T.V. mute button, jumped off the couch, grabbed my phone off the kitchen table, and checked the screen.

Pix.

"Feeling better?" I said, making my way back to the couch.

"Much. Guess what?"

She didn't give me a chance to respond.

"The Mindy Marks debate is on for tonight."

"What? I thought Dolly canceled it."

"She changed her mind. I guarantee this discussion is going to put an end to the ruckus surrounding Treasure's Trove of Lingerie."

I paused, wondering how that could ever play out.

"I was wondering—"

"Need you ask? I'll be there with bells on," I said, not believing my luck. *After the interview, I'll invite Pix over here and talk her into staying.*

She informed me that the taping would begin at the Tea Pot Shoppe in twenty minutes.

I swiped off the phone. "Well, how do you like them apples?" I questioned the three purrs staring at me. The saying was one of Aunt Marianne's favorites and once again I realized that a lot of her personality had rubbed off on me.

Before heading to the bathroom for a quick touch-up, I removed the now cold lasagna from the microwave oven. I'll give it to the kitties for breakfast. They usually didn't get people food. But they go crazy over lasagna just like Garfield, the cartoon cat, so on occasion, I'd scrape out the filling and give it to them. I took a quick peek at the purrs brushing against my legs. "Tonight," I told them, "I become Treasure Winslow's protector."

CHAPTER THIRTY

Ten minutes later, I strolled into the Tea Pot Shoppe, eager to observe my main suspects, Mindy Marks and David Regan. I wasn't disappointed. The two of them faced each other, he with a trace of a smile, as they stood in the center of the shop. Dolly Evans was nowhere to be seen while Pix and Peter stood at the back of the long room near the arrangement of wrought iron tables and chairs.

At first, I was surprised to see Peter. But then I realized that he, like me, was here to support his daughter. A glowing sense of warmth spread through me.

I hurried toward them. "Peter, hello."

He responded by wrapping his arms around me in a bear hug. When he released me, I thought he looked tired. Or was it distress? Had he drawn the obvious conclusion that Pix wouldn't be safe until the still-at-large obsessed maniac was locked away for good? I took a few backward steps and took in his appearance. Dapper, as usual, probably wearing a hand-tailored Italian suit, but his hair seemed a bit grayer, and the puffiness around his eyes, I'd never noticed before.

"This all seems a bit last minute," I said, looking from father to daughter.

"I think the timing is perfect," Pix said, "for the truth to come out."

"Truth?" I wrinkled my nose.

"You'll see." Peter took a quick look at his platinum Rolex with its diamond bezel.

I could probably purchase a three-bedroom townhouse for just the price of his watch. Regardless, I certainly didn't have anything against rich people. Heck, I wanted rich people to become interested in my paintings, so I could kiss this gumshoeing stuff goodbye.

"I've made a lovely pot of tea, so let's get in our places. Chop-chop." Dolly's voice resounded through the entire store.

I noticed a scowl jump to Regan's face. Mindy didn't seem to have heard Dolly's pronouncement since she continued to give directions to her make-up lady. By the time I looked back at Dolly, she'd placed the pot on a table decorated with a frilly cloth and arranged with shiny silver and dainty porcelain place settings. A platter of scones and a dish of clotted cream sat next to a short vase of wildflowers.

Pix was the only one to follow Dolly's instructions. *How unusual.* That could only mean one thing. She was anxious to get this show on the road. Pix appeared completely carefree as she reached for the pot and poured herself a cup of tea. After a quick sip, she brushed her silk, coral-colored shirt, which set off her golden-blonde hair flowing around her shoulders.

Pix was about to pour another cup when Regan told everyone to take their places. I noticed the worry lines disappear from Dolly's face as she puffed out, "An about time."

Mindy pulled out the chair opposite Pix, while Dolly sat on the long side of the table between them. Someone clapped the slate board, and Mindy pasted a smile onto her perfectly made-up face.

"Bayleys Landing," Mindy said, "is a peaceful little town full of corner cafes, bookstores, and art galleries. But, about a year ago, Treasure's Trove of Lingerie opened its doors, and the town hasn't been the same since. Treasure Winslow is the proprietor of the lingerie boutique, and this is a follow-up interview with Treasure where we'll debate the repercussions that her presence has brought to this once sleepy little hamlet."

"Cut," Regan said. He moved closer to the table. "Now, Miss Dolly, after Mindy introduces you and Treasure, I want you to pour the tea. Mindy will direct questions to both of you ladies, so just relax and answer as best as you can. Now," he said, pointing to a bright ruby-like point on the camera, "be sure not to look directly at that red dot. Understand?"

They both nodded.

I stood a few feet away, out of camera range, with Peter. He seemed a bit jumpy, which I found odd for a laid-back, former hippy turned environmental industrialist. Probably concerned about his little girl's worries. I refocused on the "tea party". Exactly as Regan explained, Mindy introduced them, and Dolly poured tea. I held my breath waiting for all hell to break loose. I sensed it wouldn't take long.

"Dolly." Mindy tilted her head toward the older woman. "If I understand correctly, Treasure's lingerie shop has brought nothing but havoc to Main Street."

"I wouldn't go that far," Dolly said, touching the wide brim of her navy blue hat with white piping. "However, many of my colleagues at the Merchant Association believe that Treasure's type of establishment is inappropriate. Even the president of the Bayleys Landing Historical Society agrees."

Jane Parks. I rolled my eyes. *If she had her way, we'd all be wearing hoop skirts and writing with quill pens.*

"Now, Treasure." Mindy shifted her sight across the table. "I found your lingerie shop to be a bit unusual with your collection of antique undergarments, even though you do carry a wonderful assortment of sexy lingerie. If I'm not mistaken, that is exactly what's gotten many local shop owners up in arms. On top of that, there's talk that your distinguished and wealthy father influenced the process of your acceptance into the Merchant Association."

Peter crossed his arms and glared at Mindy, but then a smile began to creep across his face. I glanced at Pix, expecting to see her eyes flaming with indignation, but like her father, a smile dominated her face.

"It's true that a few shop owners weren't exactly overjoyed that Treasure's Trove of Lingerie had found a home on Main Street," Pix said. "But now, they're appreciating the benefit of a trendy store that offers a bit of history and outrageously sexy apparel. Because it's been the catalyst needed to generate a different type of shopper—younger, vibrant, fun—into our town which has only increased sales. For all the Main Street businesses." She raised her teacup and took a sip. "You mentioned my father's influence. I hope you weren't suggesting that he offered bribes to sway the votes." She shot Mindy an icy glare. "That wouldn't fly in Bayleys Landing. We believe in what we believe, and nothing, even money, would change that."

She paused a second and glanced at Peter. He nodded as if urging her to continue.

"My father, Peter Winslow, is a pioneer in the environmental industry. I'm thrilled and proud to announce that my father is the force behind the new parking garage that will begin construction west of Main Street tomorrow. He has funded the entire project. In addition to the parking garage, he is providing three electric shuttle buses. The shuttles will ferry visitors from the parking garage, located a half-mile outside of town, to Main Street free of charge."

For a second, I thought Dolly was going to fall off her chair. Instead, she pressed her hands together as if offering a prayer of thanks. "I can't believe it. You did say free shuttles?"

Pix nodded. "Free electric-powered shuttles. Not only will visitors be relieved of the hassle of driving around hunting for parking, but the environment will also benefit."

"Wonderful. Just wonderful." Dolly beamed, lifting the platter and handing it to Pix.

"Please, dear, have one of my blue ribbon cranberry scones, and don't forget the clotted cream."

Pix lifted a scone. "The shuttles will run every fifteen minutes, every day, seven days a week." She took a bite of the tender, flakey confection.

What a bombshell, I thought. *Electric shuttles!*

Pix wasn't finished yet. "My father's generosity will cause a boon for our town. The lack of parking has always been the number one chief complaint of merchants and visitors alike."I wasn't the only one floored by the announcement. I'd never witnessed it before, but Dolly could smile—an actual—authentic —smile. In fact, she shot Peter one, so big and bright, I thought her cheeks might split. Mindy, on the other hand, looked deflated.

Satisfaction was written all over Pix's face when she handed Mindy the platter. Instead of selecting a scone, Mindy stood and glared at Regan with a scowl.

"Cut, cut, cut," He ordered.

"Did you know about this?" Mindy snapped at Dolly.

"I hadn't the slightest idea. But isn't it fantastic? If Treasure hadn't opened her shop here, we'd never have a wonderful new parking facility. Oh." She glanced at Pix. "Is this distinguished gentleman your father?"

Pix nodded, swallowing a mouthful of the prized scone. "Let me introduce you.

Peter—"

"Can we get back to the interview?" Mindy's irritated voice sounded and her face flushed an angry red. Her make-up lady hurried over with a compact and powder puff.

As the cosmetician blotted tiny dots of perspiration off Mindy's forehead and smoothed her already smooth hair, I couldn't help but worry if she was going to bring up the attacks. Though Pix had crushed Mindy's angle concerning the lingerie shop, I feared she'd trump Pix when it came to discussing Bayleys Landing crime spike.

A few minutes later, Mindy with regained composure and the camera rolling, focused on Pix. "Townspeople that I've spoken to believe it's your fault these gruesome crimes are happening in this once idyllic village. Just yesterday, I interviewed Jane Parks, a local historian, and author. She believes that the current level of violence is a direct result of, and I quote, 'you and your trashy store.'"

I edged near the table where the three women were seated, but a firm grip around my arm stopped me. I looked into Peter's face, and he shook his head. By this time, Pix was addressing Mindy.

"It's true that the recent attacks have been aimed at friends of mine. In fact, my fiancé is one of the victims. But whoever is committing these crimes is at fault. Not me."

"Could one of your jilted lovers be responsible for the crimes?"

I wanted to point my finger in Mindy's face and accuse her. Instead, I gritted my teeth and waited for Pix to respond.

"Not a jilted lover, Mindy, but maybe a lovesick specter from another era."

Oh, no, she didn't, I silently screamed.

"What?" Mindy once again jumped up. This time she walked around the table and stared at Pix. "You did this on purpose to destroy my interview and make a fool out of me. A parking garage and now this—a ghost? You've got to be kidding. But I'll get even with you. Mark my words."

CHAPTER THIRTY-ONE

"You were brilliant," I whispered into Pix's ear as I hugged her. "What great news," I said, twisting my neck so I could see Peter, "about the parking garage. You're the hero of Bayleys Landing."

"Can you believe it? Peter kept the news all to himself until right before the interview." Pix beamed at her father. "Isn't he wonderful?" She reached up and pecked his goateed cheek.

I noticed his face blush and was surprised that a successful man like Peter would be embarrassed by being able to achieve what many had miserably failed to do—tear through bureaucratic red tape—and shred it to pieces.

Dolly rushed over. Her eyes sparkled as she held a package. "These are for you, Mr. Winslow. An assortment of my fresh scones. Cranberry crumb, rustic oatmeal, and lemon blueberry."

"Thank you." He took the white cardboard bakery box.

His face had taken on a deeper reddish hue.

"Once the news gets out, the merchants will want to hold a parade for you. Right down the center of Main Street," Dolly said.

"Your thanks are more than enough." He lifted the box. "And these. Very thoughtful of you."

"I like the idea of a parade," Pix said. She looked at Dolly. "Why don't you bring it up at the next Merchant Association meeting?"

"I most certainly will." Dolly nodded. "Oh, I must thank our other guests." She hurried away moving toward Mindy and Regan, who had their heads together.

I nonchalantly followed her, aware that I'd have to employ my best eavesdropping technique since I was itching to find out what they were discussing. I stopped at a display table close to where the two of them were conversing in hushed tones. Pretending to inspect the hand-painted roses on a tea pot's lustrous surface, I strained to hear their words. Oh, why, I chided myself, have I never learned how to read lips? I lifted the pot and raised it in front of my face.

Dolly's voice boomed. "It's been ever so wonderful being interviewed for your, umm, national show."

"The word lingerie isn't a curse word," Mindy said dryly.

"Of course not. But in the long run," she said as if trying not to smile, "something great came out of the hubbub circling around Treasure's little 'unmentionables' shop. Plus, the antique pieces are of historical value." She grabbed Mindy's hand and heartily shook it. "Ta-ta!" She bounced away and started to clean up the cups and dishes left behind from the interview.

I targeted my attention back on Mindy.

"Winslow's segment is never going to air. I'll see to that," she said, not masking her anger.

"Calm down," Regan said. "You did an amazing job with the initial interview. Once the editors get hold of it, I swear, Min, it might be your very best work."

"You think so?"

"Absolutely."

"Well . . ." She fluffed her shiny blond hair as a tiny smile found its way to her lips.

"If you want to hang around this backwater a few more days

to follow up on that story about her," Regan jutted his chin in Pix's direction, "that'll be no problem."

I replaced the tea pot on the table and stepped a bit closer. So involved with each other, neither one seemed to notice me.

"I'd like that, Davey. Because when my story about Winslow— a classic example of a black widow—is aired, my career is going to skyrocket. I might even wind up becoming a national news anchor. I can just see it. Me interviewing the President."

I rolled my eyes. *In your dreams.*

"Whoa," Regan said. "I'm not sure that would be your style. I envision you hosting a national entertainment news program."

Mindy's eyes seemed to pop.

"I've talked to Channing. Channing Clarke. Senior executive, of the Hurrah Channel, and he's very interested—"

"Oh. My. God." Mindy squealed. She put her hand over her lips, looked around, and spotted me standing almost on top of them. She dropped her hand and shot me a scowl.

"Becca," Pix called from across the room where she and Peter talked with the cameraman.

Cameraman? I couldn't believe it. I hurried over to the little group.

"This is Al," she said.

I grabbed the cameraman's outstretched hand.

"We were talking about poor Nick. He and Al were buddies," she said.

"I'm so sorry," I murmured.

Al nodded. "Look, I gotta get going. Nice meeting you all." He headed to the front of the shop and joined the gaffer and best boy who were packing up their equipment.

"We're going out to dinner. To celebrate," Pix said, "at Palette de Vie."

I looked at my clothes. A mustard yellow chenille pullover, dark slacks, and a pair of cowboy boots were fine for the Crab Kettle, but not a two-star Michelin-rated restaurant.

"The reservation is for eight, so," Pix said, checking her watch, "you've got twenty minutes to change." She glanced at Peter and then at me. "I'd better go with you. I know how easily you're distracted, especially when you start playing with the cats."

"Really, Peter, that's not true," I said as Pix started to giggle.

"You seem more like sisters every day." He shook his head. "Look, you two, I'm going to head over to the restaurant. Your mom will be joining us there." He eyed Pix but handed me the box of scones neatly secured with bakery twine. "Brenda will never allow these into the house, so, please, Becca, enjoy them."

"Thanks," I said.

Pix grabbed my arm. As we headed for the exit, I noticed that every trace of *Lingerie Exposed* had disappeared from the little tea shop.

I supposed that Pix would be chattering the whole way to my apartment, but instead, we walked in silence. *She must be thinking about Chuck. Her fiancé?*

"It's a beautiful evening." She broke the stillness between us. "There's going to be a cat moon tonight."

"Cat moon?"

"Well, it's what some cat lovers on the net are calling tonight's perigee, otherwise known as the 'Super Pink Moon'. It's when the moon is closest to the earth and is really bright."

"Cool. After dinner, let's look for it," Pix said.

"It won't be hard to miss since there's not a cloud in the sky."

Pix stopped walking and looked at me. "Everything's starting to make sense."

"Sense?"

"Uh-huh. I've got to hand it to Brenda. After we found out about Chuck's accident, she said that before the day's end, everything was going to turn around for the better. I didn't believe her but now . . ." She shrugged. "Brenda must've somehow known that the celestial event was going to influence today's outcome."

"Celestial event?" I sighed. "Your dad must've been working with the county for months trying to get the parking garage contract. As for Chuck, he's in a nationally renowned hospital and receiving some of the best medical care in the state. I doubt the moon had anything to do with anything." I started walking, and it only took a couple of seconds for her to catch up.

"You may be right. But Brenda wouldn't agree. When I was young, she labeled herself a lunatic."

"Lunatic?"

"Not in the sense of someone with mental health issues, but as a worshipper of the moon. The practice goes back to the ancient Babylonians. But she's moved on from that kind of thing. She now believes in a higher power that's not a planet. One that's more like an incredible energy force."

"Then I won't bring up her days as a lunatic over dinner." I didn't know if was due to a pent-up release over the success of Pix's interview or an image of Brenda genuflecting in the moonlight, but I burst out laughing.

"What's so funny?"

"Nothing," I managed between spurts of the giggles. "It's just the look of Mindy's face when you nailed her in the interview."

"She went all bug-eyed. I think I saw steam coming out of her ears." Pix joined in my hilarity, and by the time we reached the apartment, we were still tittering, and tears streamed down our cheeks.

We stepped inside, and the purrs weaved themselves between our legs. Caspurr was trilling his usual, I want a treat sound, and Coppurr looked at us with a hint of amusement. Jaspurr rubbed against Pix's ankles until he decided to sit on her feet.

"The purrs are happy to see you. As usual." I hurried toward my closet. "They'll keep you entertained while I change clothes."

It took only ten minutes to transform myself from shabby to chic—or was that chic shabby?

I stepped out of the bathroom and glanced at Pix. Coppurr nestled in her lap sound asleep, while Caspurr and Jaspurr sat adoringly at her feet. She glanced in my direction.

"Ready?" Pix tried to move Coppurr without waking him, but the gentle movement of her hand, caused him to flash his eyes open and jump off her lap.

"How's the visit with your parents going?" I moved closer to the couch.

"Great." She stood and smoothed her black skirt, streaked with cat fur. "Except I feel guilty keeping them from their trip to Harmony Vista. They both have such busy schedules. Finally, they coordinated a time that worked for both of them. Starting yesterday. Who knows when they'll be able to work in the visit now?"

This was the opportunity I'd been hoping for. "I got a great idea."

"Oh?" Pix bent over and patted Coppurr on top of his head. He let out a happy mew.

"Chuck told me he doesn't want you to be alone. That's why he's relieved your parents are staying with you. But what if you bunked in here, with me, then your folks could still savage their trip to HV."

"Did Chuck put you up to this?" She clutched her narrow hips.

"No." I wouldn't dare tell her that Daily had ordered me to keep her in my sight at all times. "I take full credit. Anyway, it would be fun. A throwback to our dorm days at MICA. Plus, your parents wouldn't have to worry since you'd have your own private investigator at your beck and call."

"You've got a point there." She pursed her lips as if considering my invitation. "The truth is, I feel awful they gave up their vacation to keep me company. Not to mention, I've had it up to here," she said, tapping to her forehead, "with tofu and dandelion salad."

"So?"

"Okay."

I exhaled, not realizing I'd been holding my breath.

"My parents flew here in Peter's private jet. They can leave for HV as soon they want."

"Tonight?"

"I don't see why not. If they decided to leave right away, I can already imagine tomorrow's breakfast. Dolly's scones with a cup of English tea," Pix said.

"Sounds like a plan." I draped the sweater that I'd almost forgotten about around my shoulders. "We better get going. Don't want to keep your parents waiting at Palette de Vie."

"They're going to love your idea of us being roommates until Chuck is released."

"I hope so." I crossed my fingers. It was the only way I could think of to keep Pix safe.

CHAPTER THIRTY-TWO

The fancy French restaurant looked exactly how I'd imagined. The main dining room, where we were seated, wasn't particularly spacious since Palette de Vie occupies the former living quarters of a nineteenth-century Second Empire style house with a mansard roof. The square wooden tables covered with crisp, white linen were tightly fitted. Even so, an aura of intimacy lingered in the room, adorned with paintings of thoroughbred horses in heavy frames. Bronze wall sconces diffused soft light causing the gilded oval mirrors to shine. The fireplace's mantle fashioned from black marble was adorned with sculpted leaves and a shell carved in its center, which I supposed, was authentic to the original structure.

Palette de Vie is celebrated for its hearty French country food. Since I'd never been to France, or actually, out of the good ole USA, I wouldn't know the difference between a Parisian four-course dinner and one served in south-central France. But the delectable aroma wafting through the air guaranteed a heavenly eating experience.

Not sure about how the conversation would flow, I needed not worried. Peter and Brenda were gracious, as usual, and centered the conversation around me.

"So, Becca," Peter said, "Pix told us that you've photographed this year's designer house."

"I did. It was fascinating to see how each designer's creative eye interpreted and reinvented their assigned rooms. I also learned a bit of history about the house, which was fun," I remembered Jane Hunt's insistence on the presence of the ghost who liked to rearrange furniture.

"My photos will be used for marketing the event."

"Oh, I adore interior designs," Brenda said. "Has Pix told you we've recently relocated?"

I nodded. "In fact, I have a housewarming gift for you."

I touched the present I'd placed on the floor next to my chair. I'd purposely hadn't shown Geoff this piece even though I considered it one of my best experimental landscapes. I figured he wouldn't be interested since the painting reflected a different style and technique from the others he'd purchased. The colors were more vibrant, the brushstrokes looser, the paint thicker, and it expressed an energy that my careful studio renderings lacked. I couldn't help but feel a bit proud of my *plein air* painting.

I'd painted the picture with the sole purpose of giving it away as a gift. I have a long-standing practice of bestowing my paintings to close friends for special occasions—weddings, anniversaries, birthdays. But once Pix shared that her folks were coming to Bayleys Landing, it was a no-brainer who'd be the recipient of this painting. I only hoped they'd ask for more.

Even though Pix and I were dormmates for three years of college, her parents' visits, though sparse, resembled tumultuous whirlwinds. A whole lot of anticipation on Pix's part, then upon arrival a cacophony of exclamations, queries, and gossip before being swept off to dinner, and then puff they were gone. Never was there time for show and tell. So, consequently, they hadn't the opportunity to see any of my paintings, let alone either one of our student shows.

I had grabbed the painting, already tucked inside a gift bag, from the studio before leaving for the restaurant. Pix asked about it, but I'd said it was a surprise. This satisfied her since she was always big on surprises.

I focused across the table at Brenda, lifted the gift bag, and noticed how a rush of excitement flushed her cheeks. Apparently, Pix took after her mother when it came to surprises. I handed the present to Peter, who was seated next to me. Brenda jumped up and scurried behind her husband. While he held the bag, Brenda, in a ceremonial fashion, slowly removed each sheet of tissue paper like she was performing the dance of the seven veils.

The anticipation made my heart hammer. I really needed another patron. If the Winslows offered me a commission, then I'd dump the P.I. work for good and fulfill my dream of being a full-time artist. But I'd be sure to keep my private investigator's license up to date, so if it didn't work out, I'd always have something to fall back on.

"Oh, it's a painting." Brenda's voice jumped up an octave.

It seemed like a lifetime as they inspected the canvas without comment. I felt like throwing up.

Finally, Peter broke the silence. "I thought you specialized in photography. But . . . You painted this?" He peered at me above the golden frame.

"I was a painting major along with photography. Well, anyway, I thought um . . . perhaps you'd consider . . . Umm . . ." I rubbed my damp hands together. "I hope your new home brings you years of happiness." Disgusted that I'd lost my nerve about asking them for a commission, I managed to paste a fake smile on my face.

"It's amazing," Brenda said under her breath. "I had no idea." She lifted her head in Pix's direction. "Why didn't you tell us Becca could paint like this?"

The question seemed to startle Pix. She opened her mouth to respond but ended up only shrugging.

"You're quite a talent," Peter said. "You know, just recently, Brenda and I were discussing that our house in Switzerland needs a makeover. I'm wondering . . ."

My heart pounded so hard, I could hardly hear his voice above its thumps.

"Would you consider creating—"

"We'll need at least fifteen—twenty paintings," Brenda said.

"Twenty?" I almost choked on the word.

"Is that too much to ask for?" Brenda said with the beginnings of a pout.

"No. Not at all. Twenty is a good number." I nodded so quickly I probably looked like a bobblehead.

"We can see breathtaking views for miles from our balcony," Peter said. "Would that interfere with your responsibilities? I do know that you have cats. But, not to worry, we'll work something out, so you'll be able to bring them with you."

My head was spinning. "Bring them where?"

"To our chalet. In Switzerland." Brenda enunciated like I was a simpleton.

"Don't worry about expenses," Peter said. "We'll fly you over, and you can stay at the house while you're not traveling around the countryside painting."

I couldn't help it. My jaw dropped.

"You don't have to give us an answer now," Peter said. "Think about it and let us know."

Think about it?

"I'd love to," I said louder than I meant to.

"Then it's settled," he said. "We'll finalize the details after the wedding."

The wedding. I shot Pix a look I hoped expressed; why haven't you told me about the most important decision of your life?

"That'd be great," I said, redirecting my attention to the couple.

Peter squeezed my arm while Brenda kissed my cheek and whispered, "I bet you're a Pisces."

PIX AIMLESSLY CLICKED the remote control. "I can't believe you don't have cable."

I moved to the couch with a bowl of air-popped popcorn. "That's not true. I subscribe to the sports channel."

She reached for a handful of fluffy puffed-up corn. "Like I said, no cable."

I plopped down beside her. "Your parents are amazing. I still can't believe they want me to paint twenty pictures for them." An unsettling thought had been racing through my mind ever since Pix's folks had invited me to Switzerland for the painting fest. "Did you have anything to do with it?"

"Me?" She widened her eyes innocently then filled her mouth with popcorn.

"Maybe a quick hint to Brenda that I'm the proverbial struggling artist, and she offered to help out? Because really, Pix, nobody in their right mind hires someone to create twenty paintings based on a small, plein air study. Even if it was incredibly good."

She shrugged.

"I figured as much." I stared at the television but didn't pay attention to the images flashing on the screen.

"If it makes you feel any better, I took Brenda to the PPS Gallery and showed her your paintings," Pix said. "You know how she and Peter are so into nature. And when she saw your paintings, well, she was floored. At least, that's the word she used. I assumed she liked them because she bought the last two paintings you had on display there. I told Simon not to tell you since I wanted it to be a surprise."

"What?"

"She bought your paintings. The ones, hanging at the Prescott Painting and Sculpture Gallery."

I moved to the edge of the couch and twisted so I could see her better. Simon's visit last night in search of new paintings now made sense.

"When Brenda and I went to the ladies' room at the restaurant, she told me she liked the plein air painting even more than the ones she purchased from Simon." Pix glanced at the TV and switched the channel. "Brenda likes to refer to herself as a nemophilist."

"I take it that's different from being a lunatic."

Pix shot me a stare that told me she wasn't amused. "Allow me to expand your vocabulary. A nemophilist is someone who is enraptured with trees, forests, the woods. Peter's the same way. They like the way you paint trees with all the precise details and textures."

"So, they weren't kidding. Your parents really do like my painting."

"Uh-huh. You got anything to drink? This popcorn's kinda dry."

I wanted to do a happy dance. Instead, I jumped up, raced to the refrigerator, and pulled out two Diet Cokes. I retraced my steps and handed her a can. She flipped the tab and took a sip.

"Though they're off the beaten path, you're so lucky," I said. "You've got the best parents ever. If only I had . . ." I shook my head, stopping the self-pitying thought from forming. "Pride was written all over their faces after you explained how you wanted to stay with me, so they could resume their vacation plans."

"I'm over the moon they agreed. I felt terrible wrecking their trip to H.V.," Pix said, glancing at her watch. They'll be taking off in about two hours." She reached for the bowl but then let her hand drop. "Aren't you going to ask me about—about my engagement?"

I'd been dying to ever since Brenda spilled the beans. Instead of answering, I took a long draught of cola.

"Honestly, Becca. I have no idea why I said yes to Chuck. It was just, oh, I don't know, he looked helpless as a baby bird with a broken wing." She bit her lip.

The image of Chuck resembling an injured bird caused me to consider the depth of Pix's tender heart.

"I love him. I really do. But I'm only twenty-five. Plus, my business is just getting off the ground. I don't want to be tied down yet." She rubbed the center of her forehead. "I only want

Chuck to get better, recover, regain his strength, and then I'll have to—"

"Break his heart."

"I let my emotions roll over my good sense. Breaking the engagement will ruin not only our relationship but our friendship as well."

I blew out a stream of air. "This is a fine pickle you've gotten yourself into." I immediately regretted the comment when I saw Pix's eyes tear up. There'd been too much crying—sadness—and grief already. I couldn't even begin to understand how Pix managed to cope with everything that'd happened. No wonder she said yes to Chuck's proposal.

"Hey, stop beating yourself up. If I know Chuck, he'll understand. Come on." I pointed to the door. "It's nearly a quarter past ten. The perfect time to take a look at the cat moon."

CHAPTER THIRTY-THREE

As we'd planned last night, we ate Dolly's scones and shared a pot of English tea for breakfast. I was surprised how delicious the scones tasted, actually a bit shocked that Dolly was capable of producing such delectable pastries. With a sour expression to match her personality, I guess I figured everything she touched would be bitter. But, as I was discovering, I'd misjudged the tea pot queen. After our calorie-laden breakfast, we'd decided to stop by Pix's house so she could pack a suitcase and then head to the hospital to see Chuck.

Sipping the last of the tea, the chance meeting I had with Woody crossed my mind. "Have you eaten at Billy's Bagels?"

"Billy's Bagels? Oh," Pix said with a toss of her head. "I love the blueberry ones. Why?"

"I ran into Woody yesterday and —"

"How is the big, old teddy bear?"

"He was a frontier farmer circa 1880."

"I love his quirky personalities. He's so believable. That takes a lot of talent."

"Talent? Yeah, I guess. But he made a weird comment. Said that Billy has a guy working for her. Since you seem to know all the men that work on and off Main Street, I thought you might know him."

"Really, Becca? I don't know every guy. And Billy's shop is in Othello."

"Only a mile or so outside of Bayleys Landing."

She pursed her lips and crossed her arms. I imagined she was thinking.

"Nope. And it's hard to believe Billie would hire a guy after years of being a strictly feminine business. Seems out of character for her."

"I agree. But maybe she wants to be more inclusive?" I left the kitchen and found my cellphone on an end table. "I'm going to check."

"Really?"

"I'd planned on picking up some bagels for breakfast tomorrow. I'll place an order and . . ." I located the number on my contact list and tapped it. After two rings, a female voice sounded. "Billie's Bagels."

"Hi. I'd like to place a takeout order. Two plain, two raisin cinnamon, and two blueberry. Oh, and by the way, is there a guy working there?"

"A man working here? Oh, you mean Guy."

"Um. Yeah."

So a guy—Guy--does work there. One who's smitten with Pix?

"Could I speak to him?" I looked at Pix, trying to keep the surprised look off my face.

"He's not here. Guy stops by once a month to check the books. After last year's fiasco with the IRS—well, anyway you want to talk to Billie? I think she's still here."

The woman called Billie's name but then her voice faded.

"Hello? Sorry. Billie's gone over to Guy's house. A family get-together. Can I take a message?"

"Are Billie and Guy dating—"

"That's too funny. Don't you know, they're twins. Wilhelmenia and William—better known as Billie and Guy. He and his wife just had another baby—Wesley. A brother for Wendy who is going through that terrible two stage."

Must be a slow day at the shop, or this woman loves to gossip. Probably that older woman who talks you to near-death when all you want to do is pick up a take-out order.

The woman rattled on, but I'd stopped listening. "Okay. Thanks," I said, breaking into a long-winded sentence. I clicked off the phone and faced Pix. "Do you know a man named Guy—Billy's brother?"

"Guy?" Her eyes lit up. "Guy Mincello? He's like one of my best customers. Always stopping by to pick up a sexy piece of lingerie. His wife just had a baby."

"Mincello?" I pursed my lips. "Is it the lingerie or you that interests him?"

"Don't even go there," she paused, "because that's like ridiculous."

"Why?"

"He adores his wife. She had a difficult pregnancy, and the little gifts of lingerie lifted her spirits. That and the chocolates he always bought from the "Box". I wonder why he never mentioned Billy's his sister." She paused a moment pursing her lips. "I guess, he must've thought I already knew. Anyway, Guy was excited about the publicity the *Lingerie Exposed* shoot would drum up for me," Pix said with a shake of her head, "Nick and I ran into him at the Tiber Bistro. I didn't think anything of it since it was Monday night."

"Monday night?"

"Karaoke at the Winged Victory Pub. Guy likes to sing. He and Chuck are buddies."

Even though his name is *Mincello*, he's probably not responsible for the crimes. *But why in the world would Woody infer that a man working at the bagel shop could be responsible for the attacks? Unless—Woody really does know something hinky about Guy.* "I'll check him out just to be sure."

"That would be like a waste of time," Pix said. "But speaking of time, I can't wait to get home. But I don't mind picking up the bagels on the way to my house."

"Bagels?" I'd forgotten about them already.

"Earth to Becca." She stood. The sleep shirt I'd lent her last night brushed the mid-point of her calves. I'd offered her a pair of sweats. But both of us burst out with a case of the giggles with the thought of her traipsing around in my oversized clothing.

"How about another *cuppa*?" Pix said with a pretty believable English accent.

The conversation remained light while we scarfed down the last two scones and and focused on the purrs and their antics, but a thread of unease kept me on edge. The only viable plan to ensure Daily's command was to confiscate Pix's car keys. I couldn't allow her to drive all over God's green Earth, in other words, Bayleys Landing, unsupervised. The idea of slipping them out of her handbag and feigning ignorance rebelled against my ingrained code of ethics. The only other way was to persuade Pix to relinquish her Escalade key fob into my safekeeping. Getting her to agree would be a hard sell.

After we pulled ourselves together, me in jeans and a sweatshirt, and Pix—even with limited options—looked like a knockout, we headed out the door. I stopped by my Honda and stuck the key into the lock. "After we pick up the bagels, I'll drop you off at your car. Then I'll follow you to your house."

"Follow me?" Her eyebrows knitted together.

"This way, you can leave your car there."

Her frown only deepened. "Why would I do that?"

Why, indeed? The only way it would make sense is if I tell her about the threatening note. "What do we need two vehicles for? If you want to go somewhere, you can use my car." I jutted my chin toward the Civic.

A sour look crossed her face. "You want me to drive that . . . that . . . look, I don't mean to hurt your feelings but—"

"I get it. She's no luxurious SUV but is a great little ride," I said, patting the car's fender.

"Apparently, you've got a weird attachment to your . . . hey, didn't you buy that junker used when were in college?" Pix didn't wait for an answer. "But just because you like it doesn't mean I'd feel comfortable driving an old and outmoded compact car."

Pix's wealthy, privileged background was playing to my advantage. "Since you don't want to drive my burgundy beauty, I'll take you wherever you want."

She widened her deep brown eyes. "Look, I can't expect you to ferry me around like you're some kind of undercover taxi service."

"Where do we have to go besides the hospital and an occasional pit stop at the grocery store? It'll be fun."

She shook her head. "I know you too well, Rebecca Flynn. There's something you're not telling me."

Of course, she'd think that. It'd be ridiculous for Pix to give up cruising around town without a sensible reason. But I had nothing to offer.

"You trust me," I said.

She nodded.

"Then just appease me no matter how screwy it seems. Please?"

She rolled her eyes toward the crystal blue sky, but a moment later, she half-heartedly agreed. Much to my relief.

Even so, it was going to be a bear shadowing her. I could only pray that Daily would come to his senses and handcuff Mindy. Fast. Or Min-Jun-Min. Or this Guy Mincello person. I made a mental note to call the Winged Victory and check Mincello's alibi.

Out of the corner of my eye, I caught a glimpse of Father McCarthy turning the corner across the narrow street. I needed to talk to him, but this wasn't the time. I had one foot inside the sedan when I noticed Pix waving in the priest's direction. Instead of returning her greeting with a nod or a friendly smile, he crossed the street and met us.

"Good morning," he said with an easy smile.

"Morning, Father." Pix and I said in unison.

"Glorious day, isn't it?"

I hadn't considered the weather, for as far as I was concerned, a blizzard could bury us under four feet of snow, and it wouldn't affect me as long as Chris Tucker remained in custody.

"Oh, Father," Pix said, "please pray for Chuck. Yesterday, he had a terrible fall and might need additional surgery."

I chewed my lip. I wondered if the priest knew Tucker had been arrested. If he did, I didn't want him to mention that tidbit of news to Pix. I purposely hadn't told her Daily had a suspect in custody. I didn't want her hopes, once raised, to be dashed when Tucker was released. Especially if the true culprit still roamed at large.

"It's hard to believe the—"

"Father." I cut him off. "Umm." I pressed my lips together for a second. "Could you hear my confession," I said the first thing that popped into my mind.

"Of course," he said.

I handed Pix the keys. Would you mind waiting in the office while we . . ." I gestured from me to the priest.

"No problem," she said. "I'll play P.I. secretary while you're giving Father McCarthy your *looooong* laundry list of offenses. However, if you're not finished by noontime, I'll be ordering lunch from Pantheon Pizza." She winked before leaving us.

"Forgive me for lying," I said. "Pix doesn't know about the arrest of Chris Tucker.

That's what I want to discuss with you."

With a nod, he waved toward a bench halfway down the block.

We walked in silence. Once there, I dropped on the bench's wooden slats like a sack of potatoes. "So, you *are* aware Chris Tucker's been arrested for the cameraman's murder and the attack on Chuck."

"Detective Daily stopped by the rectory with the news last night."

"He did?"

"He wanted to pick my brain, I guess that's what you'd call it, about Chris's character. Bottom line, he wanted to know if I believed Chris could be a cold-blooded killer."

I didn't move my eyes from his face.

"Now about your confession."

"What? No, Father." I shook my head. "What did you tell Daily?"

"That Chris's heart is good, but only God can discern the well-being of one's soul."

"In other words, you didn't tell Daily that Chris could never have committed the crimes."

"That's for the police to investigate and a judge and jury to rule. My chief concern is for his soul. I've been praying for Chris and his little band of comrades for months now. Like them, I've placed Chris into God's hands. We must trust in our faith that the outcome shall be as God wills."

"Yes, yes." I nodded. "But Pix needs your prayers now more than ever." I shared with him the contents written inside the get-well card. "She doesn't know anything about it, but I've been watching her like a hawk. And I will continue to do so until the true murderer is behind bars."

"You think Chris is innocent."

"Yes, and I would've bet that you believed it too."

The priest placed his index finger over his lips and nodded.

"That must've been one long confession."

I flinched, hearing Pix's voice. I should've known she'd get bored waiting inside my tiny office with only an African violet for company.

"I thought confession was supposed to be good for the soul," she said, "but you two look like somebody died. Oh no." She visibly shook. "Don't tell me." She focused on Father McCarthy. "Did you get an emergency call from the hospital? Something bad has happened to Chuck?"

I jumped up and draped my arm around her shoulders. "Nothing like that." I forced a smile. "I was just completing my act of penance."

"Oh," she said with a sigh.

I glanced at the priest, who didn't look very pleased, probably because of my lies. Though I hadn't gotten the opportunity to ask him, I guessed my question wasn't really necessary. It seemed obvious that Father McCarthy believed I should tell Pix the truth.

"Thanks, Father," I said. "We better get going. Pix is bunking with me for the time being. We're going to head over to her house to pick up some clothes and stuff. Then it's off to the hospital."

Father McCarthy rose. "May our Lord protect you." He made the sign of the cross blessing us.

～

PIX PULLED her ruby red Escalade into the detached garage while I parked my Civic in the long cement driveway designed with a geometric pattern. I stepped out of the car and looked around. The location of Pix's house was beautiful. I'd even set up my easel a couple of times to paint the horses who lingered by the fence against her property. But Chuck was right. The house did stand in the middle of nowhere. Definitely, a smart decision, moving her into my place.

She walked out of the garage and headed my way.

"I don't want the mail to pile up," she said. "We'll have to swing by the post office so I can put a hold on it."

"That's a good idea."

We sauntered along the long driveway and stopped at the mailbox. She opened it and withdrew a handful of envelopes. Her mail looked a heck of a lot different than mine, which regularly consisted of junk mail, circulars, and the occasional card or letter. Hers, from what I could detect, was comprised of envelopes stamped with official-looking letterheads.

"Hold these while I find my keys." She handed me the pile and rooted inside her oversized tote bag.

I glanced through the envelopes. Microsoft, Logitech International, EnviroTech. *Dividend checks? Perhaps, I hadn't given Pix enough credit.* A pang of remorse hit me for the times I viewed her as frivolous and flirty, nothing more than a social gadabout. No one would deny she possesses some business chops since her lingerie boutique is thriving, but Pix, a savvy investor? Apparently, Peter had taught her a thing or two.

"Why didn't you park in . . ." I pointed to her residential garage. "We could've walked right into the house." I tucked the mail into my sweatshirt's kangaroo pocket.

Her eyebrows rose, widening her eyes. "Do you have to be so nosey? But I guess that's why you're a detective." She resumed looking inside her purse.

How am I being nosey?

It hit me a second later. There's something in the garage she doesn't want me to see.

"Here they are." She shook the ring of keys like a maraca.

As we headed up the driveway, a rumbling car engine filled the air.

"Hey! Pix. Becca."

We both turned as Simon hopped out of his icy blue Miata roadster. He hustled toward us, clutching a colorful bouquet of flowers.

"I thought these would cheer you up," he said, handing Pix the bunch of wildflowers.

"They're lovely," Pix said with a smile. "And thoughtful."

He looked down as if inspecting his scuffed Timberlands but then raised his head with a smile on his lips. His ruddy face has taken on a pinker hue.

"I'm about to grab some clothes because Becca and I are now roomies."

I sensed confusion by the way he lifted his hands, palms skyward, into the air.

"Why are you—"

"Because. . ." I said even though I didn't have a good explanation. "Because we like being together."

This only caused him to frown.

"You mean like . . . like . . ." His face now flamed a cherry red.

"Not like that," Pix said. She moved next to him and linked her arm through his. "Even though Becca doesn't readily admit it,

213

she really does like men. And don't forget, I *am* engaged to Chuck."

"What?" His eyes grew large. "Engaged?" He pulled away as if she possessed a deadly touch.

"We haven't made an official announcement, but yes. Chuck and I are going to be married."

A wave of disbelief rolled though me as Pix told him about the engagement. One that she was going to break. Shortly. Directly. In a New York minute.

Maybe she'd changed her mind?

Knowing Pix, I wouldn't be surprised.

"Chuck popped the question from his hospital bed," she said. "And of course, I accepted."

"Of course." Simon parroted her and shook his head. "God, this is sudden. You've only been dating for like a week? Don't you think you're rushing into this?"

"I've known Chuck ever since the Merchant Association tried to keep me from opening my business. Becca introduced us."

He shifted his gaze to me. "What do you think about this— this engagement?"

"Great. I think it's amazing two of my best friends are getting married. To each other." The words slipped out easily enough, though I believed they were running toward a lifelong commitment without giving it much thought. That is if Pix was still on board with the wedding. Simon's concern seemed understandable.

"You've really dropped a bombshell. I'm still a bit stunned," he said, shoving his hands into his jean pockets. "But the bottom line is I want you to be happy. And if Chuck's the guy who fits that bill, I have no complaints. So, congratulations." He bent over and kissed her cheek.

She turned her head and kissed him squarely on the lips.

What is she doing?

She has to know Simon's crazy about her. The totally inappropriate kiss guaranteed confusion or, at the very least, hope that maybe one day she'd dump Chuck for him. I zoomed in to gauge his reaction. Nothing. He only looked at Pix with his puppy dog eyes and crossed his arms.

"This might be a silly question, but after you and Chuck tie the knot, can we still be friends?"

"Need you ask? We'll always be friends," Pix said.

I heard him sigh and couldn't help but feel sorry for the guy. She couldn't be blind to Simon's infatuation. *And what does she do? Offer him a taste of the forbidden fruit. The sensible and kindest thing to do would be to dissuade him. Why couldn't Pix see that? Clearly, it was one of her flaws.* She craved attention from the opposite sex—and admiration. Another reason for Pix to evaluate her rash engagement plans. *Was she ready to spurn the flattery and enticement of other men?*

"You girls better get back to your packing." Simon turned and headed toward the sports car. He paused a second and called over his shoulder. "Becca, I need a couple more paintings.

Drop them by the gallery later today?"

I swallowed hard. "Sure, Simon. Will do." I couldn't put it off any longer. I'd have to tell him about the paintings I'd sold to Geoff. If only I could shrug it off but then my darn conscience wouldn't give me a moment of peace.

He tooted his horn as Pix and I headed toward her front door.

CHAPTER THIRTY-FOUR

After stopping at the post office, the farmer's market, and the salon where Pix had her nails shaped and polished to perfection, we arrived back at the apartment. I made a salad chocked full of the veggies Pix had picked up at the market and added some grilled chicken for a dose of protein. She curled up with her lunch on the couch and proceeded to give the begging brothers, Caspurr and Jaspurr, small chunks of chicken.

"You'll spoil them," I told her with my most irritated-sounding voice.

"Like they're not spoiled already."

She had me there.

"I'm going to open the store. I'm scheduled to receive a shipment this afternoon." She glanced at the cellphone she'd dropped on the cushion. "Since it's a beautiful day, the street will be filled with eager shoppers. Hopefully, some in search of racy, lacy, silky, risqué unmentionables." Pix made air quotes.

"Okay," I said after swallowing a mouthful of romaine and mushroom. "I'll go with you."

"Go with me?" Pix faced me where I was seated at the dinette table.

Before I could answer, the buzzer from my office sounded. I raised a forefinger signaling her to give me a minute, and I flew down the steps. I had a sneaking suspicion it was Daily. Hopefully, with news that he'd come to his senses.

I unlocked the door and pulled it open. Mindy Marks stood there. I stared at her with my mouth ajar but quickly snapped it shut.

She sashayed inside.

I'm downright certain Mindy's not here because she needs my investigative services.

She sat in one of the visitor chairs, crossed her long, shapely legs, and folded her hands into her lap. I pulled my eyes away in the nick of time, and slammed the door shut as Coppurr raced into the room. He'd never seen an opened door he didn't like. The last thing I needed was for him to get loose and wind up amid the dangers of a congested Main Street full of drivers looking for parking spaces, not a kitty darting into the road.

"What a cute cat," Mindy said.

Coppurr waltzed to Mindy with his tail held high like a flag. He sniffed the hand she offered and rubbed his forehead against it.

Befuddled, I watched his little display of affection, wondering what in heaven's name had gotten into him. Usually, he was an excellent judge of character. He muffed up this time.

I dropped into the adjacent chair and stared at Mindy with a guise of suspicion. A myriad of questions zoomed through my mind. The most pressing ones made me shudder. *Did she know Pix was upstairs? Was she here to harm her? Me? Both of us?*

She touched her throat with her elegant hand. "I forgot my Perrier, and I'm poached. Do you have something to drink?"

I eyed the water bottle sitting on top of the desk. Ah, so that's how she's going to do it, I calculated as my mind leaped to the notion of poison. *She'll drop something deadly into her water and do the old switcheroo.* "Sure." I reached for the lighted refrigerated beverage center against the wall next to my desk. "Would you like a diet or regular cola?"

"Water would do nicely."

"Uh-huh." I tugged open the glass door and pulled out a bottle of spring water.

"Thanks," She took the plastic container and twisted off the cap.

I frowned when she downed half the water in one gulp.

She fiddled with the cap for a couple of seconds, twisted it back on, and lifted her head.

Her eyes bore into me. I bided my time, waiting for Mindy to make the first move.

"I want to clear the air," she said.

I must've looked puzzled because she shook her head.

"Not between us." She motioned from herself to me. "But between your friend, Treasure, and myself. I hope you'll agree to be an intermediary. I couldn't face her because . . ." She took a deep breath. "Because of the shameful way I've treated her. You see, I blamed Miss Winslow for poor Nick's death. I hated her for that, and well, I wanted to get even."

Not sure I heard right, I nodded, urging her to continue.

"Jealous as a jilted lover, I hated that Nick was attracted to her. I know, it's childish."

She reached for Coppurr, who sat like a statue with his eyes glued on her and stroked his head. "I'd been dating Davey—David Regan—my director. Well, things between us had gone south, and I wanted to screw it to him so, I started dating Nick." She shifted her attention away from Coppurr and gazed directly at me. "It might be hard for you to believe, but I'm not that shallow to use another person like that."

Though I tried to keep my face like granite, I frowned because she'd pegged herself exactly that way. She *was* petty enough to use Nick as a means to get back at the director and Chuck to get at Pix.

"I liked Nick. He was sweet. Different from other guys I'd known with his off-beat sense of humor. When you talked to Nick, he gave you his complete attention. Like you were the most important person in the universe. But it didn't take long to realize

I need a man who challenges me, spars with me, forces me to take chances—like being tested in fire—so I could grow and become the best whatever I want to be."

Coppurr began meowing.

"Let me get the cat." I rose and began to walk around Mindy.

"Leave him," she said. "I love cats."

Mindy, the dragon lady, loves cats?

When I returned to my seat, Coppurr jumped into Mindy's lap. I could hear his gravelly purr. *Traitor.*

Coppurr targeted his green eyes on Mindy as if mesmerized. Her shoulders dropped, and a tiny smile touched the corners of her usual pouty lips.

"I realized," she said, "it was Davey, all along, who I really cared about. But my pride wouldn't let me to go crawling back to him. I could tell that flaunting Nick in his face hurt him, but I couldn't stop. I didn't want Nick to be sucked up into the hostility between me and Davey, so I broke up with him."

She dumped Nick?

Coppurr snuggled deeper into Mindy's lap. She stopped petting him and turned her attention to me.

"I sunk to my lowest level the day of the first interview at Treasure's Trove of Lingerie.

When I glanced at the crowd of onlookers, I saw him—tall, dark, and handsome—my kind of guy. So I flirted with Chuck Stetson, hoping against hope that Davey would take me in his arms and tell me what I wanted to hear. But he didn't. My lame attempts at jealousy failed, and I had to face the fact, I'd blown it."

I know, as well as anyone, the benefits of a good confession. *But why is she pouring out her heart to me? And even if what she's spewing on about is true, what does it have to do with Pix?*

"I was a total basket case when I found out Nick had died. That's when thing changed between Davey and me. He admitted to being stupid. That we'd wasted precious time playing games by letting our egos rule us instead of our hearts. So we put the past behind us and made up."

NoNoNoNoNoNo. This can't be right. Mindy was jealous of Pix and wanted to see her suffer by killing Nick and Chuck. David Regan was her partner in crime. I grabbed my water bottle and took a few deep gulps. The water wasn't fresh or cool, but it was wet and moistened my dry throat. *This could be a ruse. Something she told Daily to get her off the hook.*

"I would've staked my life on it. Treasure Winslow had something to do with Nick's death."

What?

I'd had enough of Mindy Marks and didn't want to hear another word coming out of the lingerie reporter's mouth. She was like a wind-up toy that kept talking and talking but not making sense.

"Though I still grieved for poor Nick, something deep inside," she said, tapping her chest, "pushed those feelings away."

I pursed my lips. *That thing deep inside her is called ambition.*

"I needed to find justice for Nick," Mindy said. "The amazing thing was I could solve two puzzles—Nick's death and the scam surrounding the lingerie shop—with one story. A big story. *The* story. One that could make my career. I had no choice but to pursue it."

This I understood. *This is the Mindy Marks I'd seen in the hospital and at Pix's follow-up interview. Damn anyone's feelings, pain, and loss. Take any means necessary to get a story.*

"But then the news reported the person responsible for the attacks had been arrested—"

"Wait. What? Chris Tucker's arrest has been made public?"

Mindy nodded. "My chance of breaking the story went up in smoke." She twisted off the bottle cap and took a sip of water. "My theory— dead as roadkill. Nick lost his life in a robbery gone wrong. My golden story with its intrigue and glamour," she said with a sigh, "kaput."

"Well, I . . . I . . . ." Pressing my lips together stopped my stuttering.

"Your friend did get back at me. She ruined my investigative report with the news of her daddy resolving the biggest problem plaguing this town." She shook her head. "Who would've thought? A parking garage," she huffed. "I guess Treasure will be the darling of all the merchants in this dreary little two-bit backwater."

I smiled, realizing Mindy wasn't quite the penitent she'd made herself out to be.

She gingerly lifted Coppurr from her lap, looked into his sleepy face, and set him on the floor. Instead of heading to the scratching post or racing up the stairs, he rubbed his forehead against Mindy's leg. With a tinkle of a laugh, she rose and smoothed an imaginary wrinkle from her emerald green satin blouse. A bit envious, I noticed how the fabric made her blonde hair even blonder.

"Oh, by the way," Mindy said, facing the door. "That interview with Treasure is my last with *Lingerie Exposed*. I've been hired as the co-host for a new entertainment news program. *Celebrity Files*." She reached for the knob, pulled the door open, and glanced over her shoulder. "Davey and I are a team once again." She waved her left hand in the air.

I don't know how I could've missed it. The humongous-gorgeous diamond sparkled in the sunlight. She slammed the door shut behind her before I could say a word.

CHAPTER THIRTY-FIVE

I dropped back into my seat and stared at the cream-colored wall behind my desk. Coppurr circled around the chair. Only half-aware of him, I jumped when he leaped into my lap.

Mindy hadn't stopped by to apologize for anything. It was her way of sticking it to Pix. I bet she dropped by the lingerie store, and not finding Pix, remembered where I worked. That whole little song and dance routine was an act. Her goal was to let us know that her ruined "headliner" didn't matter. She only wanted to gloat. Wield her triumph that she'd managed to snag a plumb job and the man she desired. Disgust filled me. How small can a person be?

"But if Mindy wasn't the driving force behind the attacks. . ." I shook my head. The little voice in my head told me not to scratch her name of the suspect list yet. Even only if I wanted her to be guilty.

The touch of Coppurr's fur helped soothe my agitation as I rubbed the M-shaped marking on his forehead and traced the stripes along his cheeks. He purred with contentment. The mystical alchemy cast by the cat's soft trills and luxurious fur enfolded me within a peaceful calm. Until . . . I jumped up, and a startled Coppurr sprang onto the linoleum-titled floor. "If Mindy's story is true, could I've been mistaken about Chris Tucker?"

My lunch roiled in my stomach as I whispered the suspects' names. Mindy Marks, David Regan, Min-Jun-Min, Guy Mincello. . . Chris Tucker? I rubbed my aching temples. I'd left Pix alone way too long. Leaving Coppurr, curled up on a cat bed in front of the beverage fridge, I raced up the stairs and entered the apartment. I found Pix where I'd left her, on the couch, but now she was stretched out fast asleep. I tiptoed to the kitchen area, looked at my half-eaten salad, and shook my head. I grabbed the bowl, scooped the contents into a Tupperware container, and placed it in the refrigerator, along with the rest of the boxed leftovers.

"Becca."

I heard the sleepiness in Pix's voice. "I'm heading to the studio to dig up some halfway decent paintings for Simon."

"There's a ton of work I have to do at the store. Inventory, a new window display, and a shipment is due soon," she said, leaning up on her elbows.

"Treasure's Trove isn't going anywhere. What you need is a good snooze. I'll wake you in about an hour."

Her eyelids drooped. "Okay," she murmured and stretched out once again.

After cleaning up the kitchen, I grabbed my keys and locked the door leading to the office staircase. I wasn't going to take any chances with Pix's well-being and knew she'd be safe, bolted inside the apartment.

In my closet studio, I flipped through a stack of stretched canvases leaning against the wall. I pulled out a couple, hooked them on the display board, and gazed from one to the other, analyzing the compositions, colors, and textures. The finished landscapes evolved from a compilation of several plein air sketches I'd made during a road trip to Western Maryland. About a year ago, I labored for hours in my studio, striving to recapture the glow of the afternoon light and the fresh scent of the air—the very atmosphere of the wooden glen nestled between sloping hills dotted with the rebirth of spring foliage. And now, after not viewing the paintings for months, it was like seeing them for the first time. In all honesty, I'd forgotten about these two. I thanked heaven I'd rediscovered them because now I'd have something terrific to offer Simon.

I sunk onto my stool and glanced at the canvas sitting on the easel. A painting I'd started weeks ago, of the purrs. I'd worked hard on the composition in an attempt to convey each cat's personality; Caspurr with his liquid blue eyes and unabashed friendliness, Jaspurr's playfulness, and Coppurr's intuitive nature. I picked up a brush from my work table, stared at the frayed bristles, and tossed it back onto the wooden surface.

I exited the studio and moved into the office. I glanced at the chair where an hour earlier, Mindy Marks unburdened her soul to me. If Mindy and Regan weren't behind the attacks and Chris Tucker was innocent, then who? Min-Jun-Min? I wrinkled my nose. Guy Mincello? I paced across the room before dropping into my fake leather swivel. A tapping sound filled my ears. It took a few seconds to realize the drumming sprang from the sole of my boot, slapping the floor.

I grabbed the telephone and called the pub. Hopefully, Irene was working. I pumped the air when she answered.

"Hey, this is Becca. Quick question. You work on Monday nights, right?"

"Yup."

"Do you remember if last week a man named Guy was at karaoke night?"

"Guy Mincello?"

"Uh-huh."

"We were jammed-packed as usual. Guy, seemed a bit lost without his buddy, Chuck, well, until he took hold of the mic."

"So, he was there."

"Yeah. But the funny thing is he tore outta here like a house on fire."

"What time?"

"I don't know exactly. I guess, around eight-thirty. Does this have something to do with a case you're working on?"

"Sort of. Thanks, Irene."

"Glad to help. How's Chuck?"

"He's doing good. Should be out of the hospital soon."

"Tell him we all miss him here."

"I sure will. Bye." I cut the connection.

Questions buzzed around my brain. I need to organize my thoughts, I decided. On a legal-sized pad, I drew a line dividing the paper in two. At the top of the columns, I jotted, Suspects/ Not Suspects. The Not Suspect space filled up fast as I wrote the obvious: Pix, Daily, Simon, Ralphie, Dolly, Jane, Woody. I dropped the pen.

"Woody? No. He couldn't be the Pawcattawaye River Killer."

I shook my head, trying to dislodge the crazy idea that an elderly historian with a fanciful imagination could be responsible for the murder. *After all, he's harmless. Doesn't have a mean bone in that roly-poly body of his.*

But then the little voice in the back of my mind nudged me. What about all the killers who hid their bloodlust behind a façade of respectability? A list of murderers flitted through my mind— John Wayne Gacy, Ted Bundy, Dr. Michael Swango, Jeffery Dahmer—killers who blended seamlessly with the rest of humanity. Now I wished I hadn't spent endless hours in front of the TV watching the true-crime channel.

But Woody?

I dropped the pen and stood. Coppurr looked at me. "Woody has a bunch of alter-egos. Does one belong to a serial killer?"

Coppurr tilted his head as if considering my question.

"Woody goes into some kind of trance when he's in character. Claims he doesn't recollect what goes on. So, if he attacked Chuck and killed Nick, he wouldn't remember?"

Coppurr raised a paw, washed his white furry toes with his fastidious tongue, and wiped the little mitt across his face.

"That's hard to believe. How could he not remember?" I paced back and forth, careful not to step on the purr, who sat in a yoga position with a hind leg behind his head and the tip of his pink tongue poked out between his lips.

"I have no choice. I'll have to confront him."

Wondering if I had a screw loose for thinking Woody could be a killer, I headed for the outside door. Coppurr walked beside me, his striped tail straight up. In a flash, he changed course and darted between my feet, weaving around one and then the other. His unexpected movement almost caused me to trip.

"What are you doing?" I scolded him. He stopped, mewed, and parked himself on top of my feet.

"So, little purr, you don't want me to leave. I promise. I won't be gone long."

I glanced into the short hallway leading to my studio and checked his food and water. He had plenty, enough to last for hours. I carried him to the food bowl. After an indecisive look in my direction, he lowered his head and began to dig into the pile of kibble. The sound of food crunching filled my ears as I slipped outside.

Not dressed for jogging, wearing jeans, a pullover, and cowboy boots, I half-ran, zigzagging through alleyways. I took an uphill shortcut through a renovation site of an 18th century stone house —one of the oldest standing in Bayleys Landing— and bounded past a stain glass studio, old Doc Andrews's dental office, and a law firm. A few minutes later, I entered the Archeological Museum.

A couple, arm in arm, strolled in the main room, but besides them, the place appeared empty. Until I heard a familiar voice.

"Just the person I want to see."

I turned and faced Jane Parks. She appeared schoolmarmish as usual, with her eyeglasses resting above the tip of her nose and a pencil sticking out of her black hair arranged in a tight bun.

"Hi, Jane. Is Woody around?"

"Woody?" Her forehead collapsed into a sea of lines. "He was here. Oh, yes. He's out to lunch, and then he has something, oh, now it's slipped my mind."

I should've looked for him on Main Street.

"At least," Jane continued, "that inappropriate lingerie shop reaped something good for the town, after all."

"Uh-huh." Wrapped up in my own thoughts, I only caught a couple of Jane's words. *I could run back to Main Street, but there's a good chance we'd cross paths.* I didn't want that to happen.

"I understand that Treasure's father is quite a distinguished and successful businessman.

It's wonderful he's donating solar-powered buses. And the parking garage. I really don't know where to begin singing his praises over that."

"What?" *Solar-powered buses?* The last thing I wanted to discuss was what type of energy would shuttle tourists to old town Bayleys Landing.

She patted her 1960 style hairdo. "There's been talk that he's a bachelor," Jane said. "A very eligible bachelor. Will he be in town long? I'd love to give him a private tour of the museum. That way, he'll gain an insightful look into the sterling history of our much-beloved town."

I blew out a stream of air. I didn't want to be the one to burst Jane's bubble, but someone had to tell her the truth. "Peter is traveling back to California with his wife. Pix's mom."

"Oh, dear. Dolly believed he was unattached."

She seemed to be talking more to herself than to me.

"Dolly?" I purposely widened my eyes to feign surprise. In reality, I wasn't a bit surprised she'd been spreading rumors. "She probably jumped to that conclusion because Brenda wasn't at the Tea Pot Shoppe interview. Truth is, Pix's mom is young, vivacious, and . . ." I smiled innocently as I twisted the knife deeper, shredding Jane's hopes into ribbons. "Frankly speaking, gorgeous."

"Ah, well," she said with a little shrug.

I felt a stab of guilt. Apparently, Jane was used to her hopes for romance going up in smoke.

"I have something to show you," She strode to her massive desk, lifted a folder, and withdrew the contents. "These are the photos the historical society has chosen to publicize the Designer House. And Burl—Burl Johnson—vice president of the society, hoped you'd design the posters. Like all of us, he's seen your paintings at the Prescott Painting and Sculpture Gallery and is impressed by your talent. We're trusting you'd do it pro bono."

How many times have I been asked to volunteer my artistic ability to local charities, from the scouts to the Church, in the form of designing posters, leaflets, and signs? Fortunately, by now, I had my answer down pat. "Sorry. I'd love to help, but I'm not a graphic artist. But I'm sure Jase over at BL Graphics could assist you splendidly."

She licked her lips. "I think Burl already stopped by there."

I held back the smile that wanted to break across my face. *Jase White is no pushover. He established his graphics business to make a profit.*

"Do you expect Woody soon?" I glanced at the photographs Jane had handed me. They'd turned out better than I'd expected. I handed them back.

"Oh, dear me. We were so hoping you'd whip up a little design we could run off at the printers. They're giving us a twenty-five percent discount."

I guessed she hadn't heard me. I raised my voice a notch. "Woody. Will he be coming back soon?"

She waved the air in front of her face as if swatting a pesky fly. "Woody?" She glanced at the photographs in her hand. "No, dear. I thought I told you. Oh, where is my mind today? He's taking the afternoon off. He *volunteers* here so much. It's a rare sight when he's not around, playing docent to a group of school children and enthralling them, I might add, or cataloging items. He understands the value of giving back to the community."

Ouch! Could Jane have been any less tactful?

"I need to see him. Do you have his cellphone number?"

"Cellphone? My, my, my." She tsked with a shake of her head. "A cellphone is the last thing Woody Weygant would ever own." She paused a second to reposition the pencil that dangled from her hairdo. "He has important business to take care of."

"Important business?"

"That's what he said. I'm sorry to say, I hardly paid much attention. The Designer House poster has been on my mind." Jane squeezed her eyes shut so hard her forehead wrinkled. "Oh, now I remember. I'm such a silly goose to have forgotten. He's developing a new character." Her eyes popped open. "Based on a little-known fact. I wasn't even aware of, but Woody brought it to my attention. We decided to—"

"What kind of character?" I knew Jane well enough that once she started talking, she could blather on.

"A clown."

"Clown?"

"He's planning to purchase all the necessities. Wigs, pancake makeup, big floppy shoes."

I swallowed hard.

"Woody's research is impeccable, and that's how he unearthed this little gem. We're going to create an exhibit to run throughout the summer."

Jane's enthusiasm assured me that her anxiety over the Designer House posters had taken a back seat.

"In June of 1897, the circus arrived in town via the railroad. It was quite a spectacle, I presume, with all the hubbub and frenzy it must've generated. Because back then, the circus *was* the greatest show on earth. There were parades down Main Street and the thrill of seeing exotic animals, bearded ladies, trick riders, clowns, and acrobats captured the imagination of the townsfolk from the youngest tots to gray-haired grannies."

Her rambling made my head spin. "Look, Jane, I've gotta go."

"But Becca." Her face fell.

"Sorry. I'm late for a meeting with Simon." I tapped the watch on my wrist.

I didn't wait for a response and turned away, racing out of the museum. The pounding of my heart filled my ears but couldn't drown the frightening thought running through my mind. *John Wayne Gacy used to amuse children dressed as a clown. He was an entertainer . . . volunteer . . . serial killer.*

"Just like Woody?"

CHAPTER THIRTY-SIX

The idea of Woody being the Pawcattawaye River Killer struck me as ludicrous and, at the same time, horrifying. I paused a second to collect my thoughts. What did I know about him, anyway? Barely a thimbleful of facts. Woody's a friendly, endearing, sweet guy plagued by a dissociative identity disorder. But could he also be a killer? "No," I said firmly as I raced past the Crab Kettle, keeping my eyes peeled for him. I stopped at the corner of Caesar Lane and surveyed the street. I took another peek down the lane before continuing my trek along Main Street when I couldn't believe my luck. Woody. Exiting the cosmetic boutique, Marlene's ~ Maven of Make-Up.

I yelled his name. He didn't hear my call since, even to me, my voice sounded thin. He continued walking along the street's gentle incline. I called again before realizing it was useless. I'd have to catch up to him. Jogging diagonally across Caesar Lane, a horn blasted, but I kept running.

I pulled the cellphone from my back pocket and scrolled on the screen that bounced in my hand, ready to alert Daily. I hesitated a second before tapping his number. If I told him my suspicion, he'd laugh. And if Woody wasn't the perp, he'd never let it drop that I considered an eccentric old codger a murder suspect. No. I'd confront Woody on my own. I slipped the phone away.

I'd reached the make-up shop as Marlene stepped outside arrayed as usual, in a flowing colorful frock. Her filmy dress resembled a garden with a black background and giant red roses.

"Hey, Becca," she said. "How you doing, sugar?"

I slowed long enough to offer her a nod and a wave. Her mouth turned downward. I wasn't surprised since she loved to gab. As I resumed running, my spirit flagged since Woody had disappeared. I wanted to scream or cry or do both, but instead I backtracked to question Marlene. Facing her wasn't a pretty picture. She'd set her hands firmly on her thick waist and her exquisitely made-up face twisted into a frown.

"Sorry." I tried to look contrite but with every ticking second, Woody moved further away. "Forgive me? Please." I prayed to God she knew something.

"Well, alright." She broke out into a smile. "I'm fixin' to pour me some sweet tea. You up for a glass? We can sit out back on the veranda."

I ignored her invitation. "Did Woody just leave your shop?"

Her face softened. "Yessum, that big old jelly-baby 'bout bought all my face paint." The lilt of her slow Southern draw lingered in the air along with the sweet scent of magnolia. "I keep it in stock for Halloween, and turned out the face paint was buried in the back of my storage area. I had a dickens of a time finding it. When I finally did, I said to Woody, "Sugar, what do you need all this make-up for? And you know what he said?"

I was ready to pull my hair out.

"Well, he said, and I about laughed myself silly, Woody-bear said he's fixin' on becomin' a clown. You believe that? Said the circus has right come to Bayleys Landing, and he's gonna join the party."

"Party?"

"Gonna be a big shindig at the museum. A fundraiser."

I frowned. Jane mentioned an exhibit, not a fundraiser. I shook my head, wondering who really ran the museum—Jane, the curator, or Woody, the volunteer—probably a combination of both. I glanced down the street, hoping against hope, but he was nowhere to be seen. *Had Woody ducked inside a shop or gotten into a car and driven away?* The sorry fact surfaced—I'd lost him. My first impulse was to castigate myself for being such a rotten private investigator, but there wasn't time for incrimination.

"Did he happen to mention the recent crimes—"

"Oh, lordy me," Marlene said. "Isn't it a crying shame what's been going on? Heartbreaking." She moved closer and lowered her voice. "From what I've heard, Treasure, bless her heart, is the reason a jealous lover killed that poor cameraman and landed Chuck in the hospital. All of this violence is about to give me a conniption fit." She waved her hands, fanning her face as if overcome by a hot flash. "Mercy me." She pulled a lacy hankie from her voluminous muumuu and gingerly touched it against her forehead. "But to answer your question, no, we didn't talk about anything ugly." She slipped her arm through mine. "You're pretty as a peach, but . . ." She hovered a finger over my cheek. "I've got the most luxuriant moisturizer that can take care of that dry skin. After our tea and gossip, I'll let you try a dab or two."

"I'd love to, but right now, I'm working on a case." I extricated my arm.

Her eyes grew. "How exciting. Anything I can do to help?"

"Umm-not really." I took a few steps away from her. "But I need to catch up with Woody."

"You'll have to hurry 'cause he took off faster than a hot knife through butter. She flashed me a bright smile and fluttered the hankie shooing me away.

I moved down the block, peeking into shop windows and doors, but nothing. I stopped at the street corner where the commercial zone ended, cupped my eyes, and squinted. The sidewalk flanking the row of gingerbread Victorian houses adorned with an abundance of towers, turrets, and dormers stood empty.

I pivoted around, and noticed Marlene fussing with the flowers overflowing from the boxes attached to her shop's windowsill. I hurried back.

"My, y'all are pretty as a picture." She cooed at the flowers.

"Um, Marlene," I said, imagining her embarrassment of being caught talking to her assortment of red, white, and blue wave petunias.

She twisted her neck in my direction. "Becca?" She straightened up and brushed her hands together. "Aren't they gorgeous?"

"Uh-huh. Very pretty." With no time for chit-chat, I forged ahead. "Did Woody mention where he's headed this afternoon?"

"Why, he sure did. Now that he's got the proper make-up, he needs a genuine clown suit. Said he'd be heading into Baltimore to a top-notch costume store."

"Hmm." I tilted my head, "Does Woody have a car?"

Marlene half-shrugged. "I didn't ask how he was gonna get there."

"Of course not, thanks." I changed direction and walked to Main Street, intent on stopping at the Tea Pot Shoppe. Dolly might know something since those two seem chummy despite her domineering personality. I glanced at my watch, surprised so much time had ticked by. Dolly will have to wait since I need to check on Pix.

I hurried to the apartment, poked my key into the lock, pulled the door open, and paused.

Voices. "Sorry, I've been gone so long," I said, stepping into my living area. The words hadn't come from the T.V. as I'd imagined.

Pix, seated crossed legged on the couch, faced Simon, who stood with a silly grin on his face. They glanced in my direction. Relief flooded through me since it was Simon and not Woody in the apartment.

"I stopped by to pick up some paintings," he said. "And was surprised to find Pix here.

It'd slipped my mind you two are roomies."

My eye, he forgot.

"We were talking about Chuck," Pix said. "And the engagement."

"Oh?" I raised my brow.

"How she rushed into accepting Chuck's proposal," Simon said. "But, like I told Pix, engagements are meant to be broken."

"Not usually, they aren't," I said.

"Well, in this case, I think you . . ." He shifted his sight to Pix. "Shouldn't feel pressured to marry Chuck. He's a levelheaded guy. He'll understand."

"It's not like Father McCarthy is going to perform the ceremony tomorrow in Chuck's hospital room," I said.

"I love Chuck," Pix said. "But we're both career-minded and maybe this isn't the right time. I'm not sure—"

"When Chuck's better, you'll have plenty of time to review your plans," I said. "After all, there's no rush. But you don't want the best thing that could ever happen to slip through your fingers."

"You should make a clean break of it now," Simon said.

Pix shook her head. "That wouldn't be right."

"I agree." *Why is Simon pushing her to dump Chuck? Usually, he's chill about everything—except art. Lately, he's been obsessed with Pix. Weird. Could he? No. Simon is above suspicion—as any of our Main Street friends. But still—why does he want Chuck out of the picture? Simon and Pix—nah, that would never happen.*

"You okay?" Pix asked.

"Yeah, fine. I was just thinking—"

"Take off your thinking cap and . . ." Pix patted the space next to her on the couch.

"Can I get you guys something to drink?"

"A beer would work," Simon said.

Pix lifted her Mountain Valley Spring water bottle. "I'm good."

I moved to the refrigerator, pulled out a Natty Boh, and twisted off the cap. Stepping into the living area, I pressed my lips together. Simon had claimed the spot next to Pix. She rested her head against his shoulder. I handed him the bottle. She sat upright when he raised it and took a long swig.

"Thanks," he said, looking at me. "Hey, is something wrong?"

I must've been frowning. *When is Pix going to stop being such a flirt?* "No, it's nothing." But it wasn't, I thought, realizing Simon's preoccupation with Pix was way over the top. I pushed the notion to the back of my mind needing to sort out my suspicion regarding Woody.

"I'll run downstairs and grab those paintings while you finish your beer."

Once in my studio, I called Dolly Evans. She picked up on the first ring.

"The Tea Pot Shoppe. May all your cups be refreshing. This is Dolly. How may I help you?"

Give me a break.

"Hi, Dolly, this is Becca."

"Becca?"

"I was wondering, does Woody own a car?"

"A car? Why do you want to know that?"

I chewed my lip a second, trying to think of something reasonable. As usual, I hadn't quite worked out all the details. "Well, um, Marlene told me he was planning to head to Baltimore, and I thought if he didn't have transportation, I could give him a lift."

"That's quite generous of you." Her voice had taken on a friendlier tone. "But don't you know, he owns several automobiles. Some people might even consider him a collector of antique cars. His vehicles match up with some of the characters he portrays at the Archeological Museum. He has a beautiful dusk rose '57 Chevy Bel Air, a 1932 Model B Ford roadster, and a sweet baby blue convertible, a 1964 Mustang, which is my favorite, by the way. But he runs errands in his brand-new Mercedes Benz."

"Mercedes?" I felt a headache coming on.

"You do know that Woody is a San Francisco Weygant. The hotel people."

No. I didn't know.

"With his privileged upbringing, he never had to work a nine to five. He spent all of his time studying. That's why he's an expert in history," Dolly said.

"So those stories about him chopping wood as a child——"

"Oh, that Woody. He's such a card. I believe he started that rumor."

A tap sounded on my studio door. "Look, Dolly, I have to go," I said as Pix peeked around it. I said goodbye and ended the call.

"I'm going to hang out with Simon at the gallery for a few minutes," Pix said. "He wants to discuss a Merchant Association memo that, for some reason, I never received. Could you go to my shop and wait for the delivery? I got a text. It'll be there, like, in ten minutes."

I nodded.

"Thanks, Becca. You're the best." She turned to go back up the staircase.

"Wait. Give these to Simon." I walked to the display wall and removed the two landscape paintings.

"I might want to buy one of those. They're really good."

I refrained from rolling my eyes imaging I'd become the Winslow's family pet charity.

"I guess you'll have to paint another one for Simon."

"Simon." I pursed my lips. "Don't you think he's acting way too protective?

"What do you mean?"

"Seems like every time I turn around, he's hovering over you. He shows up at the Hot and Chilly Bean when you're there, stops by your house to check up on you, dropped in here with the pretext of picking up some painting. And why is he adamant about you dumping Chuck?"

"Now that you mentioned it——"

"What?"

"I'm feeling a little uncomfortable around him. Simon keeps pushing me to date him. I like him and all—but romantically?" Pix shook her head. "I tell him I love Chuck, but he blows me off."

"To you, flirting is an innocent game. But some guys think you're serious."

"I'm beginning to understand what you mean."

"How about Woody? Have you ever—"

"Woody?" Be real. I don't flirt with men old enough to be my father. I like all those quirky characters he portrays, but flirt with him? I don't think so."

"I had a notion about Woody—crazy, I guess. It's just that I'm so worried about you."

"About me?"

I bit my lip. "Chuck didn't want me to tell you."

The color drained from her face. "He wants to call off the wedding."

"Call off? No, nothing like that," I sighed in relief. "We think that you might be driving someone to commit murder. He wants out of the hospital to keep you safe."

"I've believed all along that I'm the reason my friends are being targeted. But I can take care of myself." She paused. "Don't tell me that's why you insisted we room together?"

"I don't want you taking any chances. Discuss the memo with Simon, then hightail it directly to your store."

"If it will make you feel better." Pix reached into the little pocketbook sitting on her hip. "You'll need this to get into the shop." The keys jingled as she handed the metal ring to me. "It's the one with the F marked on it. For front door."

She picked up the paintings and headed up the staircase.

∾

As I WALKED to Treasure's Trove of Lingerie, the revelation hit me that nothing about this case made sense. *A television cameraman murdered after having dinner with Pix. A homeless man arrested for trying to kill Chuck when he actually saved his life. A threatening get-well card.* "How does Woody fix into the mix?" I mumbled under my breath. I prided myself on my level head, an eye for details, and not jumping to conclusions. Desperate to keep Pix safe, I'd lost perspective. *Woody is probably the last person to be considered a suspect. And who would've thought he's some kind of heir to a hotel fortune?* I brushed a strand of hair off my face the wind had blown there. *At least I hadn't embarrassed myself by telling Daily. I'd never hear the end of it.*

I slowed, reaching the Prescott Painting and Sculpture Gallery. I considered ducking inside to get Simon's take on the paintings. But glancing through the opened door, I saw that he and Pix were in the middle of something. She was talking, and his arms were folded across his chest. He didn't look too happy. *She's probably telling him to back off from trying to take Chuck's place.* The sound of a truck's engine startled me. The delivery truck.

I picked up speed even though Treasure's Trove stood only a couple stores away.

I jogged passed the wide window adorned with gold stenciling, Tomes from the Past Secondhand Book Store and reached Pix's shop just as the delivery guy braked the lumbering truck. He doubled-parked, which instantly caused havoc, snarling up traffic.

I'll have to make this quick, I realized as blasting horns filled the air. I greeted the delivery guy with a smile.

"Treasures Trove of Lingerie?" He looked as if he'd sucked a lemon.

"Yep," I said, pulling out the keyring.

He retreated to the truck's cargo area while I opened the door, flicked on the lights, and waited. It took him only a minute to stack the boxes on a trolley and wheel them inside. "Where to?"

I directed him through the showroom. He navigated the trolley through the door propped open with a stepstool and stopped inside the storage area. It took him no time to unload the boxes. He only slowed down when he gave me a slip of paper to sign and handed me an invoice. "Thanks," I said. He grunted and bolted out of the lingerie shop like the place was on fire. I doubted it was because of how he'd parked. Probably used to backing up traffic and most likely didn't give a hoot.

But why would anyone want to rush through this store, I wondered. *Sure, it offers lingerie, hosiery, shapewear, and my favorite shopping area tucked into a back corner, cotton and flannel sleepwear. I think Pix added that section just for me.*

I walked through the storeroom, into the kitchenette, and stopped at the doorway. I peered into the shop and caught my breath, again in awe of the elegant design. Damask wall coverings, ornately carved moldings and cornices, and the stylish displays reflected Pix's art background.

The very idea of ghoulish fiberglass mannequins dressed in her exquisite lingerie made Pix cringe. Instead, she draped garments across tables covered in velvet, satin, and silk. When a customer showed interest in an item, Pix would retreat to the storage area and find the appropriate size and color. Just like the workings of a shoe store.

Pix believed the bedroom with its dimensions of lovemaking, a tactile and beautiful encounter, even if the couple had been married for thirty years. She wished to offer her clientele an extravagant and lavish adventure in preparation for the ecstasies of the bedroom. I believed she'd hit her mark dead center.

I dropped on the stool and breathed deeply of the calming lilac and lavender-scented air.

It offered a sense of serenity I didn't want to disturb. But I figured I'd better head down to the gallery since Pix should've been here by now.

I stepped inside the kitchenette, reached for the keyring I'd dropped on a countertop, and spied a cookie tin. It reminded me that I hadn't eaten much lunch and could do with a quick snack. I wiggled off the box's lid. "Yummmm. Berger cookies." The chocolatey aroma of the thick layers of fudge wafted under my nose and enticed my taste buds. I grabbed one and headed for the door. My cellphone sounded. I took a quick bite of cookie and swiped the screen.

"Where are you?"

Daily.

"I'm fine. Thanks for asking." I swore I heard his eyes roll.

"I stopped at your place earlier, but no one was there. I need to talk to Pix."

"You've located Woody?" I bit my tongue a second too late.

"Woody? What?"

"Never mind. What do you want with Pix?"

"I've decided to tell her about the threat. We don't think it's a hoax. She needs to be made aware of the situation."

"You can't do that. Chuck doesn't want her to know."

"I assume she's with you."

"Didn't you hear me? Chuck doesn't—"

"I don't care what Stetson wants. Let me speak with Pix."

"Umm. Well . . . uh . . ."

"Don't tell me," he barked.

I pulled the phone away from my ear. "She's fine. So, relax. She'll be here any second."

"Where is here?"

"Treasure's Trove."

"Alright. I'll meet you there in ten-fifteen minutes." Daily cut the connection.

"If he isn't the most infuriating man," I said, chewing the last bite of frosted shortbread. I reached for another cookie but stopped, noticing a greeting card lying on the counter. I lifted it and grinned at the cute smiley face flower design. "Thinking of you," I read the caption and opened the card. The red ink handwritten message wasn't centered and filled the top quarter of the inside panel. *Forgive me for being direct but marrying Chuck would be a stupid move on your part. Reconsider. Please. Simon*

I closed the card and glanced at the cover illustration. It reminded me of Chuck's smiley face card with the cryptic message. Actually, I mused, the two of them could've come from the same box of greeting cards with their similar artwork, graphics, and textured paper. I turned the card over, looking for the trademark. The company that had produced Chuck's card had a unique name. I swallowed hard. Four Paws Greetings. *The same logo on the card Chuck received.* "A coincidence," I said, pushing away a thought I didn't want to surface. I flipped the card open again. The words had been written with a fine-tipped marker like the message in Chuck's card. *And with an unusual shade of red—a wine-colored crimson—that matches the pen Simon uses to indicate a painting has sold by marking a dot on its tag.* A sick feeling clutched my chest.

I dropped into a chair and stared at Simon's handwriting. The sinister message on Chuck's card had been written in block letters. Simon had written his message in cursive. Except for his signature. A mixture of small and capital letters—just like the words in the threatening message.

My outgoing, off-beat, art-loving friend is responsible for the crimes? I wanted to push the idea out of my head but couldn't. I imagined Simon as a lovesick puppy when it came to Pix. *But had he harbored a deadly obsession?*

Simon wasn't like the other guys, who have crushes on Pix. Along with them, Simon shot adoring looks in Pix's direction. But his unfailing pestering for updates about her every move and his over-the-top interest in everything Pix seemed weird. I'd chalked that up to his artistic personality, prone to feel things deeper than the ordinary Joe.

Had I closed my eyes to Simon being a suspect because I didn't want to believe a friend could commit the unbelievable? Was I grasping at straws attempting to pin the murder on Mindy, Mr. Min, Woody, or even Guy Mincello who dashed out of the pub probably because his wife had gone into labor? What motive would any of them have to want to kill rivals for Pix's affection? And threaten Pix?

It only makes sense by adding Simon to the equation. *Pix had rebuffed his advances. In an attempt to level the playing field, he decided to eliminate the competition. His pride, injured once again by Pix's engagement, decides he'd rather kill Pix than lose her to another man.* I chewed my lip, questioning if this motive was as thin as the one I imagined for Mindy Marks.

Except the little voice in the back of my mind told me, this time, I was on the right track.

I should've seen this from the get-go. What a rotten detective I've turned out to be.

I jumped up from the chair, determined to get Pix away from Simon. Voices filled the air.

I'd left the door unlocked. *Customers?*

I stepped into the sales area and froze.

CHAPTER THIRTY-SEVEN

S imon turned the lock, stepped deeper into the showroom, and stood next to Pix. It took a minute to decipher his words since he talked so fast, but I picked up the phrase, "being lied to." I screwed up my face and slipped back inside the kitchenette, lingering inside the doorframe.

"You misunderstood," Pix said.

"Misunderstood?" He flayed his arms around like a maestro conducting an orchestra.

She took a few steps away, moving closer to the kitchenette. "Please leave. We'll talk when you've calmed down."

"I'm not going anywhere until things between us are straightened out."

She turned away.

He grabbed Pix's arm and pulled her back so that she faced him.

My stomach dropped. But before I could move, Simon pressed his lips against hers. For a second, I believed Pix owned this, confusing him by batting her long-lashed eyes, running her fingers through his coppery hair, rubbing his shoulders. No wonder he's perplexed about her feelings toward him.

Perplexed enough to kill?

She struggled within his tight bear hug. "Let me go," she said. And he did.

"You gotta know how I feel." He tugged the tip of his beard. "I love you, Pix."

"Love?" Color sprung to her cheeks. "I don't understand. We're friends."

"Friends." He spat the word. Can't you see, you're everything to me. Without you, my life is empty."

"I don't know what to say."

"Do I have to spell it out?"

She raised her palms outward, urging him to stop.

"I'm asking for the chance to make you happier than you've ever been."

She wrinkled her nose, shook her head, and turned away.

"You can't deny the special bond between us. The way you smile at me. Your touch—your kisses." He ran his fingertips across his lips.

"I'm sorry if I led you on. I always thought my flirting was harmless. But now, I know different. Let's just put this misunderstanding behind us and go on as usual.

"Like drinking coffee and talking about your precious collection of antique underwear."

"Well, yeah."

"Sorry, Pix. That ain't gonna cut it. I want more."

"This is getting old. How many times do I have to tell you? I'm in love with Chuck."

"Chuck." He sneered. "I can't believe you're that shallow. But I should've guessed.

That damn cameraman was a pretty boy just like the candy maker."

"I don't judge people by their looks. The attraction might've been physical at first, but it boiled down to personality. Chuck and I—well, we clicked."

"And we don't click." He made air quotes.

She sighed.

He pounded his fist on a table displaying lacy teddies, knocking several to the floor.

"Get a grip," Pix said. She touched his arm. He shook her hand away.

"After everything I've done for you." He opened his fisted hand, splayed his fingers, and closed it again.

Pix glanced at the kitchenette, and our eyes met. She moved her hand, gesturing for me to come into the showroom. I shook my head, placing a finger over my lips.

"Are you listening to me?" His voice rose.

"How could I not, the way you're shouting?" She took a few steps in my direction. "But I've heard enough."

"Babe, you haven't heard the half of it." He raked his fingertips through his hair stopping at the man-bun on his crown. "You will hear me out." He stuck his hand into the back pocket of his jeans.

I couldn't make out what Simon pulled from his pocket. But with a flick of his thumb, it shot open and revealed a two-inch utility blade. A tool he uses in his frame shop for cutting picture mats. I swallowed hard. All my mistaken hunches evaporated like the morning dew in the summer sunshine. The final piece finally fell into place. *Tucker hadn't heard Min but—mon—*

Si-mon. He hadn't caught the entire name. Not Mindy, Min-Jun-Min, or Mincello. But Simon.

I inhaled a deep breath. *Daily is on his way. But when he gets here, what will he find?* I grabbed my cellphone and texted him: *Hurry. PRK is here. Simon.* I stepped from my hiding place, but neither one of them seemed to notice. She was focused on the utility knife and Simon on Pix's horrified face.

I fought the urge to race over and pull Pix away. With a slow, steady gait, I approached them. "Simon," I said a hair louder than a whisper.

His eyes flicked in my direction. "Where the hell did you come from?" He took a step closer to Pix and waved the blade near her throat.

"I understand you're angry. But if you love Pix—"

"Love her? I would cut open my own heart for Pix. My Treasure."

I have to deescalate the situation or else . . . "It's because of your love for Pix," my words tumbled, "you stopped her from making terrible decisions. Choosing the wrong man to spend her life with."

"The way she looked at Rizzo with desire in her eyes." His head snapped in Pix's direction. "Why can't you look at me that way?" He shouted.

Pix trembled.

"Nick would only cause Pix heartbreak," I said, hoping he wouldn't detect the fear in my eyes.

"Yeah. So, I kicked his ass and killed the loser." He turned his gaze back to Pix. "I had to protect you. Can't you see that cameraman and Stetson were bad news from the get-go. I couldn't let them hurt you."

"Like I'm not hurt because you almost killed my fiancé?" Pix's eyes flashed as her voice rose.

"I did you a favor." He lunged at her, swiping the knife.

Pix jumped back and the blade missed its mark.

"That's enough, Simon. Give me the mat cutter," I said.

He turned so fast in my direction, I feared he'd knock me over.

"What do you take me for? A complete idiot?" His eyes looked black, wide open, menacing.

He didn't give me a chance to respond.

"If I can't have Pix, nobody will." He stepped closer to me with a wicked smile. "My promise to Chuck in a get-well card. I wouldn't want to disappoint him." A rumble of laughter burst through his lips.

"It doesn't have to be—"

His face went solemn. "You're gonna have to find a new gallery because," he said, slicing the blade across his wrist, "Pix and I are going to the hereafter together."

"That's crazy. Get a grip, Simon, and stop this madness," I said as Pix edged closer to the front of the store.

She bumped into a marble-topped lyre table, and the silver candelabra on top crashed to the floor.

He dashed to Pix and pressed the blade against her neck.

A rush of adrenalin surged through me. I reached for his arm. Pulling it away from Pix's tender flesh, the knife tumbled to the floor.

"Leave me the hell alone," he yelled at me.

He bent over, reaching for the blade. I kicked it away and the mat cutter slid underneath a display rack. His face, blood-red, twisted into a mask of hate. He lifted the lyre table and raised it staring at me with cold eyes. I crouched, shielding my head with my arms and squeezed my eyes shut, anticipating the impact of the solid wood table hitting me. After what seemed like an eternity, a crash shattered the tense-filled air.

I dropped my arms and stood upright, surprised by the scene facing me. Simon lay sprawled on the floor with the table straddling his body like a cage. Trying to figure out what happened, I looked at Pix. Her eyes gleamed and a proud smile filled her face. "Oh my gosh, you're amazing. What did you do? Trip him?"

"I didn't—"

"An act of sheer bravery on your part. Thanks for saving me from being whacked with that." I pointed at the table. "Looks like he's out cold."

"He fell alright. After being belted in the gut."

I focused on the silver candelabrum she gripped with its broken candle stubs still in the holders. "You hit him with that?" I moved to the entryway's short staircase, sunk onto a step, and ran my fingers across the soft Turkish carpet covering it.

"I didn't hit him."

I rubbed my temples. "You're confusing me. If you didn't hit him—"

"It was Robert Sullivan who came to our rescue."

"Wait." I squinted. "What?"

"Robert dropped the table over Simon before disappearing."

She must've noticed the confused look on my face.

"It was great the way you stood up to Simon. But once Robert showed up and knocked the knife out of Simon's hand, there wasn't anything to worry about."

I lowered my head between my knees, trying to ward off dizziness. The ramification of going toe-to-toe with a cold-blooded killer hit me like a ton of bricks. Both of us could've been murdered. Thank God, Simon tripped and hit his head on the marble floor. I glanced at Pix from the corner of my eye. "What were you saying about Robert Sullivan?"

"You didn't see him?"

"All I saw was a madman with a knife who wanted to kill you."

Loud, insistent banging filled the showroom.

"Police. Open up." The words rang out.

I twisted around and saw Daily, with gun in hand, through the door's glass window.

A burst of energy shot through me. "Not a word about ghosts to Daily. Understand?" Still a bit shaky, I stood and moved next to Simon's unconscious body.

"Okay." She ran to the door, flipped the deadbolt, and opened it.

Daily rushed past her with quick strides. He stopped and pointed at Simon. "You two did this?" He looked from me to Pix.

"Becca did. Simon had a knife at my throat."

"After he admitted to killing Nick and assaulting Chuck." I nodded with a touch of a smile.

A low whistle escaped his lips. Daily returned the gun to its holster as Simon began to stir. He removed the set of handcuffs from his belt. "I'm impressed. Really impressed, Rebecca.

Maybe you're a better P.I. than I ever imagined."

"She's the best," Pix said with a wink.

CHAPTER THIRTY-EIGHT

Coppurr, a furry ball in my lap, purred in his sleep as I completed the online registration for the cat show. Luckily, I'd made the deadline for the annual *Easter Eggstravaganza Cat Show* by the skin of my teeth. I needed a change of pace from the mayhem of last week and being surrounded by beautiful felines and my cat lover friends would surely do the trick. Jaspurr will be showing, and the other two will be there for support.

As if he needs it, I thought with a shake of my head. Jaspurr lives to take center stage at cat shows. Even so, Caspurr and Coppurr will enjoy the extra attention, hugs, and pettings from the visitors. My purrs have always been "pet-me-cats" unlike the bulk of the pedigrees whose owners would just about bite your head off if you tried to touch one of their pure breeds.

I tickled Coppurr's chin and rested in the blessed ho-hum normalcy of everyday life. Pix had resumed living in her "starter castle". I'd spent relaxing days painting *en plein air* by the river and even picked up a new client who wants me to get the goods on her cheating husband. The best news by far was that Chuck was recovering so well, he'd be out of the hospital by Easter. Coppurr

251

looked at me with an intense gaze, meowed, and jumped to the floor.

The only downside was that after a century of showcasing the spectacular work of local artists, Prescott Painting and Sculpture Gallery had closed. Yesterday, I'd collected my two landscapes—they hadn't made it to the gallery wall—but sat in the middle of the queue waiting to be framed. A deep sense of desolation filled me as I brought them home. Such a waste. Simon, stealing a life and throwing his away for unrequited love.

I closed my laptop, eyeing the couch. It must have been the fresh air and sunshine that zapped my energy. But so had the rollercoaster of a murder case, from which I hadn't completely recovered. A long nap could only help.

Loud banging jerked me out of my dreamless repose. Even if I wanted to rush to the door, I couldn't. Apparently, the purrs believed I looked lonely on the couch, so they'd decided to join me. Jaspurr, curled up on the armrest, had extended his front legs entangling them in my hair, Coppurr had sandwiched between my legs, and Caspurr, all twenty pounds of him, had stretched out across my chest like the crushing weight of a sandbag.

The knocking awakened Caspurr, and he looked at me with questioning eyes while Coppurr popped off the sofa. As I attempted to sit up, Jaspurr shifted his position and parked his derrière on my forehead. The banging grew louder. "I'm coming," I called. After a good forty-five seconds of shifting cats, I freed myself and made it to the door.

I yanked it open, and Pix breezed past me, holding an oversized notebook.

"I'm so excited, I could dance a jig," she said.

"Well, try to control yourself." I shot her a playful grin. "What do you have there?"

She plonked herself on the couch. "I solved the mystery."

"Mystery?"

"Of Robert Sullivan."

Robert Sullivan. The name I wanted to eradicate from my memory.

I racked my brain trying to come upon a logical explanation

for what happened three days ago at Treasure's Trove of Lingerie but came up empty. I decided the best way to deal with an unexplainable phenomenon was to forget it. *But now what? Pix wants to upset the apple cart?*

"This is the ledger for my period underclothing purchases." She tapped the top of the leather-bound binder. "Where I keep meticulous records. Provenance. Very important when it comes to antiquities." She opened the book and moved her finger across the top of the page pointing out the categories, including item, owner, location, price, and notes.

"Very professional," I said.

"It was quite the adventure traveling across the country putting together my impressive collection. Didn't we have a ball the time you came with me?"

I nodded. "Pennsylvania. Brandywine Valley. You visited a few old homes searching for underwear treasure while I explored the art museum and the Wyeth house and art studio. Didn't you find an amazing piece there?" I squinted, trying to remember.

"The nightgown that's displayed in my shop's window."

"That's right. It's one of my favorites. Victorian. Woven from cotton imported to England from Southern plantations and adorned with beautiful hand-made lace details. I always spend a moment or two looking at that one in your window display."

Pix nodded, flipping through a few pages. She ran her fingers over an inked-in sheet and looked at me. "I can't stop thinking about Simon and what happened."

"I know. Who would've ever thought mild-mannered Simon had a vicious side? I patted her hand, resting on the book.

"It took a lot of courage for Robert to save our lives from that madman."

"Look, Pix. I believe that you believe you saw Robert Sullivan. Being under a tremendous amount of stress can cause our brains to play tricks."

"You still doubt that Robert saved us?"

I shrugged.

"I know what I saw. What I don't believe are those stories

about Robert being a coward and going AWOL during the Civil War. He was so brave to take on Simon."

"I wouldn't exactly call it being brave," I said. "A ghost or a spirit doesn't have a physical body. It doesn't feel pain. It's not like Simon could've hurt him or anything."

"Well, that may be true. But he did save our lives, and in my book, that makes him a hero."

"As it should." I hoped being agreeable would end the topic of Robert Sullivan.

"I got to thinking about what you said about ghosts not having crushes on living people. So if Robert wasn't infatuated with me, there had to be another reason why he always hangs around my shop."

Coppurr jumped into my lap. The cat didn't distract Pix, though she did rub the spot between his eyes causing his gravelly purr to sound.

"When I was talking to Brenda, oh, my gosh, she wanted to fly right back here when I explained want happened," she said with a shake of her head. "Anyway, she suggested that there could be an item that fixated Robert."

"Item?"

"Psychometry. I didn't understand all of it, but what got my attention was the bit Brenda explained about objects possessing an energy field. Through this energy field, the object can transmit facts about the object's owner—what the person was like, how they felt about stuff, how they died."

Brenda and her off-beat ideas. I wasn't about to make a comment either way but decided to listen to what Pix had to say and stay neutral.

"Brenda suggested that maybe one of the pieces in my shop window belonged to Robert Sullivan. That couldn't be right since I only have female undergarments. But then I started thinking maybe Robert was married. Could something in my display window have belonged to his wife?"

I recalled the letter Woody had shown me in the Civil War

room. "Robert Sullivan did have a wife. Bridget. She died from complications of childbirth."

"How do you know that?"

"Remember? I volunteered to find out about the Civil War ghost for you."

"So, you really did investigate Robert." Pix shook her head, and a lock of golden-blonde hair brushed against her cheek. She swiped it back. "Your research confirms what I discovered. Look here," she said, sliding her finger midway down the page.

I focused on Pix's precise handwriting.

"Underdress. 1860. Cooperstown, New York. Owner: Lois Boyle."

"Underdress?"

"Sort of like a slip with short sleeves that fit over the many layers of underwear."

"So, that's an underdress displayed next to the Victorian nighty? Looks like a white dress to me."

"Uh-huh. But the amazing thing is *that* underdress belonged to Robert's wife."

My mouth dropped open.

"The piece was part of an estate going to auction. To make a long story short, the elderly lady who owned the underdress turned out to be the great, great-granddaughter of a Civil War Corporal named Robert, who she believed was killed in the war. His wife, Bridget, died in childbirth. The owner of the underdress' name was Lois Boyle, but her maiden name was—"

"Sullivan?"

"Bingo."

I inched closer to Pix with budding interest.

"When I reviewed my records last night, I about passed out. It explained why he's been a fixture outside the shop. Apparently, the underdress' energy field transmitted the information to Robert that it had once belonged to his wife. There's a good chance she may have been wearing it when she died."

I shook my head, not knowing what to say.

"That's why Robert came to my rescue. I've preserved, cherished, and displayed his beloved wife's garment. I guess when he looks at it, he remembers their life together. And it brings him joy."

"That is the most farfetched story I've ever heard," I said. "But fascinating."

A knock sounded, and the purrs ran to the door.

"You expecting company?" Pix said.

"No." I pulled the open and Daily faced me.

"I was passing by the Hour of Roses when I saw these. They reminded me of you." He held a bunch of white flowers. Gerbera daisies, orange blossoms, roses, and carnations.

I looked at him wide-eyed and a bit dumbfounded.

"I know we tend to be at each other's throats sometimes, well —most of the time—but I hope you'll accept them as a peace offering." He handed me the bouquet.

"They're beautiful," I said, inhaling the fresh citrusy aroma. "Thank you."

He turned to go but stopped and faced me. "Would you like to go out to dinner?"

"Of course, she would," Pix said.

I hadn't noticed that she'd moved next to me.

"Hi, Pix," Daily said. "Prescott's been arraigned. I wasn't surprised that he pled not guilty."

"Has he been released on bail?" Pix's voice went low.

"No reason to be concerned. Look, everyone is innocent until proven guilty but in this case, Prescott was remanded, placed in protective detention until his trial because of the likelihood of him committing future crimes."

"They think he'd come after me?" Pix grabbed my arm. "Or Chuck?"

"Don't worry. Prescott is never going to see the light of day as a free man again. Especially after you two testify at the trial."

"When is that going to be?" I asked.

"As you probably know, the criminal justice system moves at a snail's pace. It can take a long while to resolve a case. Years, even. So, don't stress-out about it. Take care of Chuck," he said to Pix and shifted his sight toward me. "Keep chasing cheating spouses."

I rolled my eyes upward but couldn't help but smile.

"So, what about it? You up for a pizza at Pantheon?"

"Yeah. I guess. Give me a minute," I said, looking at my paint-spattered jeans.

"I'll be down," he said, thumbing over his shoulder in the direction of the street.

I watched as he descended the metal staircase and shut the door.

"You don't have to hang around here," I said. "Go home. Spend some quality time in your Jacuzzi."

"I'd rather spend time playing with the purrs. And I want to hear all about your date when you get home."

"Going out for pizza is hardly a date."

"It's a start. Remember when I sensed chemistry brewing between you two? I might've been right all along." She reached for the bouquet. "I'll put these in water."

"Thanks." I headed to the closet, pulled out some clothes, and raced into the bathroom, intent on making myself look presentable. "Living is much less complicated when the "men" in your life are four-footed, covered in fur, and have whiskers," I said through the open door. "I bet if Caspurr was a man, he'd look like DJ. Tall, strapping, crystal blue eyes, thick blond hair, a bit mischievous, but playful and resourceful. Didn't you say Caspurr is your best mouser?"

I stepped out of the bathroom dressed in a gray pencil skirt and a light peach cashmere sweater. One of my best outfits. "Caspurr is also neutered."

"Well, DJ sure ain't. Anyone who's met DJ Daily knows he's a true blue, red-blooded, all-American male."

He's also egotistical, irritating, opinionated, conceited, chauvinistic... But then I remembered the warmth and safety I found within the tender strength of his arms. "That's what I'm counting on." I winked at Pix.

"You go, girl," she said as I closed the door behind me.

THE PAW PRINT MURDER

BOOK 2 OF THE BECCA FLYNN SERIES

Chapter 1

I plopped a stuffed bunny on the cage next to a woven bamboo basket filled with plastic grass and marshmallow Peeps—yellow chicks and black cats with white whiskers. Where's Pix, I wondered, tapping my foot. My diminutive friend, Treasure Winslow, nicknamed Pix, short for Pixie, should've arrived a half-hour ago. Judging starts in fifteen minutes, and she promised to help decorate my benching area for the last cat show of the season —the Bayleys Landing Easter Eggstravanganza. I took a deep gulp from my to-go cup from the Hot and Chilly Bean and eyed Jaspurr. He paced in the 22 x 22 x 44-inch cage, eager to get to a ring and strut his stuff.

The event is hosted by the oldest and most distinguished cat fancier organization, if I'm not mistaken, started in England sometime during the reign of Queen Victoria. Determined to win the prize for the best decorated show cage, I nodded, inspecting the little Easter "village" I'd set up with a bunny conductor and the cars holding brightly colored eggs. I smoothed a wrinkle from the curtain falling over the top of the cage, still not believing my luck that I'd found fabric online of kitties wearing rabbit ears holding Easter baskets. The only drawback was the background color. A pastel pink—and my "purrs"—Caspurr, Coppurr, and Jaspurr—are boys. My friend, Marlene, owner of the beauty supply shop Maven of Beauty, whipped up the cage curtains and sewed a sky blue ruffle along the fabric's edge and the bottom of the skirt that hides the paraphernalia we lung to the shows—crates, food, toys, grooming supplies, blankets, litter boxes . . .

Now stretched out on his hammock strung across the cage, I popped open the door, and Jaspurr rubbed his cheek against my hand. I placed a pillow inside that Marlene had stuffed with catnip. It took him a nanosecond to leap from hammock to pillow. Even with all the surrounding hubbub—announcements blaring from the PA system, exhibitors chit-chatting, and vendors setting up shop—Jaspurr's purrs tickled my ears. By the time I filled his bowls with kibble and water he was rolling from side to side like a drunken sailor.

"Your cage looks very Eastery, Becca. You might win this time."

I looked over my shoulder into Taffeta's face. Her expression didn't match the sound of her cheery words.

Taffeta MacIntyre and her husband, Tartan, are what I consider super-exhibitors traveling way beyond the states bordering Maryland to show their two kitties. Their lives seem to revolve around their Scottish Folds, Tutu and Tweed—and all things Scottish. And for as long as I remember, their cage always won the best-decorated award.

"What's wrong with Jaspurr?"

I noticed a slight upturn in her lips.

"He's relaxing with a touch of catnip before the show starts." Jaspurr and Tutu are neck and neck on the leaderboard—tied for first place.

"Aren't you showing your other two purrs?"

"Jaspurr doesn't need the competition—and neither does Tutu," I said with a knowing glance at the matronly woman. "But they'll be here tomorrow as Pet Me Cats." I noticed Taffeta eyeing the basket with the Peeps. "Spectators love to pet kitties, and my purrs love to be petted."

"Visitors may admire our two 'folds' but absolutely no touching is allowed. Who knows what kind of icky germs they could spread to our kitties."

"That's the reason we offer sanitizing hand wipes and—"

"Ours save all their purrs and loving for the judges. Tutu's favorite, Gary Galbraith, is in ring four. He always places Tutu first." She beamed, then pulled in the corner of her lips, squelching the smile itching to form. "Oh, but anyway, I hope you have a good show." Taffeta grabbed one of the yellow Peeps and bit off the chick's head. "Mm-mm," she said under her breath.

My heart sunk when I discovered Gary Galbraith was one of the show judges. He wasn't crazy about either of my red with white cats. Gary preferred Tutu's calico coat and her upturned ears. Unlike Tutu, Tweed's coat is chinchilla silver—white with black pointed hairs on his back—and ears tucked close to his round head. Both cats are purebreds, but because of Tutu's ears, a quality that made her ineligible for show, she wound up in our camp—the household pets. The HHPs are cats without papers, mainly rescues or cherished family cats.

Gary Galbraith usually placed Jaspurr in the middle of the pack with a fifth-place rosette. If the judge is true to form, this will be a close race between the two contenders.

"Hey," Pix's voice chased my thoughts away.

I faced her. "You're late, Treasure." I only use her given name when I'm peeved with her. A look of contrition crossed her face. But a second later, it vanished.

"I brought you doughnuts from Sweet Kneads. She placed two white boxes tied with bakery twine in front of Jaspurr's cage.

I shook my head. How could I stay mad at her? After all, she is my BFF. "How many doughnuts did you—"

"I thought you'd like to share with your fellow cat friends." Pix faced Taffeta, who popped the final bite of a cat Peep into her mouth. "Oh, hi, Taffy."

No, she didn't. Taffeta despises being called Taffy, and Pix knows it. She likes nothing more than getting a rise from the mother of "T 'n T."

Taffeta pressed her lips together as if trying to swallow her aggravation along with the marshmallow.

"Where's Tartan? I picked up his favorite Scottish-ish doughnut—chocolate with a confectionary custard filling." Pix pulled the string off the top box, opened it, and with a napkin, grabbed one. "I just love a man in a kilt."

"He's busy. Preparing for the opening ceremony," Taffeta said. "So don't distract him with . . ." Taffeta said to Pix's receding figure.

I'd believed that Pix learned her lesson and had quit flirting. Especially now since she's engaged to Chuck Stetson, our town chocolatier. But I guess old habits are hard to break.

"We're benched there," Taffeta said, pointing down the long aisle flanked on both sides by long tables crowded with show cages —many decorated with an Easter theme.

I knew which cage she meant since their fan club had already crowded around their pop-up cage and additional grooming space. I thought it kind of sweet that folks from the MacIntyre's Scottish club supported Tutu and Tweed. "I'll stop by to wish T 'n T good luck. Want a doughnut?"

She shook her head as she grabbed another Peep. "Oh, there's the mayor. Goodwin Meyer is a close friend. Yoo-hoo, Goodwin," she called as she hurried away.

I dropped into my chair with a quick look into the open doughnut box, noticing Pix had filled half the box with my favorite chocolate covered crullers. My mouth watered with the thought of decadent chocolate on my tongue. I reached for one, just as Pix returned with a big smile and eyes bright, a sight I missed when her fiancé was brutally attacked and wound up in a trauma center. The good news is that Chuck is scheduled to be released from the hospital any day now.

"I'm glad I bought a couple of those chocolate creamed-filled doughnuts. Gary wants one."

"Gary?"

"The judge. With a name like Galbraith, what else?"

"Scottish?"

"Uh-huh."

Somewhere in the show hall, she'd located paper plates and placed the doughnut on one.

"I'll be back in a sec," she said. "Keep an eye out for Dolly and . . . and DJ."

"Daily? It's hard enough to believe that you invited Dolly Evans but Daniel James Daily?"

"Dolly's not that bad once you break through her outer coating of snobbishness."

"She only thinks you're the cat's meow because your dad is donating electric shuttle buses to the town. With the parking situation under control, Dolly's probably betting on more people attending afternoon tea at her shop."

Pix shrugged. "She's bringing Woody along."

"Of course she is." I took a bite from a cruller.

"They want to cheer Jaspurr when he receives his first-place ribbon—best Household Pet in the Southern Region."

"Daily too?" I narrowed my eyes.

"DJ really likes cats. You wouldn't think a guy like him would go for the little furballs."

"Cats, yes. But cat shows?"

Pix answered with a half-shrug. "Ah-oh, looks like Tartan is about to start the show. I better get this doughnut over to Gary." Pix hurried down the aisle, squeezing between little clusters of people littering the tight space. Even though the Exposition Hall at the Bayleys Landing Fairgrounds is spacious, with two hundred exhibitors, venders, a food court, and the judging rings, it was more than a bit close.

A bagpipe's high-pitched skirl filled the air. The hum of voices quieted, and all eyes focused on Tartan decked out in his kilt and plaid. Later on, he'd change into his Highland outfit consisting of dress shirt, tie, vest, tweed jacket, in addition to his kilt, knee-highs, and a little pouch. I'm not sure what the pouch is for, but I guess it's where he keeps T 'n T's treats. Taffeta stood next to him, her eyes shining with pride.

Tartan is a talented bagpipe player, I conceded, as the crisp notes of the Star Spangled Banner filled the hushed show hall. After the last trill, rousing applause erupted, followed by a staticky voice from the speakers requesting Premiership Longhair Alters numbers 109-121 to ring five.

The show had officially begun, but Mayor "Goodie" Meyer took the mic and welcomed everyone to the show. It didn't take him long to start tooting his own horn and solicit votes for the upcoming fall election.

I strained to hear over his booming voice, hoping that our class would be called soon. Even though I enjoy showing the purrs, the downtime between rings could be maddening. I lifted my coffee, ready to wash down the last bit of cruller, when Taffeta's voice cut through the hall.

"Tutu is missing!"

ACKNOWLEDGMENTS

On a blustery New Year's Eve in a local bookstore, the first kernel of a story sprouted as I discussed a "cozy" mystery idea with my dear friend and cousin, Karen Smithson Esibill. I envisioned a P.I. who'd rather be an artist and lived in a place that resembled the quaint and quirky Main Street of Old Town Ellicott City. And cats—there had to be cats—and my three "purrs" would work perfectly in a small-town, cozy mystery. When the floods swept through Ellicott City, Maryland, in the summer of 2016 and again in 2018, I knew it was time to write this story. But it wasn't until a couple of years later that I put ink to paper. And what a fun time I had, creating the colorful characters who live and work in Bayleys Landing. A very special thanks to Karen for her insight and encouragement.

My deepest thanks to Michael Dolan, who liked my pitch on #PitMad which led to a publishing contract at Winding Road Stories. His enthusiasm, expertise, vision, and availability make him the publisher/editor authors dream about—it's been a privilege working with him.

ACKNOWLEDGMENTS

A special thank you to my critique group members, R. Lanier Clemons, L.R. Trovillion, Kim Hamilton, Mike Sage, Missy Burke, and P.J. O'Dwyer.

For their unfailing support, I'd especially like to thank my siblings; Roy, Patricia, and Thomas. Thanks also to Shirley Pratt, Pegi Taylor, and Amy Harke-Moore. Above all, thanks to my husband extraordinaire, Chuck Smithson.

268

ABOUT THE AUTHOR

Karen Leigh Charles has been a child advocate, human rights commissioner, and an art educator. Once the writing bug bit her, she found the creative process magical. In addition to writing, she is a professional artist whose paintings are showcased in local galleries. Karen has been known to pop up as an extra in Baltimore-based movies and television programs. She also writes the award-winning Beth Getty Mysteries under the name Karen Neary Smithson. She lives with her husband and three rescued turned show cats in Ellicott City, Maryland.

CPSIA information can be obtained
at www.ICGtesting.com
Printed in the USA
LVHW100034280922
729418LV00003B/182